MW01688747

Table of Contents

Chapter 1

When I was little and watched the Olympics on my family's television in our humble, middle-class living room, I'd get lost in my thoughts and would dream that I'd be the next great figure skater like Tara Lipinski or a great gymnast like Shannon Miller. Then I would go outside and attempt to ice skate on the pond behind our house and fall flat on my ass with my ankles going in opposite directions. I couldn't even do a cartwheel in our backyard and was far from graceful; I was lucky I could manage a somersault.

My parents always said, "You can be whatever you want to be, Aubrey. You just need to apply yourself." Yeah, that's the story of my life. Since I was a twenty-five-year-old college graduate with my Master's Degree in Journalism and Creative Writing, I should have been able to handle whatever came my way. At least that's what my mom said when my parents sold my modest childhood home and moved to their ritzy chateau in Paris. To say my mom had changed was an understatement. Apparently, my grandparents had invested wisely, and when they passed away, they left my mom everything. Now that my parents were well off, Mom decided she wanted to live the life of the rich and glamorous. I couldn't fault her really. My parents worked their asses off and deserved a great life. I just didn't expect them to move to Paris. *Oh well, I'll survive on my own.*

At my age, I knew I should be applying the education I earned by joining the workforce. I should also be partying with my girlfriends, meeting guys, and just having fun. Was I doing that? No. Instead, I sat in the small apartment that my parents rented for me in the city and I read. Life was going on right outside my window, but my nose was stuck in a book. My life came down to romance and mystery novels—some good, some just cheesy, some that just got me hot and bothered. Who was I kidding? It was all just fiction. That stuff couldn't possibly happen. That was how I thought of my life sometimes—full of fiction. I didn't have an ounce of romance in my life and had no clue how to remedy that.

I looked around my small bedroom at the pictures: my parents and me at Jones Beach, my best friend Julie and me just goofing around, but none of me with a man. I realized I hadn't had a true boyfriend . . . well . . . ever. At one point, I thought I did. His name was Garrett Reed. We were good friends, and I thought we had something special. He told me I was special, and I believed him, but once I slept with him, that was the end of the relationship. Maybe that was all he really wanted, or maybe I just didn't get his rocks off. I don't know. Honestly, he didn't do much for my rocks either. I snickered at the thought; although, it still made my heart ache a little. I really liked him, or I wouldn't have slept with him. I wasn't that kind of girl, and he knew that. Maybe that's what hurt me the most. The feeling of being used is a horrible feeling, and that was how I felt. I had Garrett to thank for being guarded.

After graduation, I hoped to be an editor for the Times,

but my secret aspiration was to write a romance novel. I had a problem though; I didn't know a thing about romance. That wasn't a slight problem; it was a huge problem.

My friend, Julie, knew about it, though. She was confident, beautiful, and she turned heads everywhere we went. I was known as the pretty girl's friend, which was fine with me. I didn't exude the confidence that she did. I had been in school, so inundated with classes and homework and wanting to be the best in my class that I never took the time to apply makeup or spend a lot of time on my hair. Sure, I had great clothes because Mom sent them or the money to buy them to me and I loved to shop, but that was about it. I was going to have to confide in Julie to get her to help me with this. I trusted her with my life. We had been best friends since the sixth grade, and I knew she could help me. I just had to find the courage to tell her without sounding like a complete head case.

I looked in my bathroom mirror at the person staring back at me: long dark hair, empty light blue eyes, and skin that desperately needed some makeup or a spray tan. Exhaling, I picked up the phone to call Julie. She answered on the second ring.

"Hey, *chica,* what's shaking?"

"Hey, I need to talk to you about something. Are you busy or can you stop over?"

"I'm not busy. I can come over in a few. Is everything okay? Are you okay? You sound weird."

"Yeah, I'm fine." I knew I didn't sound convincing. "I just need your help with something." I felt like Sandy in the movie *Grease* calling Frenchy for a makeover. I guess in a way I was.

"Say no more. I'm on my way."

Julie really was the best. She showed up less than an hour later. We sat on the couch, had a soda, and I tried to muster up the courage that was needed to tell her why I needed her help. I ran my fingers on my microfiber couch, creating a figure eight pattern, around and around and back again.

Julie stared at the shapes I was nervously making. "So are you going to tell me what's going on, or are you trying to hypnotize me?"

Julie was tall with perfectly highlighted blond hair and big, gorgeous green eyes with sweeping lashes. She was taller than I was, probably about five foot seven, and had a gorgeous figure. Her personality was even more beautiful. She had the entire package. It was no wonder men loved her.

I took a deep breath and cleared my throat. "Well, I've been thinking about writing a book—a romance novel to be exact." I looked up at her through my thick eyelashes to gauge some sort of reaction. I didn't know why, but I felt embarrassed and a little shy. This was my best friend. I should have been able to say anything and know there wasn't going to be any snarky attitude.

She grinned ear to ear. "I think it's an awesome idea! You majored in this stuff, right? From what you've told me, you've read hundreds of those books, so, yeah, right on!" Then Julie's brows furrowed and she looked confused. "Why do you need me? I practically failed English, so writing a story is totally out of my realm of expertise."

Okay, here comes the hard part. "I know my studies prepared me, and I aced my writing classes, and, yes, I've read a ton of books, but when it comes to actual heart-melting, making-me-want-someone-so-bad-I-can-feel-it-in-my-legs romance, I'm clueless."

I looked down at my hands, which were now twisting in my lap. "I haven't had a boyfriend in years, and the last one was crappy at best. I want to feel romance, the swept-off-my-feet-I-can't-believe-this-is-happening-to-me type of romance."

Realization dawned in Julie's eyes, and they grew bigger. She bounced up and down on the couch cushion and clapped her hands as if they were on fire and she needed to extinguish them. "Oh my God, we are so going to do this! I'm so excited! We need to find you a muse and get you a sexy outfit! Then we need to make sure that you're trimmed everywhere if you know what I mean!" She winked after that.

I wanted to smile at her enthusiasm, but instead I felt a little nauseated. Maybe this wasn't a good idea. "Okay, so the outfit seems easily attainable, and, uh, I don't need a trim anywhere, except maybe the ends of my hair, but finding a muse will not be as easy." I made sure to use finger quotes when I said "muse."

"That's where you're wrong, Aubrey. We can totally do this. As a matter of fact, I'm working at a Speed Dating event tomorrow night at a hot club called The White Orchid. Walker-Stone is in charge of its marketing and advertising. It's a sold-out event, but I can get you a ticket. I'll be there with my boss, Brian, to make sure everything goes as planned, so you'll have a wing man, well, wing woman."

Julie laughed; apparently, she found humor in my despair. I suddenly felt as if we were no longer Sandy and Frenchy, but now Maverick and Goose from the movie *Top Gun*.

"What the hell is speed dating and why doesn't that

sound romantic?" *Top Gun* flashed in my head again. "I feel the need, the need for speed." I almost laughed out loud. What was next? Going to a bar and singing "You've Lost That Loving Feeling"?

Julie rolled her eyes. "It isn't romantic. Well, I guess it could be if there were such a thing as love at first sight, but the goal is to meet a guy, right? Not necessarily fall in love. You just want someone to make your panties a little damp."

Julie enjoyed this banter a little too much. She was so comfortable with guys and sex. She wasn't a slut by any means; she just knew how to have safe fun and not get heartbroken.

"Look, I don't need my panties damp. Knowing me, I'll have an anxiety attack and probably pee a little; that'll make them damp."

We both laughed. Although, I inwardly cringed; it really wasn't that farfetched. I was known for my anxiety attacks. They started in middle school when I was picked on for not having the right brand of clothing or something like that. I ended up at the nurse's office, and that was where I met Julie. She didn't feel well that day. Well, that's what she told the nurse. She really didn't want to go to Algebra. She confided in me that day, and we'd been inseparable ever since. Julie was one of the cool girls, so my being picked on was instantly over. Back then, I was so thankful for Julie, as I am now.

"How does it work anyway?" I felt my anxiety building already.

Julie adjusted herself as if she were going to give me a marketing presentation. Her posture was perfect; she flipped her hair over her shoulders and flashed her perfectly white teeth. "There will be tables lined up, and each of the ladies picks one and sits down. Every six minutes or whenever the bell rings, a new guy will sit at the table. Both the men and women will have rating cards where they can make notes on whomever they meet. At the end of the night, Brian and I will collect the cards to see if there are any matches and take it from there. Voila! You could have your muse!"

I was shaking my head in disbelief, and my head was spinning. I felt as if I just drank a pitcher of margaritas. "So I'm going to be rated by men I've only spoken to for six minutes? And you expect me to find a match? What the hell do I say in six minutes that gets me a high rating? 'Hi, you're hot. Want to have sex?' Will that do it?"

"Oh, Aubrey, you're so dramatic! Listen, you'll never know if you don't try. What do you have to lose? If all else fails, we'll call it conversational practice. It's a win-win!"

"Yeah, win-win or lose!" I covered my face with my hands. I couldn't believe I was considering doing this.

Julie pulled my hands down and looked at me. "What do you have to lose? If you don't meet Mr. Romance Hero, you don't lose anything. But you could meet someone. You won't know if you don't give it a shot. Just have faith."

Julie was right; I had to admit at least that much. If I really thought about it, the idea wasn't that bad, and I really didn't have many other options. I was just trying to think of what to say that would be so amazing in six minutes. Worse yet, what would a guy say? And what were these guys like? They were probably creepy losers, and this was the only way for them to talk to women. Or worse yet, they were players looking for their next piece of ass, like Garrett. Either way, I couldn't believe I was going to do this. Did that make me a loser too? *Oh hell, who cares? I need to do this.* "Okay, I'm in. What do we need to do first?"

"First, we call the spa and make appointments for tomorrow, and then we shop and figure out what questions you're going to ask in your six-minute time frame." Julie was so excited; it was as if she were the one who would be speed dating; she definitely had faith.

"How come you never told me about this event or club?"

"I don't know. Honestly, it never dawned on me. I never thought you would do this or even want to."

"You're right. I wouldn't have done it if I had any other choice. I really need this for my research, or I wouldn't be going."

"Yeah, about that . . . What happens if you do meet a great guy? You know that's a possibility."

I shook my head and rolled my eyes. "I honestly don't think anyone who would attend an event like this would be my type—no offense. And what do you mean by 'what would I do?'"

"I mean if you meet some delectable, stunningly handsome, want-to-make-you-strip-naked creature of a man and you end up dating him, will you tell him about the book, about him being your muse, or will you keep it to yourself?"

I shrugged, "I don't know. I never thought about it. Anyway, I highly doubt I'll meet someone who'll make me melt and be gaga over. Do you know what kind of guys signed up?"

"We ran limited background checks on the guys. They have to be gainfully employed, between the ages of twenty-five and forty, single, and not on any sex-offender registries."

My eyes went wide. "I guess those last two would be

quite important!"

We both laughed. We called the spa to make appointments for nails, hair, and makeup for the next afternoon, and then we were off to find some nice little boutiques off the beaten path.

I had money, but I didn't want a cookie-cutter outfit. I didn't want to look as if I tried too hard, but I definitely didn't want to look like a mall rat. I purchased a black pencil skirt that came just above my knees and a tasteful blue, sleeveless top that had a scoop neck and just grazed the top of my cleavage. I didn't have much in the breast department, but the padded black lace bra Julie picked out for me helped fill me out nicely. She also made me buy a matching black lace thong and confirmed that I was okay in the waxing department. She wanted me to wear a garter belt and silk stockings. I just laughed and told her that I was all set. We finished our day with some good food and wine.

That got me thinking. *I'm probably going to need wine to get me through tomorrow night. I should stop and pick up a bottle—no, a case!*

Chapter

2

MY TAXI PULLED UP TO The White Orchid, and there were a decent amount of people entering. The club-goers were dressed to the nines. I was thankful that I decided to take a cab so I could be dropped off in front of the door. I wore my five-inch Jimmy Choo black pumps, and I felt wobbly just because of my nerves. If I had to park and walk for God knows how many city blocks, I probably would've fallen on my ass, broken an ankle, and ended up in the emergency room. Come to think about it that may actually have been a better alternative.

I paid the driver, exited the car, stood on the sidewalk, and stared at the entrance. The door seemed as if it were screaming at me to run and run fast. *What had I gotten myself into?*

Still outside the club where there was a gently calming breeze that washed over me and calmed my nerves, I looked at the list of questions I wanted to ask the guys. I figured by the tenth guy I would have it down pat, but I wanted to memorize them so I wouldn't look too rehearsed. Julie and I went over the list, and we thought it was okay. I thought I would ask these questions: What do you like to do on dates? Do you like to travel? Do you like sports? Are you close to your family? Have you ever been married? Did you go to college? When was your last relationship and how long did it last? That last one was important to me. If by chance I met someone who I wanted to get to know better and he'd just gotten out of a long relationship, I didn't want to be involved. That could lead to nothing but bad drama. I didn't need some psycho ex-girlfriend, or worse an ex-wife, coming after me. I know that when I read a romance novel there is always that twist, but that was one I didn't want to experience. I just wanted to experience the romance, love, tender kisses, moonlight strolls, and the sound of his voice before I fell asleep. Yeah, that's what I wanted. I blocked everything out, closed my eyes, and could almost picture it all.

I jumped as my phone vibrated. It was a text from Julie.

> ***Julie:*** *6:55 p.m.—I saw you get out of the cab over fifteen minutes ago! Get your ass in here! It is going to start soon.*

I felt embarrassed that I was standing on the sidewalk alone staring into nothing. *God, I am such a loser, and I am worried about meeting losers?* I laughed to myself at the irony. I straightened my skirt, adjusted my top, took a deep breath, and made my way inside.

The club was gorgeous and looked very posh. It was different from most of the clubs I had been to. The décor was comfortable and enticing at the same time. There was a mild floral scent permeating the air. I couldn't put my finger on what flower it was. It was dimly lit, but I could see the small round tables surrounded by cozy crushed-velvet chairs, which were silver and burgundy. There were high-top tables with stools scattered around. The dance floor looked like glass and was huge. It could easily accommodate over a hundred dancers, and the DJ booth behind it was encased in glass. It was a really stunning setup. I looked over at the bar made of dark wood. Its glass shelves were gently lit and displayed bottles of top-shelf liquor. This definitely wasn't your run of the mill nightclub. It was perfect and opulent down to every detail, and all the glass made you feel as if you were floating and could see through everything. It was really pretty.

Julie saw me gawking at the club. She walked over to me, grabbed my arm, and started dragging me next to her. "You look beautiful, Aubrey. Just relax. Everything will be fine." I smiled and took a deep breath. She handed me a ticket and a name tag. Thankfully, last names weren't on there. With my luck, I'd meet a stalker or worse a murderer. I had a really bad feeling about the guys who were going to be here.

Julie led me to a small room adjacent to the bar where the event was going to be held. There were about twelve tables with two chairs at each of them. Each table was covered in a crisp white linen tablecloth and decorated with a single white orchid in a small vase. It dawned on me that that was the scent I smelled—orchids. It was still early, so the rest of the club wasn't busy yet, but this little room was bustling with daters. I hurried and scoped out those in attendance.

Julie's boss, Brian, who was married, in his fifties, and had salt and pepper colored hair, didn't look as if he wanted to be there. He gathered the group and told us the rules. "You get six minutes together. Make them count. Write your date's name on the scorecard. When you hear the first bell, your date begins. You are not allowed to touch or ask for last names, phone numbers, or addresses. I will ring the bell when your six minutes are up. At that time, all gentlemen stand and move to the table to your right, and ladies, stay where you are. You will have one minute to complete the required scorecards, which are on your table. This will reoccur until the dating has concluded, at which time you will hear the sound of two bells. At that time, you can move about the room, and you will need to bring your scorecards to myself or my colleague, Julie." Julie gave a small wave so people would see who she was. She was so damn cute. I couldn't help but smile.

I stared at the scorecards as if they were laughing at me. I had a thought that made my stomach turn. *What if no one gave me a good score or rating? How embarrassing would that be?* I have to say the ladies in this group were attractive and maybe slightly older than I was, but most twenty-five year olds would be coming to the club later to hang out and have a good time, not attending a Speed Dating event at seven in the evening.

Brian continued with the instructions. "We will review the scorecards and introduce you to your best match for the evening. If there aren't any questions, we will begin." No one said anything. "Ladies and gentlemen, welcome to the Speed Dating event sponsored by Walker-Stone Marketing at the beautiful White Orchid. I hope you find a match tonight." People began applauding; I joined in and felt like an ass. "Please take your seats."

Once we were all seated, Brian rang the bell.

Holy shit! Here we go, time for the crazy Speed Dating to begin. I was starting to sweat . . . fantastic! I noticed that most of the guys were a lot older than I was. Most of them were going bald or had gray hair, and I was sure the wrinkles weren't smile lines; they were full-blown I-am-old-enough-to-be-your-father wrinkles. There was no way all these guys were under forty. Note to self: remind me to kill Julie later. She had to have known this and most likely didn't share because she knew I'd prefer to be home on my comfy sofa rather than here. Fuck!

The first man who sat with me reminded me of my late Uncle Charlie—not a great start. He liked going to movies on dates. He liked watching horseracing, which I really never thought of as a sport, and when I mentioned that, he started lecturing me on the mental awareness and muscular strength a jockey needed. I just nodded and prayed for the sound of the bell. I continued with my questions, and found out that he had never been married. He was about to explain why when the bell rang. Thank God! He stood up to move to the next table. That was when I noticed why he got so defensive about horse racing; he had to be about five feet tall. He was probably a jockey. I almost started laughing, but then another man sat down.

As the night wore on, I got pretty much the same answers to all my questions from the guys, and it seemed as though the answers were exactly what a girl wanted to hear: I haven't been in a long relationship in quite some time. I like to go out to dinner on my dates. I enjoy watching sports, as long as it's with my date. That one was such crap! I didn't know any guy who wanted to do that unless his date loved sports, and even then it was suspect. I was getting a bit frustrated, since it was all starting to feel phony—not that I was helping the situation with my fake smile—I responded with all crappy answers to make sure I didn't get paired up with anyone who I didn't think would be a good muse, which pretty much meant everyone. None of them sparked anything that would make me want to know them, let alone write about them. This whole thing was not going well. I wouldn't have even filled out a scorecard if it wasn't mandatory for me to turn it in at the end of the night.

The bell rang twice, which meant it was over. Thank the

good Lord! That was the longest hour and a half of my entire life. I was just about to get up when a shadow cast over my table. I was exhausted and didn't want to go through this torture anymore. I looked to my right, ready to tell whoever was standing there that the bell had rung and to move on. However, I found myself staring at a man's waist, a very nice trim waist. My eyes continued upward, downward, and back up again. Our eyes connected, and I couldn't help staring, that is until I lowered my eyes to his lips. Holy hell, he was gorgeous! He was tall, about six foot two; his hair was cut short on the sides, but longer and wavy on the top and styled perfectly. He had deep blue eyes, which almost looked navy, a well-trimmed beard, not a full beard, but a little more than a five-o'clock shadow. His body was teasingly god-like in his black fitted and most likely custom-made suit. His cufflinks were platinum and were adorned with diamonds. He definitely had money. He smiled at me, and I think I melted a little in my chair. *Where the hell was this guy earlier tonight?* My heart raced as if I'd just run the New York Marathon. I wondered if we'd run out of time and he was supposed to be my last speed dater; that would be my totally my luck if that were the case.

"Hello there. May I join you?" He said in a deep sexy made-for-radio kind of voice.

Smiling and trying to continue breathing at a normal rate, I motioned my right hand toward the empty chair at my table. "Please." I sounded so formal; although, I was surprised and not to mention happy that I could say anything.

He had the sexiest smile I had ever seen, and his voice . . . It had to be the hottest thing I had ever heard. I pictured him next to me naked, touching me and kissing me. My eyes fluttered shut, and I think a moan may have escaped my throat.

His voice broke my reverie. "Do you do this often, because you don't seem like the Speed Dating type? Not to mention, I think you are ten years younger than every other woman here." His eyes pierced mine. Could he see through me? Was I still breathing? I wondered what the hell was going on with me.

I cleared my throat, and my fingers started playing with the tablecloth. Since my eyes were still grazing his suit-clad body, I noticed he wasn't wearing a name tag. "Actually, this is the first time I've done this and didn't realize there was a specific type that utilized Speed Dating. I notice you aren't wearing a name tag. Did you arrive too late to get one?" I was starting to get nervous now. Who was this guy?

He laughed. "No, you're right; I don't have a name tag." He looked at mine, which was placed over my almost non-existent left breast. Thank God for the padded bra I wore. "Aubrey." He extended his right hand, and I met his with mine. "I'm Alex Logan." We shook hands, but it was more like a hold than a shake, and I felt his touch all the way through me. I felt completely and utterly captivated.

"It's nice to meet you, Alex Logan. I'm Aubrey Ryan. Well, you know I'm Aubrey. You just didn't know the Ryan part. Well now you do because I just told you. I mean . . ." *Oh my God, I sound like an idiot! Christ, get a hold of yourself, Aubrey* "I don't mean to be rude, but if you aren't here for the event, then why are you here?" I couldn't wait to hear his answer.

"I own the club. I happened to be checking in with the bar staff to make sure everything was in order for the evening. I knew this event was going on, so I popped my head in and saw you." He shrugged his shoulders. "I hope you don't mind. I don't want to keep you from these eligible men." He was looking around the room and had a shit-eating grin on his face. He knew there was no one of interest to me there.

That was not the answer I expected. Yeah, I minded that this gorgeous man took it upon himself to come over to me and wanted to sit down. "No, not at all." *Actually, this is the best conversation I've had all night.*

He laughed. "Not many good conversationalists?"

Holy shit! Did I say that last part out loud? I couldn't believe I'd said our conversation was the best of the night! *This is why I am single!* Total brain-to-mouth malfunction!

I smiled and tried to play it off. "No, and my best friend is going to kill me. I purposely tanked most of my answers because the guys were all losers. I could tell their answers were all fabricated, and if they weren't, they should have been. I figure if they were going to lie to me in six minutes what would they do during an entire real date?" I made sure to finger quote "real." "And the truthful ones just weren't my type."

"So these questions of yours . . . Hit me with them. Let's see if I'm your type." Amused, Alex leaned back in the chair and crossed his arms in front of his chest. And what a chest it was, not to mention his arms. I could have stared at him for hours. The span of his back covered the entire chair; he was a phenomenal specimen of a man.

"Okay." *God, why am I so nervous?* "Are you ready?" I tried my best to be as cool as Julie and prayed I could pull it off.

"Yup, hit me!"

I nervously laughed, squirmed, and shifted my ass in my chair. I straightened my back to appear confident. Clearing my throat with a smile, I asked, "What do you like to do on dates?"

He was just about to answer when Julie came over to get me, apparently not realizing I was content where I was.

She looked at me and then at Alex. She extended her hand to him. "Mr. Logan, I didn't know you were here. I don't know if you remember me, Julie Michaels with Walker-Stone Marketing."

He shook her hand. "Of course I remember you, Julie. You were just here last week." He smiled that ridiculously sexy smile.

"Right, excuse my interruption, but can I borrow Aubrey for a moment?" Julie actually blushed.

"By all means, I'll be waiting, Aubrey," he said with a grin. I couldn't help but smile back.

Was Julie just as affected as I was? She sounded so odd around Alex, definitely not like my confident best friend; that's for sure.

"Aubrey, what the hell are you doing with Alex Logan, and how do you know him?" I moved further away from the table to ensure Alex didn't hear us and Julie followed.

"I just met him, Jules." I looked over at him; luckily, he was looking at his cell phone and didn't appear to have heard anything. "He's totally hot though, right?" She looked stunned, mouth agape and eyes wide.

"Aubrey, we need to talk about that, but right now I could smack you because you rated the lowest on all the scorecards. What did you do? Tell them you had an STD? No one wants to be your match." She looked disappointed and a little pissed.

I laughed and snorted a little. "Of course not, you saw the guys—they were wretched. Alex, on the other hand, is amazing, and if you don't mind, I'd like to get back to him and my research."

I walked away from a shocked Julie. I actually shocked myself and went back to my table. I apologized to Alex and told him that I was right: I didn't score well and Julie was on to me. I shrugged my shoulders because I really didn't care. I was hoping for that outcome.

"Okay, back to my questions, I believe you still need to answer the first one."

"Ah yes, what do I like to do on dates?" He rubbed his chin. "Well, that all depends on the woman and what she likes. If she hates Chinese food, I guess going to a Chinese restaurant is out of the question. But I guess in general, I like doing things that allow us to talk. That's why I never go to a movie on the first date. I like a nice quiet dinner or something that allows me to get to know her, like a nice walk in the park."

Hmm, okay, that was a decent answer. I hit him with the second one. "Do you like to travel?

"I do. I prefer to travel the States and Europe, primarily France."

Good, while we're there, we can drop in on my parents. Why the hell did I think that? Holy shit, I really was losing it!

I started rattling off the other questions. "Do you like sports? Are you close to your family? Are you in a relationship?"

He rubbed his jaw as he answered each question in order: "Yes . . . No . . ." He paused and looked concerned and said, "That's complicated." He rubbed the back of his neck. He suddenly seemed completely stressed.

What the hell did that last answer mean? I had to mentally think of the order of my questions. He liked sports, wasn't close to his family, that one made me sad, and his relationship status was complicated. Was he still in one? I felt the smile fall from my lips and my chest hurt a little. I couldn't continue this . . . whatever this was, if he were in a relationship, complicated or not. That totally went against what I believed in and was definitely not romantic. I would never be the other woman.

I took my purse off the back of my chair and stood up to leave. I stretched out my right hand. "It was nice meeting you, Alex." He didn't put his hand out. He looked up at me as if he had more to say.

He ran his hand over his shoulder and around his neck. "Was it something I said?" He looked confused. The neck rubbing must be his tell for being nervous. I'd have to remember that.

Yeah, how about complicated—complicated because you have a wife sitting at home? I noticed he didn't wear a wedding band, but that didn't mean anything. "Yes, as a matter of fact, it was something you said. I'm not interested in complicated."

"What are you interested in?"

"I'm interested in dating someone who isn't complicated. I made sure to use finger quotes when I said "complicated."

"Let me buy you a drink and explain what I meant by that." His deep blue eyes stared at mine; they pleaded for me to comply. I felt something in me when he looked at me, a feeling I'd never felt before.

Chapter 3

I FELT APPREHENSIVE, YET INTRIGUED and interested in hearing his explanation. *Who knows? It may help me come up with a title for my book.* I reluctantly nodded and agreed to hear him out. He led me to the bar where Julie was wrapping up the night's events over an apple martini. She smiled when she saw us. I knew that smile; it wasn't authentic. She was nervous. I wondered why. Was she nervous that I would blow this, or did she know something more about him?

Alex asked what I wanted to drink and gestured for the bartender, who walked over. "Tyler, would you please get this lovely woman whatever she'd like?"

"What'll it be, hon?" His voice was almost as deep as Alex's.

"I'd like a chardonnay, please."

He winked. "Sure thing, babe."

Alex glared at Tyler, who looked as though he'd just stepped out of a male modeling magazine. I wondered what that glare was about. Maybe he'd broken a rule by calling a customer "hon" and "babe."

Tyler came back, set my wine down on a silver cocktail napkin, and did the same with Alex's beer. He shook hands with Alex and went to help more people. I leaned toward Alex to thank him, when a leggy blonde sidled up to him right between us, forcing me to back up. She was stunning and tall with perfect curves; she could have just stepped out of the same magazine that Tyler did. She rubbed Alex's arm, ran her pointer finger behind Alex's ear, following his hair line to his neck, and in a sexy voice she said, "Save me a dance tonight, okay, lover?"

"Not tonight, Leah, I'm kind of in the middle of something." He nodded toward me. She turned up her nose and said, "You know where to find me when you get bored." She strutted away. My eyes followed her as she strode back to a table at which I could only guess were her friends, apparently also models or wannabes.

Does this happen to him all the time? Was he this woman's lover? Is that what he meant when he said, "It's complicated?"

"If you'll excuse me, Alex, I'll be right back." I needed to escape the funky feeling that engulfed me. He stood when I left and looked a little concerned. Maybe he thought I wasn't going to return. He could be right. I decided I would head to the ladies' room to collect my thoughts.

Julie saw me get up and walk away, so she followed me. The club was getting crowded. There were more women than men; it almost looked like a cattle call. Some women were dressed provocatively, trying to look older and attract men, and then there were older women trying to appear younger. The guys didn't really seem to have a preference; they probably all just wanted to get laid. As I walked through the club, I noticed that lovely scent again. I figured it was piped through the vents since it was everywhere.

We finally made it to the ladies' room, and as soon as the door closed behind us, Julie immediately started in on me. "What is going on with Alex, Aubrey? Do you realize who he is?"

I glanced at another woman in the room and looked at Julie, almost embarrassed that a stranger heard her scold me. I tried to whisper, but I was getting agitated. "Other than just finding out he owns the club, no, I don't know who he is since we just met. How is it that you know him so well?"

"Aubrey, he is *the* Alex Logan."

"Is that supposed to mean something to me?"

The other woman continued to fix her lipstick then smirked and looked at me. I felt like saying, "What? Do you have something to say too?" But I refrained for fear that she did. Maybe she was one of his complicated women or something.

"He's loaded and he owns this place! His Dad is Jack Logan, one of the richest business men around. He owns Logan Industries. Alex is a great catch, but he's a total player. You did see that blonde who strolled up to him, not giving a shit that he was with you, right? Well, she is Leah Pierce, a rich bitch from the city who lives off her trust fund and who feels superior to everyone else and entitled to whatever and whomever she wants. And to answer your question, he's a client of Walker-Stone Marketing, the company that employees me. We prepare all the marketing for the club, but you knew that. I don't know him outside of business and what I've heard and seen here at the club."

The other woman walked into a stall. Maybe she felt uncomfortable; I sure as shit did.

There was so much to absorb; my brain was on overload. "Okay, I get it. Maybe he won't be good for my romance research, but when I talked to him, he seemed a little more genuine than the way you're portraying him.

Plus, every romance novel has a villain, right?" I shook my head and exhaled. "You're right. I should just move on. We're at a club, right? There are a lot of guys here. I noticed some real winners on the way in here, or better yet, maybe I can catch that five-foot-tall awesome specimen of a man from earlier." My sarcasm was obvious.

"I have to say that when I saw him I thought there goes her high-heeled shoe collection!" Julie looked at me and we both laughed.

"Look, if you think that Alex is what you want, go for it. Just remember everything I said." She made it sound like a warning.

I tried to look happy, but apparently didn't pull it off, since I could feel my face drop. Julie looked at my reflection in the mirror.

"I'm sorry to burst your bubble about Alex. Maybe he is a decent guy. Maybe he's changed and I'm way off base. I can only go by what I've heard and seen. I just don't want you to get hurt."

I shrugged and nodded. "Remember the purpose of this: the novel I want to write—that's all." I tried to sound convincing, pulling my shoulders back and smiling. What I was really thinking was that I needed to get to know Alex. There was something about him that made my heart expand.

We turned to walk out of the bathroom when Leah and her entourage strolled in, making us back up. They smiled at the woman who'd just walked out of the stall. Apparently, they traveled in packs, and they were friends with her. Leah gave me the once over from head to toe with her big brown eyes and smirked. "So you're Alex's playmate of the night?" *What is with this chick?* She leaned in and whispered in my ear, making my skin crawl. "Here's a tip. Don't get too attached." Then she smiled the fakest smile I had ever seen. I was floored and tongue-tied.

"Why, Leah, is it the lighting in here, or are you turning green?" Julie was definitely not a fan of hers, and her tongue was definitely working.

"Go to hell, Julie. You know that I can have any man, anytime, anywhere."

Holding the door open for Julie, I looked at her with pleading eyes to end the verbal battle that was about to commence. I just wanted to leave before it got worse.

Maybe Julie was right. I seriously doubted every emotion Alex brought out in me. Maybe I was stunned by his looks, but when he touched my hand, I really thought I felt something indescribable. Maybe I forgot what it felt like to have a man touch me and I mistook that feeling for something more.

We walked back to the bar. Julie stopped me and could see that my expression had done a one-eighty. "Don't listen to her, Aubrey. She's a total bitch. Forget what I said before. Go for it. Go for him. Fuck her. You are so much better than she is. She's been around the block so many times that if she had an odometer it would be broken from spinning too much." We both giggled.

Back at the bar, Alex was talking to a hot guy and Tyler. I looked over at Julie and noticed she appreciated the group as much as I did. She looked at me and winked. Alex looked our way and smiled; he stood and pulled out bar stools for us.

He introduced us to his friends. "Aubrey and Julie, I'd like you to meet my friend, Brett, and, Aubrey, you already met Tyler." I noticed Alex was curt when he spoke about me having already met Tyler.

Brett was extremely attractive, about six feet tall, with light brown hair and hazel eyes, and he had a great body. I could appreciate Tyler even better now since he wasn't behind the bar. He was tall and slim. He had the body of a runner. I pictured him strutting on a catwalk. Julie began to blush when she shook Brett's hand. I knew that look of hers. He must have sensed it too because he asked her if he could buy her a drink, and she shyly nodded. What happened to my outspoken friend? He had her resorting to nodding. I looked at her and raised my eyebrows. She just shrugged and grinned.

I turned back to Alex and smiled. He returned the gesture, laid his hand on my shoulder, and whispered in my ear, "Would you like to dance?"

I loved to dance. "Sure, I'd like that."

We weaved through the crowd. The beat of the music was intoxicating. There were people everywhere. It took us a while to get to the dance floor since everyone stopped Alex on the way over. He had men wanting to meet him and women wanting to touch him and get a moment with him. He took my hand in his and laced his fingers with mine; we fit together perfectly. He brought me to the center of the dance floor. There were quite a few couples dancing. I was a little nervous and grateful the music had slowed down a little. It wasn't what you would classify as a slow song, but it was slow enough that Alex held me close to him. Our hips connected, and my knee slid in between his. We swayed to the beat of the music as he led me through our first dance. I wondered how many dances we would share. I hoped this wasn't the first and last.

His arms slid around the small of my back while mine were draped around his neck. He pulled away a little and looked in my eyes. "I'm sorry about the woman at the bar.

That's what I meant when I said it's complicated."

I just looked up at him. I realized I was playing with the back of his hair, so I stopped and moved my hands to his shoulders.

"This club consumes my life, and I'm here all the time, so relationships are hard to keep because of that. It's not that I haven't had a girlfriend; it just makes it complicated." He shrugged his shoulders. "If I had a girlfriend, she'd have to put up with my hours and the women who are constantly here; they aren't exactly shy. I'm sure Julie told you that I don't have the best reputation."

I hated to admit that Julie and I had talked about him, but I nodded.

We were dancing slowly to the music and never realized the music changed to something faster. We glanced around and noticed the floor started getting really crowded and the dancing got a little crazy. He took my hand and brought me back to the bar where Julie was talking to Brett. I looked around and noticed that Tyler was at Leah's table and that they were practically in each other's laps. Leah was running her fingers up and down his chest, and I swear she had her tongue in his ear. Alex grabbed my hand and my glass of wine and told Julie and Brett to follow us.

I needed to know, so I asked. "Does it bother you that Tyler is with Leah?"

"No, what they do is their business; it doesn't affect me. Leah is just well . . . Leah and Tyler is a guy, so . . . yeah, that about sums it up. So I don't care who they're with."

That was good to hear.

He brought us all upstairs to a VIP area, which was much quieter, and we could actually hold a conversation. It was very nice: plush jewel-toned couches and chairs with a table in the middle and an arrangement of white orchids in the center. Julie sat down next to Brett, and we sat opposite them on a different couch. That's it. There it was again, that scent. It was definitely orchids.

"So The White Orchid. What made you pick that name? Don't get me wrong. The flower is beautiful, and they smell lovely, but it doesn't seem like a typical name for a club."

Alex's eyes fell a little. "They were my mom's favorite flower. She passed away when I was twelve, but I remember that she always loved her orchids. It's just a way for me to keep her close to me."

I felt tears prick my eyes. *Holy shit, why did I bring that up?* "I'm really sorry, Alex." I felt awful.

He rubbed circles on the back of my hand that he was holding. "It's okay. It was a long time ago."

I forced a smile and nodded. I still felt like crap.

"I'm glad you came to the dating event tonight, and I'm glad that I met you. I would like to get to know you better if that's okay with you. You're so different from the women who usually come here. You're like a breath of fresh air."

My mind was trying to comprehend that he was talking about me. He wanted to get to know me?

"Let me take you out sometime." That was more of a statement of fact than a question.

I literally shook; my knee bounced a mile a minute. "That would be great, Alex." My heart told me there was something special about him. I also knew I wasn't naive and that I was not the type who would tolerate dating a man who was tempted to be with multiple women, not to mention worrying about how many women were trying to attach themselves to him. But I shouldn't get ahead of myself. He asked me out on a date, not to marry him. Then I thought about my original purpose . . . research. *I can do this. I just won't get attached.* I wondered if he was a romantic. He obviously didn't have to woo a woman to get her attention.

"Great. How about tomorrow? It's Sunday and the club is closed. We can grab lunch and then go to the park."

"Okay, that sounds great, Alex. I should probably get going, though; it's getting late, and I have to call a cab."

"I have a driver here; I'll have him take you home."

"That's okay. I wouldn't want to impose."

"It isn't an imposition. A car is always here for people who have a little too much to drink. I don't want anyone driving while impaired."

He really was a good man. Maybe he wasn't as bad as Julie said he was. "Thank you. I appreciate the ride."

I glanced over at Julie, who was now in a lip lock with Brett. I rolled my eyes. *That didn't take long.* I didn't want to interrupt them, but still needed to get her attention. I looked back at Alex, and he just laughed as we stood up. Alex cleared his throat rather loudly. Brett looked up at us first while Julie blushed and dropped her head. She finally looked up while wiping her bottom lip with her thumb.

"Julie, I'm going to head home." She started to get up. I put my hand out in a stop gesture. "You stay and have fun. I'll call you tomorrow." Brett stood, shook my hand, and said it was nice to meet me. I took note that when Brett shook my hand I didn't feel anything, not like when Alex touched me. I waved bye, and Alex told them that he would be back after he walked me out.

He interlaced our fingers again, and we made our way

to the front door. I watched people look at him as he walked me through the club. Alex walked with confidence. He nodded at the patrons and received different looks from men and women. He was so self-assured, and his movements were effortless. I wish I had his confidence.

We continued through a door that led to a private hallway, which was apparently for employees, so I didn't have to witness any more women appreciating Alex's looks. Needless to say the way people looked at him and the way they looked at me with him were extremely different; they looked at him with wonder, but looked at me and just wondered. However, we did run into Tyler, who had Leah pinned up against a wall. Her right leg was bent and practically around his waist, which made her Band-Aid of a dress hike up, leaving little to the imagination. Tyler didn't notice us, but Leah did. She looked at Alex and winked. What a slut! It was women like her who gave women like me a bad name or no name at all. Alex didn't pay any attention as we made it to the door. My heart raced. This feeling was so foreign to me. Tonight definitely didn't go as planned, but you can't plan for everything.

We stopped right at the door and turned to face each other. Lost in my own thoughts, I wondered what it would be like to kiss him good-bye. I felt myself stare at him, but couldn't stop. His lips looked so soft, yet strong. What did he taste like? Would his kiss be forceful or gentle? He licked his lips. His tongue . . . What would that be like? I pictured our mouths connected and was mesmerized at the thought of his lips devouring mine. "Aubrey? Are you okay?"

"What? I mean, yes, I'm fine." Paging rock that I can crawl under please! How long did my stare fest with his lips go on for? I needed to gain back some control. "It was really nice meeting you tonight, Alex, and I look forward to seeing you tomorrow."

Alex pulled me into a gentle embrace. His hands rested on the middle of my back, and my arms slid under his, which made my hands rest on his shoulder blades. My cheek rested on his chest. He smelled so good. I would never forget his scent, and I knew I would never forget about him. He put his hands on either side of my face and tilted it up to look at him. Oh my God, was he going to kiss me?

"It was nice meeting you too." He gently kissed my right cheek. My eyes fluttered closed, and I willed my brain never to forget this moment—how he felt and how he made me feel. It was just a kiss on the cheek, but I felt it in my core. He definitely made an impression—a very good one.

He pulled out his cell phone and asked for my number. I gave it to him, and he called it immediately, so I had his number and he had mine. We walked out of the club hand in hand, and he led me to the car he had on call. He opened the back door for me, leaned in, and gave me a wink. Good God! I could have melted right there. He told the driver to take me anywhere I needed to go. He closed the door and the car drove away. What an incredible night! I had to buy Julie a thank-you gift for making me go to this ridiculous event tonight. I needed to get home and write in my journal.

Ready for bed, I grabbed my journal, which I entitled *Romance Research* out of my side table and began writing. I read my objective over again to keep my thoughts in line with my mission.

Romance, what is it? It is flowers, dinners, hanging out? Is it a look, a touch, or a memory? I need to find a man who will not only perform romantic gestures but is a true romantic. He needs to have a good heart. I don't want to hurt him, nor do I want to be hurt, but I will not fall for this man. I may tell him that I have strong feelings to see what comes next, but I cannot let myself fall for him. I know from experience that I'll get crushed in the end.

Things to consider: Does a man act differently when he gets the woman? Does he put romance aside once the chase is over or does it continue? Will he try this method on just me, or will there be several others to determine if this is an effective method of play. This may take a while, but it will be worth it in the end, I hope.

Entry 1—Alex the Player

Today, Julie brought me to a Speed Dating event, which was horrible. All the men were older and gave pre-rehearsed answers to try to score a real date. I have to say, though, I gave bogus answers too, and I didn't like any of the men. None of them were swoon worthy until the event ended, when I met a guy, and not just any guy, a wonderful guy, a guy worthy of being a romance hero. Even though he had women falling over themselves to look at him, he picked me. I don't know why he picked me, but I was glad he did. His name is Alex, and he is beyond beautiful and seems to have the whole package. He's charming and incredibly handsome, has drop-dead gorgeous eyes, and he smells amazing. He asked me to go out with him tomorrow.

Julie says that he's a known player. Maybe she's wrong – maybe not. Could I use someone like that for my book? Why not?

What I could do without is Leah. I know that a good-looking man is hard to resist, but when he is with someone else? Bitch. And he wasn't that put off by it. Player. I think Britney Spears sang "Womanizer" in his honor.

I will be continuing my research. Let's see what romantic things he'll do. I guess time will tell. One thing is for sure: I need to guard my heart.

Until tomorrow . . .

I'd forgotten that my phone was in my purse, and I wanted to make sure it was charged for the next day. I didn't want to miss Alex's call, so I grabbed my phone and plugged it in, noticing that I had two text messages.

***Julie:** 11:20 p.m.—Hey, I'm still at the club. Brett is awesome! I want the scoop on Alex. He came back to our table with a huge smile on his face and turned down all the women who came up to him. Brett said that's not normal for Alex to do! Can't wait to chat! Love you!!!*

I re-read her text about three times. *All the women who came up to him?* How many were there? I guess it says something that he turned them down, but could this really happen all the time? And would I always be wondering what he was doing? I wasn't going to go to the club every night to check up on him. I shook my head, realizing I was totally getting a head of myself. *Oh my God, I just met this man! I'll wait to talk to Julie about it tomorrow.*

Alex: *11:50 p.m.—I enjoyed tonight and am looking forward to tomorrow. I'll pick you up at one o'clock. Will that work for you?*

Me: *12:10 a.m.—Hi, Alex. Thank you for a nice evening, I enjoyed it as well. Tomorrow at one sounds perfect. I need to give you my address.*

Alex: *12:11 a.m.—I got your address from my driver.*

Me: *12:12 a.m.—You're very resourceful.*

Alex: *12:12 a.m.—You have no idea.*

I almost thought about asking how his night was going, but then thought better of it. I didn't think I really wanted to know.

Me: *12:13 a.m.—Lucky me.*

Lucky me? Really? I sounded like a Lolita! *What is wrong with me?*

Alex: *12:13 a.m.—The luck was all mine tonight. I'm glad you had a good time. My night has not been as good since you left. See you tomorrow.*

Wow, his night hadn't been as good since I'd left? That was a good sign, right? Or was he just saying that? I lay down and stared at my ceiling. I really needed to get some sleep. Every time my eyes closed, I could see Alex, replaying tonight's events over and over in my mind. I smiled and finally fell asleep.

Chapter 4

I WOKE UP FEELING REFRESHED and happy, which was rare for me, but that day I had something to look forward to. It was nine in the morning, and I had a few hours to get ready for my date. I was dying to talk to Julie, but having no idea what time she got home, I decided to wait for her to call me.

I checked my phone before I got in the shower, but there was nothing from Julie. I enjoyed the steam and hot water falling over me. I took extra time on my hair to make sure it looked as good as it did last night. After applying a little bit of makeup, I walked in my room to pick out my clothes for the day. Alex said we were going to a park and to lunch, so summer casual would work. White shorts, a black top, and a cute pair of wedges should do the trick. I felt good about myself and was ready for my afternoon with Alex.

I heard my phone vibrate on the nightstand; it was Julie, so I answered, "Well, good morning, sunshine." Julie just sighed. I was laughing inside my head. I knew that sigh. Julie must have had a really good time with Brett. "I take it you had a good night?"

"Oh, Aubrey, Brett's amazing. We talked and danced

and talked some more, and then we kissed. Boy did we kiss! He's great. We're going out again today. We actually might meet up with you and Alex later for drinks. Now tell me all about Alex. What do you think?"

I smiled just hearing his name. "Julie, first, I'm glad that you met Brett. You guys look really great together, and I could tell that you both hit it off. As for Alex, I get what you were trying to tell me about him. We couldn't turn a corner without some woman looking at him as if she wanted to rip his clothes off. Not that I could blame them, it was just weird. It wasn't like he was mine, but we were walking hand in hand, and these women didn't care. Even when Leah was wrapped around Tyler in the hallway, she had the nerve to wink at Alex. She'll really be a thorn in my side if anything develops with Alex. However, it'll be okay for my research. I just didn't think I would find someone last night. I owe you one. I just have to keep reminding myself that this is mainly about my book and try not to totally fall for him."

"No way can you tell me that he is just research. Granted, he would be delicious research, but come on, Aubrey. I saw the way you looked at him and the way he looked at you."

"Whatever . . . We'll see what happens today." She was totally right. He'd made me feel things that I'd never felt before, and I needed to see what came next.

"Hey, *chica,* I gotta go. Brett's calling my other line. Have fun today, and maybe we'll see you later. If not, call me when you get home."

My buzzer rang, and I knew it had to be Alex, but I checked anyway. I pushed the intercom button and tried to sound alluring. "Yes?" I giggled to myself because I sounded about alluring as a brick wall.

"Hey, it's me." Ah, that voice—now he sounded alluring. I couldn't wait to see him, but reminded myself that he was research—*research, Aubrey, just research.*" Yeah, as if that was going to work. I buzzed him up and opened my door a crack. I ran in the bathroom to quickly check myself. I heard a knock, peeked out, and saw him as he walked in. One look at him made my heart race and heat pool in my core. He was wore beige cargo shorts and a blue golf-style shirt that showed off his broad chest and muscular, tanned arms. He was a gorgeous man. I went to greet him.

"You look great, Aubrey." I smiled, and he kissed me on the cheek. He handed me a bouquet of flowers. I hadn't even noticed that he'd had them in his hand.

"I bent, smelled the flowers, inhaled their scent—that lovely familiar scent—and noticed a white orchid in the center. These are beautiful. Thank you, Alex." Score one for romance! I began making mental notes in my head. "Would you like something to drink?"

"No, thank you. If you're ready, we can go to lunch." His hands were in his pockets, and he was shifting and moving side to side. *Was he nervous?*

I grabbed my cell and purse, and then we headed out the door. He brought me to a little bistro not far from Creek Side Park, where I imagined we would be going afterwards. The bistro was quaint. It had about fifteen tables of various sizes with red-and-black table linens and a candle in the middle of each. The lighting was dim, almost making you forget that it was the afternoon. It was lovely.

We were greeted by a man in a black suit followed by a beautiful woman also in black, but she wore a black miniskirt and had legs that never seemed to stop. She also had a white blouse that displayed her ample breasts. I noticed Alex shift when she approached us. "Alex!" The man kissed him on both cheeks. "It is so good to see you." He had an accent, which I imagined was Italian. "Who is this lovely lady?"

"Anthony, this is Aubrey, a friend of mine."

He kissed the top of my hand. "It is a pleasure to meet you. You have a good man here in your friend, Alex. He's a good-a boy. Come, your table is ready. I show you."

He was too cute the way he called Alex a good boy in his Italian accent. I giggled a little when he said it, and Alex covered his eyes with his right hand. He looked a tad embarrassed, which made me giggle a little more.

Anthony seemed to know Alex well. Was this a regular place Alex brought dates? My heart started to race. "Thank you, Anthony."

We sat down, and the woman sauntered up to us with menus in hand. She batted her eyelashes, handed us menus hardly looking at me, and put her hand on Alex's shoulder. "Hey, handsome, it's good to see you. Can I get you something to drink?"

Alex looked at me. I tried to keep my face neutral; although, I was getting a tad annoyed. Was this going to happen everywhere? I could understand the club since he was the owner, but did he really bring me somewhere where one of his conquests worked? I made a mental note for later; I didn't want to forget anything. "Aubrey, would you like a drink?" I felt like ordering a bottle of Jack, but decided on a glass of white wine.

"A glass of chardonnay, please."

Alex smiled that beautiful smile of his, turned to the woman, ordered a bottle rather than a glass, and told her to bring two glasses. She smiled at him and said, "Anything for you, sweetheart."

Gag! My head was down, and I bit my lip and prayed I didn't draw blood. I started to think this wasn't a good idea. *Who needs this? Not me, that's for sure.* I just wanted to meet someone and get some ideas for a romance novel. I didn't want to meet someone and get information for a book entitled *How to Juggle Multiple Women at Once* or *How to See Your Exes While Out with Someone Else.*

"Aubrey, are you okay?" I looked at him. I had a quick decision to make: shrug it off as if it didn't bother me or ask him about her and this place.

"Yes, I'm fine. I take it you come here often? You seem to know the staff here." I really tried to keep my voice even, but I knew that I was going to start sounding irritated and on the side of bitchy.

He looked apprehensive. "I've been coming here since I was young. My mom and I used to come to lunch here after we spent the morning at the park. The man who greeted us knew my mom, and he knows how much I miss her. As for our waitress, Valerie, she is his daughter. We've known each other a long time; we sort of grew up together."

My head seemed to nod on its own. "I can understand why you'd want to come here. I know I probably don't have a right to ask, but Valerie seems—how should I put it—attracted to you. I assume there's a story there."

His shoulders slumped forward. Then he sat up straight and looked at me. "Yes, I guess you can say there's history, but not much of a story. We dated in high school and hooked up a couple of times in college. I don't think of her as more than a friend though. And you do have the right to ask. Since I brought you here and after what you witnessed at the club last night, my reputation isn't stellar. I'm really not that guy. I suppose I once was, but I'm twenty-eight now, and I want more than just a hook-up."

"Well, trust me, Valerie thinks you're more than just a friend; call it women's intuition, but that is how I see it." Just then Valerie sauntered back over with our wine.

She opened the bottle and poured a small amount in Alex's glass. He tasted it and nodded his head. She poured our wine and finally looked at me. She had a weird grin on her face as if she knew something that I didn't. She asked us if we were ready to order. I hadn't even looked at the menu yet. Alex asked if it was okay if he ordered for us. I nodded. "We'll have the chicken scaloppini with a side of ziti, and if you could bring us both a house salad to start, that would be great." He looked at me. "Does that sound good to you?"

"It sounds great. Thank you." Valerie took our menus, positioned them under her arm, and looked at me. "Would you like some bread?' Then looking at me, she smirked and said, "You seem the type who enjoys eating carbs."

What the hell did that mean? That I was fat? I keep hearing how bad carbs are, but what the hell? *Screw her.* "Actually, bread would be great." I looked over at Alex and then back to her. "I think I'll be able to burn it off later today." I winked and she walked away.

Alex just looked at me as if he wanted to ask me what that was about, but he just raised his glass. I raised mine. "To getting to know each other . . ." We clinked glasses and took a sip. This was exactly what I needed. I made sure not to gulp, but sipped. Valerie glared at us from the host station. She started to irritate me, but I tried not to show it.

Our salads came, and we had nice conversation. "Do

your parents live in town?"

I shook my head. "They live in Paris. They just moved there last month." He looked at me with sad eyes. "Don't feel bad about it; it's fine. I've been on my own since I went to college. I mean they paid for the portion of my education that wasn't part of my scholarship, but for the most part, I haven't lived with them in over four years. My mom is . . . Let's just say different. She and I have contrasting views. She has her own ideas on what I need and should want in life, and they are the complete opposite of what I envision. She's a little snobby and has bought into the idea that money talks and bullshit walks. I'd rather be living paycheck to paycheck and have a happy life. I'd rather be happy and poor than rich and miserable."

Alex looked at me as though he understood what I was talking about. I doubted he lived paycheck to paycheck, but maybe he wasn't as happy as he appeared to be. There was something about him—I didn't know what—but I hoped to find out. "What about siblings?"

I shook my head. "Nope, it's just me." "Does your dad live in the city?"

"Yes. He has a place close to his office." He didn't seem fond of his dad.

"Do you get to see him often?"

"No, not really, after my mom died, my dad really dove into his business. I think being around me too much reminded him of what he lost. My mom and I were close. I was definitely a mama's boy."

How sad. "I'm sorry, Alex. Do you have any brothers or sisters?"

"I had a sister. Ellie was five years older than I was. She was with my mom in the car when a drunk driver hit them.

They died at the scene, so . . ." He shrugged his shoulders.

Holy crap! The conversation got worse by the minute. I felt like bursting into tears for him. He looked up at me and could tell I was getting upset. He reached for my hand and held it across the table. "Aubrey, I'm glad you're with me today. It's nice to remember my mom and sister." I smiled and picked up his hand and kissed it. I don't know why I did that; it just felt right. I looked at him and he just smiled.

Valerie came and cleared away our salads. It was as if she was watching and wanted to interrupt our moment. Alex took that moment to introduce us, and we both smiled insincerely. As soon as she walked away, he came to my side of the table and put his hand out for me to stand up. I stood and faced him. He pulled me into him and hugged me. He held my head to his chest and kissed the top of it. There was that scent again. It was everywhere he was. It seemed as though we were standing there forever. We heard plates and noticed Valerie was placing our lunch orders down. Still holding me and not looking at her, he said, "Thank you for being here with me."

We let go of each other and sat to eat the rest of our lunch. The rest of the conversation was light. He asked where I was working. I told him that I was in the process of job hunting and that I wanted to be an editor. I couldn't tell him about my book, but part of me really wanted to. He wished me luck and told me he really hoped I got what I wanted. I was starting to think he was what I wanted. This was supposed to be research, but instead, I knew I was falling for him.

He paid for our lunch and shook hands with Anthony. I waved to Valerie and this time gave her my best smile. We left hand in hand and made our way to the park. This man was not at all the way Julie described. I hoped this was the real Alex and that I wasn't being played. I really didn't think I was, but I couldn't be sure.

He stooped and looked at me. "I'm really having a good time. Remind me to thank Julie for bringing you to the club last night and all the men who attended the event for being losers." We both laughed at that thought.

"I already thanked her for that. Hey, can we talk about last night? I have a couple of questions." I hated bringing up other women, but since this was technically research and I wanted to know what he really thought, I decided to move on with my line of questioning.

He looked at me with a nervous look and said, "What do you want to know?"

"Well, you said that relationships were complicated because of the club life. I like you, Alex, and I don't want to sound like 'that girl,' but I need to know about the women, about Leah. Seeing your popularity firsthand . . . You're a good-looking guy. You probably get your share of propositions, and . . ." Ugh! How could I phrase this without sounding possessive and awestruck, like a girl crushing on a guy for the first time? I hung my head. I couldn't put a single thought together, and I wanted to write a book? I slowly shook my head.

Alex must have sensed my discomfort with what I was trying to say. He brought both my hands up to his mouth and kissed my knuckles. "Aubrey, first of all, I'm glad that you think I'm good-looking." He smiled and I blushed. *As if he didn't know that already . . .*"You're different than the women at the club. I don't think you know how beautiful you are. I watched the guys last night. They all wanted you, which is why I made sure to sit and talk to you. I know what my life at the club seems like, but right now, you're the only woman I want to dance with, kiss, and hold."

His words were not exactly what I was hoping for. It all sounded good, except for the "right now" comment. I wasn't sure how I felt about that. *Did that mean that tomorrow or the next day he would want to dance with, kiss, and hold someone else?* I didn't see that as romantic at all. I was even more confused. My brain was on overload. I started to think this was a bad idea. I stared off in the distance, lost deep in thought, and decided that I didn't want him kissing anyone else.

"You're being quiet, Aubrey. Do you not want me kiss and hold you?"

Going on my tiptoes, I brought my lips to his. Why did I feel so brazen with him? His lips were soft and gentle. Although it was just a whisper of a kiss, it was still a good kiss. This was either going to go very well or end very badly. He wrapped his arms around me and kissed my temple.

His phone buzzed. It was Brett asking if we wanted to meet him and Julie for drinks at his place. He asked me and I nodded. It would be good to see Julie. I needed perspective. This seemed as though it was going either nowhere fast or my heart was going to end up shattered. I'd known Alex for less than twenty-four hours, and in that time, I'd had to deal with multiple women gawking at him, not to mention meeting two women whom he had slept with. I wondered how many more there were, but I didn't want that answer, not now anyway.

Chapter

5

WE WENT BACK TO THE restaurant to get Alex's car, a black Maserati GTS. It was beautiful, just like the man who drove it. The leather seats felt as if they hugged my body. Alex drove us to Brett's apartment building. I found out on the way there that it was also Alex's. It was a beautiful brick building with about twenty floors. Brett lived on the fifteenth floor, and Alex was on the twentieth. I could only imagine how gorgeous the view had to be from there. He tossed his keys to the valet, who addressed Alex as Mr. Logan. I could only guess how much this place cost. It was incredible.

Alex nodded to the doorman as we passed, and we got in the elevator. The energy between us was palpable. Alex turned to me and pulled me in for a hug. I could really get used to his arms wrapped around me. I felt so safe—comfortable—as if I were made for his arms and they were made for me. I reviewed the mental notes I would write in my journal: *flowers, ordering lunch for me, honesty, walk in the park, hugs, and kisses.* What else would this day bring? I silently prayed for the elevator to get stuck. That thought would normally send me straight into a panic attack; instead, it calmed me. Being stuck with Alex would be like a chocoholic being trapped in Hershey Park!

We reached the fifteenth floor, and Alex released me as we made our way to Brett's apartment. Julie opened the door and grabbed me for a hug. She whispered in my ear, "Brett's totally awesome! I really like him!" I think she squealed a little; all I could do was laugh.

She released me and said hello to Alex. Brett came to greet us. He shook Alex's hand and gave him the "bro" hug and then kissed me on the cheek. I liked Brett. He seemed normal, not a player type, and Julie seemed happy. That was really all that mattered to me.

Brett's apartment was bigger than most others I had seen. It was decorated in earth tones. It was comfortable. The floors were a rich-colored hardwood and were covered by a plush area rug in the living area under the sofa and coffee table. The kitchen cabinets were dark and rich in color and were lightly lit by the recessed lights in the soffit above them.

We all sat on the balcony outside of the living area, drinking margaritas. That and the wine I consumed at lunch were starting to do a number on me. I stopped after two, knowing I was getting way past my limit. We talked about normal, everyday things; it was relaxing. I enjoyed watching the interaction between the guys. They seemed close, but different. Brett seemed like the boy next door, lighthearted and free, whereas Alex seemed more serious and hardened in a way. I thought maybe it was due to all he had been through at a young age.

Julie stood and gestured for me to follow her. I excused myself. We ended up in the kitchen out of earshot of the guys. "How are things with Alex? Did you have a good lunch?"

"Everything is great. We talked about the women who seem to always be around, since he was approached during our lunch date."

Julie almost yelled, "No way!" then covered her mouth with her right hand.

My eyes darted around and quickly scanned the area. "Shhh, really, Julie, lower your voice. He explained about Leah and Valerie, the woman I met today in the restaurant. Although, if she hadn't come on to him, I could have seen us hanging out with her; she seemed as if she could be nice." What was I saying? Ugh! "I don't understand, Julie. These women were movie-star quality; it makes me wonder, ya know? I keep trying to remind myself this is for research, right?"

Julie grabbed my hands in hers. "Aubrey, someday you will look in the mirror and see what others do. You are beautiful and kind. Leah and the others I see him with are fake and nasty. I can tell you like him and he seems to like you. Maybe you should tell him about the book and bag your research. He'd probably give you chapters of romantic notions." She winked and giggled.

I didn't giggle. I didn't find that remotely funny. "No way! How will I know what romantic gestures he does for me are real? Not to mention I don't want to know what romantic things he has done for, with, and to other women. The thought is nauseating, so I say again . . . no way!"

Julie nodded. "Just be careful. I can't imagine him being happy about it if he thinks you're using him once you tell him about the book. It looks like I could have been wrong and he could be the real deal, Aubrey. He already knows how you feel about other women. Your journal is like the other man!"

Well, I'd never thought of it that way. "I'll tell him . . . soon. Let me see what all of this is before I mention it."

Julie took a sip from the glass of water she just poured for herself. "Suit yourself; just remember everything we talked about."

I nodded, and we walked back to the balcony to rejoin the guys. The rest of the afternoon was great, but I felt this tremendous weight on my chest. We were all comfortable together. It was as if the four of us had been hanging out forever rather than for hours. Alex stood up and extended his hand to me. "Ready to go?"

I easily put my hand in his and still felt the connection that we shared. "Yes." I stood and gave Julie and Brett a hug and thanked Brett for having us over.

We took the elevator down. This time we weren't alone, so there was no hugging. The others looked at us as though they knew there was something going on. It felt as if I had a sign on my forehead that read, "I want this man!"

We walked to his car when it dawned on me that he was already home. "Alex, I can call a cab. It's silly for you to drive me home when you're already at yours."

"I'll drive you. It isn't a problem really." Another note . . . *chivalry is still alive and well.*

"Okay, well then you need to come in for coffee; it's the least I can do."

He looked over at me and smiled. "You got it." Then he drove to my place.

We walked in, and I started toward the kitchen to make the coffee. I looked back, and he was surveying my place. He had a smile on his face, so I guess it wasn't too bad. I mean in comparison to his it wasn't grand or palatial, but I wasn't a millionaire and my parents had paid for the apartment.

I turned back to start the coffee. As I was counting the

scoops and putting them in the filter, Alex came up behind me, put his arms around my waist, and rested his chin on my shoulder. "Do you think it's weird that I feel this comfortable with you already?" I didn't know if it was the smell of the coffee, the drinks I had earlier or just Alex, but I was beyond the feeling of comfortable.

I turned around so I was facing him and brought my hands up around his neck, rubbing my fingers and nails through his hair. "No, it's not weird. I feel the same way." Book or no book, it was true. "What's weird is that you feel this way about *me*."

He leaned back still holding me and dipped down so we could be eye to eye. "Why?"

His look seared me. It was as if he could see into my soul. I felt flush and prayed my eyes didn't fill with moisture. "Well, I've seen your type, and since I'm not like them at all, it's surprising. I'm not a blonde, I don't have the body of a model, and I don't throw myself at you."

He stared into my eyes, making me feel as if I could take on the latest cover girl. "Did you ever think you are the type I like—what I want?"

Actually, no, I didn't. Was this guy for real? It was as if he was in my head and was writing my book for me. If I hadn't known better, I would've thought Julie told him everything. It was as if he knew what I wanted to hear. Julie would never betray me like that, yet I couldn't shake the feeling that he somehow knew. He was saying all the right things.

He was everything I wanted in a man, minus all the women, of course. After his response, I hugged him. His head was in the crook of my neck, and my head was on his chest. My hands were rubbing his sides and his back. I could feel every rippling muscle through his shirt. He looked at me. "I'm going to kiss you now."

I smiled and shyly nodded. I felt my breathing pick up its pace, and I prayed that my anxiety would stay at bay.

His lips softly but urgently met mine. There it was—our first real kiss. I felt an explosion of emotions: happy, excited, mesmerized, and a little scared. Our tongues entwined with each other, and it was amazing; we were savoring each other. His hands went from my lower back into my hair. Meanwhile, my hands were tracing his abs, and what abs they were! I felt every ridge flex under my fingertips. I could have melted right there on the spot. He broke the kiss. I actually think a whimper came from my throat. "Aubrey." His breathing was ragged, and I just looked at his beautiful eyes. "I don't want to rush this; I don't think you do either. How about that coffee?"

I looked at him, smiled, and nodded. I couldn't give a crap about coffee, but okay, I'd never felt this way. I guess it was good that he stopped, because I didn't know that I would have. Then I'd be lumped in with every other woman who ever looked at him. No wonder there were so many. I made a promise to myself to try not to think about how many he had kissed that way.

We sat on the couch and watched *Field of Dreams* while we had our coffee. We both loved that movie and apparently both loved baseball. "So Alex, tell me, which major league baseball team is your favorite?"

He looked at me and said, "The Yankees."

I exhaled. "Thank God. If you'd said the Red Sox, I would've had to ask you to leave!" We both started laughing.

That was how our evening went. We laughed, talked, and snuck in a few gentle kisses here and there.

Alex stood and I immediately felt alone. "I better get going. I have to be at the club early tomorrow morning to confirm a delivery, and Brett has tomorrow off."

"Oh, Brett works for you?" He didn't mention that earlier.

"Yes, technically, he's my silent partner, but he just went through a divorce, so he wants to become more involved. It's great because then I don't have to work six nights a week." He grabbed his cell and keys and headed for the door.

I silently wondered if Julie knew Brett was divorced.

I stepped around him and opened the door. I leaned against the doorframe and looked up at him. "Thank you for a wonderful day, Alex."

"Thank you. I'll call you tomorrow."

I smiled. He gave me a swift kiss and left.

Chapter

6

I CLEANED UP THE KITCHEN and got ready for bed. I pulled out my journal and prepared to write my notes.

Entry 2 – Alex – benching the player?

What a day! Alex is the most romantic man ever. He brought me flowers, we went to lunch (he ordered for us), met yet another ex, not romantic, but he handled it well. Plus I hate to say it, but I felt as if I could like her and we could all be friends.

We took a walk in the park, met Julie and Brett for drinks, and then came back here where we shared our love of baseball and the most amazing kiss I've ever received.

He is definitely the perfect muse for my book. I couldn't have found anyone more suited to be my leading man, but not only for my book . . . for me. He has everything: looks, brains, a gorgeous body, and a beautiful face. His kiss made me forget my own name. I'll have to see what tomorrow brings. I am trying not to fall for him, but I can't pretend that I don't have feelings.

We'll have to see if this leads anywhere or if he is still just research. I wish I could shake the feeling that Alex knows about my writing.

Julie called just as I finished my journal entry to tell me all about Brett. Apparently, she was still at his place, and she was spending the night. I was a little jealous knowing Alex was probably upstairs in his apartment.

"Hey, I need to tell you something." I wasn't sure if this was the right time, but I wanted her to know. "Do you know about Brett's past relationship?"

"Do you mean about his divorce? Yes, I do. He told me last night. It's no big deal. He was young, and she tried to trap him. He wised up and got out."

She sounded so sure about everything. "Okay, as long as you know and are fine with it. Sorry, Julie, I just needed to make sure that you knew."

"I know, and I love you for telling me."

"Have fun, Jules, and stay safe."

Julie sighed and sounded a tad sarcastic, no very sarcastic, "Yes, Mom. I'll call you tomorrow morning; maybe we can hang out tomorrow. I want to hear about the rest of your night. I love you."

"Love you too. Talk to you tomorrow." I set my phone on my side table and tried to fall asleep, but my phone chimed indicating that I had a text message.

Alex: *10:15 p.m.—I just wanted to tell you that I had a great time today. Sweet dreams.*

Me: *10:25 p.m.—I did too. Thank you for a wonderful time and a great day. Sweet dreams.*

And what sweet dreams I had. I dreamed of Alex, and the things he was doing to me were amazing. I actually woke up feeling sated and refreshed, when I should have been exhausted after all the action I had in my dream. I smiled and thought of the past couple of days and couldn't believe how much had changed in such a short amount of time.

My job hunt began that day. I made coffee and grabbed my laptop to search the career websites and local online job boards. I had money saved, but I needed to make sure I had some sort of income. My parents set up an account for me, but I really wanted to do this on my own.

I decided to call my parents. It was afternoon in Paris, so I gave them a ring. My mom answered, "*Bonjour,* Aubrey." I just laughed.

"Hi, Mom, how are you and Dad doing?"

"We're fine. How is everything there? Is the apartment okay? Did you find a job yet?"

"The apartment is great, Mom, and everything is fine. I am actually starting my job hunt today. I'll let you know how it goes. How is Paris?" I needed to change topics and make it about her, since I really didn't have anything to report—that I wanted her to know about anyway.

My mom sighed, and I could hear the smile in her voice. "Paris is beautiful, honey. The stores and restaurants are to die for. I decided the reason there are so many boutiques is because people keep gaining weight from eating so much!" She laughed. "We miss you, sweetheart. What would you think if we bought you a ticket to visit us?"

Wow, going to the most romantic city in the world would be great for my research, but that would mean that I'd be away from Alex and unable to look for a job. "Let's see how my job search goes today. But, yes, I would love to visit you. I just don't know when."

"Okay, baby, I have to go. Your father and I have dinner plans. We love you."

"Love you too, Mom, and be sure to kiss Dad for me."

I started my search with the local papers; there were some intern positions that didn't pay anything, so they were out. The positions were limited. I probably should have done this a lot sooner. Most of the college graduates had started this process, months ago. I don't know what I was thinking. I should have too. I was getting beyond frustrated. I signed up for a few email alerts and hoped something would come up. I was just about to close my laptop when I decided to "Google" Alex. I opened the search engine and typed in "Alex Logan." I started to feel creepy about the entire thing, not to mention nervous, so I never hit search.

I called Julie, figuring she had to be at work by now. She answered on the third ring, sounding exhausted. "Hey, Aubrey . . . yaawwwn."

"Gee, did someone stay up a little too late last night?" I couldn't help but laugh.

"Yeah, I did . . . yaawwwn . . . but it was so worth it. Brett's amazing and really nice. I'm going to go see him at the club tonight. Want to come with me?"

Did I want to go with her? I thought I should stay away from Alex for a little bit to see if he had any romantic gestures coming my way, but I did want to see him. "I don't know, Julie. Won't it make me look too, I don't know, eager?"

"No, it won't, but it's your decision. Text me later and let me know if you're going to stay home alone or come hang with your best friend."

"You know that I would rather hang out with you. I'm just really stressed about finding a job. I talked to my mom, and you know how she can get. I need to stand on my own. I'm thinking of calling an employment agency if all else fails."

"You just started looking. Give it some time. You already have yourself failing. Think positively and positive things will happen." Julie was always so optimistic. A glass-half-full kind of girl, me on the other hand, not so much.

"Yeah, from your lips to God's ears . . . I'll let you know about tonight. If I don't go, have fun, and, Julie, you better go drink some coffee and wake up!" I laughed and hung up the phone.

I decided to curl up on the couch with one of my books. I would read some of them over and over again trying to figure out what it was that the author wrote that grabbed me so much. I didn't know if I'd be able to do this or not. UGH! I went to my journal to start making some notes. I sat cross-legged on my bed, propped myself up against my headboard, and started writing things I didn't want to forget.

Questions . . .

What is romance?

Flowers? Affection? Texts? Calls?

When is it enough? Do we always want more?

If a guy seems too good to be true, is he?

Is Alex that guy, too good to be true?

Does he really like me or is he playing me?

He chose me. Why?

I don't think I'm being played, but how can I be sure?

I am sure of one thing. I'm falling for him.

I closed my journal and put it in my side table drawer. I flopped back on my bed, definitely not feeling like going to the club tonight. Still I couldn't stop wondering if Alex's women were there. Should I go and not let him know? That would be very telling, but that wasn't me and that wouldn't be honest. I stared at my ceiling and rummaged through my brain, looking for guidance or a sign; it didn't happen.

I dragged myself off my bed and into the bathroom. I needed to get into the shower and let the hot water pour over me. I tilted my head back and let the water beat on my scalp; it had to be one of my favorite things. I washed my hair, shaved, and rubbed my body wash all over; even though I wasn't going anywhere, it just made me feel better. The bathroom was all steamy after I turned the water off. I threw on my soft, white, terry-cloth robe and wrapped my hair in a towel. I started applying my face cream when I heard my phone ring. Alex? I hoped so. I ran for my phone and hoped I wouldn't go flying on the wet tile. It was Julie.

"Hey, didn't I just talk to you?" I smiled.

"Yes, and guess what?"

"You woke up?"

"Ha-ha, very funny. No, God's ears must have been open because Brian just told me that Jack, our copywriter and sometimes editor, is leaving the company and we need to replace him. He wanted me to look at the posting before he submitted it to Human Resources, and I told him that we didn't need to post it in the paper or online because you would be perfect for the job. If you're interested, he'd like you to come into the office tomorrow afternoon at four o'clock for an interview."

"No way, that is awesome! Thank you so much, Julie! I'm definitely interested, and I will be there tomorrow. I can't tell you how much this means to me. I guess that means I won't be joining you tonight at the club. The last thing I need is to go into the interview hung over and dragging."

Julie sounded sad. "Yeah, I don't know if I'm going to go either. I'm exhausted. How about if we go tomorrow night to celebrate? It's ladies' night, and the drinks will be cheaper, not that Brett or Alex would let us buy our own drinks."

The mention of Alex's name made my insides melt, and I felt my heart rate accelerate. Was it wrong to already miss someone I just met? *Ladies' night. I wonder how many ladies would want Alex?*

"Sounds great, Julie; hopefully, we'll be celebrating. See you tomorrow. I'm going to make sure I have something to wear to the interview and get my writing samples in order. Thanks again. I love you."

"I love you too. Bye."

The rest of my day went by in a blur. I ended up going shopping and bought a navy-blue pantsuit with a silky cream-colored top. I figured I could remove the jacket when I went to the club with Julie for drinks and it would look like a sharp outfit rather than a business suit. I was getting really excited. When I got home, I made a salad for dinner and sat down to go through my resume and the paperwork I needed for the next day. I looked at my cell phone and was a little depressed that I hadn't heard from

Alex. It was already nine o'clock, and he had to be at the club. He was probably busy. I hated to think that he was busy with other women trying to hit on him, or worse that he was dancing with someone, but I put that in the back of my mind. He was just supposed to be research. I didn't want to fall for him, but that wasn't working out the way I had hoped. I couldn't stop thinking about him, so I thought I'd send him a text to tell him about my interview.

> ***Me:*** *9:16 p.m.—Hi there. I just wanted to tell you that I have an interview at Walker-Stone Marketing tomorrow afternoon. Keep your fingers crossed for me. Hope you're having a good night.*

After I pressed send, I started having second thoughts. Should I've not texted him? I hadn't heard from him all day. I honestly thought I would. I waited about thirty minutes before getting ready for bed, but didn't receive a text. I drifted off to a restless sleep.

Chapter 7

I WOKE UP LATER THAN I usually do, but I slept like crap. I wasn't sure if it was because I was nervous and excited about my interview that day or because I'd never heard from Alex last night. After checking my phone again, I still hadn't. Maybe I'd read something into our weekend together that wasn't there. I dragged my ass out of bed and started getting ready for the day.

I was just about to eat my lunch when the buzzer to my door rang. "Yes?"

A man's voice bellowed, "Delivery for Aubrey Ryan."

Who could be sending me a delivery? I hit the buzzer and let him in. I opened the door, took the most gorgeous bouquet of flowers from the young man, gave him a tip, and thanked him. The flowers were a mixed arrangement of Gerber daisies, lilies, a few roses, and a white orchid in the center. They were beautiful. I read the card.

GOOD LUCK TODAY ON YOUR INTERVIEW.

YOU'LL DO GREAT!

ALEX

So, he did get my text last night. I smiled; although, in the back of my head, I wondered why he didn't text me back. I decided not to dwell on that and just enjoy the flowers.

> ***Me:*** *1:05 p.m.—Thank you for the flowers. They're beautiful.*
>
> ***Alex:*** *1:08 p.m.—You're welcome. They reminded me of you.*

I decided not to text anything else after that. I wouldn't even know how to respond. I felt as though my smile was stretching from ear to ear. Did he really think I was beautiful? I put the flowers in the center of my coffee table, since the other bouquet he gave me sat on my kitchen table. I decided to write in my journal. I didn't want to lose the feeling I had.

> ***Entry 3—Alex—A working project***
>
> *If flowers are a romantic gesture, then Alex definitely is a romantic. I've received flowers twice now and they keep getting lovelier. He called me beautiful. It's hard for me to accept. I really want to hope this is the real him and not the player coming out. I guess time will tell. I still need to guard my heart. Does one ever know if someone is genuine? Will I be able to tell the difference? At this point, does it really matter? I know I've fallen for Alex.*
>
> *Time will tell. Until tomorrow . . .*

I took the elevator to the fourth floor of an exquisite office building and walked into Walker-Stone Marketing at three forty-five, I had fifteen minutes before my interview to try and relax. I approached the reception area; it was a nice, understated office. There was a comfortable atmosphere. The walls were an inviting tan color, and the receptionist sat at a cherry desk. She appeared to be in her early fifties and was on the phone when I approached. She held her right index finger up to show that she wanted me to wait. When she finished the call, she said, "I'm sorry about that. How can I help you?"

"Hi, I'm Aubrey Ryan; I have an appointment with Brian Stone."

"Ah, yes, Ms. Ryan. Please have a seat." She waved toward the sitting area. "I'll let Mr. Stone know that you're here. Would you like something to drink?"

I sat down. "No, thank you." I was afraid I would spill something on my outfit, and I really needed this job.

A man approached me. "Ms. Ryan? I'm Mark, Mr. Stone's assistant." I stood and we shook hands. Wow, he was h-o-t, HOT! I'd have to guess he was in his mid-twenties. He had tanned skin, surfer-styled blond hair, eyes like the ocean, and even though he was wearing a suit, he still looked beach worthy. If I hadn't fallen for Alex, Mark would have been just my type.

I found my voice. "Hi, Mark. It's nice to meet you." This was another guy Julie had hidden from me. How many more were there? First Alex and now Mark—two gorgeous men! We walked through the office; it wasn't too big. There were offices on the perimeter and desks facing each of them, which I could only guess were for the assistants. There were cubicles with drafting tables, and storyboards hung on the walls. It looked serene and formal at the same time, sort of like Mark. We walked into the conference room, which had a large table with probably about twenty chairs surrounding it.

Brian and Julie were sitting at the table chatting. Mark cleared his throat, and Brian stood to greet me. We shook hands, and Julie just smiled at me as she stood. "I was just leaving." She whispered in my ear, "Good luck," smiled, and walked out with Mark.

My interview took about an hour. We went through the examples of my writing and editing notes. "I know you don't have any marketing experience, Aubrey, but I really like what I'm seeing here, and I think you could be a definite asset to Walker-Stone Marketing. I'd like to offer you a full-time position." He explained the salary and benefits. "There is also a ninety-day probation period for all new employees." He handed me a packet from Human Resources that outlined everything that he mentioned.

I was happily surprised and tried to hide my shocked expression. "I would love to accept your offer. I really appreciate this opportunity."

"Great. How soon can you start?"

"I can start as soon as tomorrow." I tried not to sound overly anxious, but I was excited.

Brian smiled. "That's great. We can use the rest of this week to get you acclimated to our office and our procedures. I'll have Mark make sure to leave you a badge at reception." We shook hands, and he walked me to Mark's desk. Mark stood and smiled. "Mark, will you escort, Ms. Ryan to reception and then come and see me in my office?"

Mark nodded to Brian and walked next to me through the hall to reception. "So, Ms. Ryan, how did it go?"

"Please call me Aubrey, and it went well. I start tomorrow." I wasn't able to hold back my excitement. I knew he could tell that I was really happy.

We made it back to reception, and Mark shook my hand. "Welcome to Walker-Stone." I noticed that when my hand was in Mark's I didn't feel anything, not like when Alex touched me.

"Thank you, Mark, see you in the morning." He turned and left. I couldn't help but look at him; he was just as delicious walking away. *I wonder if he's a romantic.* I'd have to ask Julie, who was running up to me.

"Congratulations, Aubrey! Brian told me the news. I am so excited! It is going to be so cool working with you! We must go celebrate. The White Orchid, here we come!" I remembered it was ladies' night, and I imagined the women who'd be there. I took off my blazer, making my appearance look more appropriate for drinks than business.

I was suddenly very nervous. We headed over to the club. "Julie, did you tell Brett we were coming?"

"No, but I should text him and tell him to get out a bottle of champagne!" She went to get her phone out of her purse.

I grabbed her hand. "No, don't!"

"What's wrong, Aubrey?"

"Please don't text him; I don't want to be expected." My heart was beating, and I swear it was going to jump out of my chest. "I want to see how Alex acts when I'm not around." I hung my head. I couldn't help but think what an awful person I was.

"Seriously? You need to reconsider your research; just let this be what it is. If you feel like writing about it after that, then come clean with Alex and tell him."

"What happened to my carefree friend? Where is the

Julie who hates players and warned me off Alex?"

"All I am saying is that you could have something with him. I jumped to judgment. Even Brett said he saw a difference in him since he's met you. Let's just have fun tonight, okay? We're celebrating you. Let's do it!"

I smiled. "Okay. I'm sorry, Julie. If you want to text Brett, go ahead."

"No need. We're here."

Looking out the window, I spotted Alex's car. My hands shook as I grabbed the door handle. I paused and took a deep breath; I stepped out of the car. I straightened my outfit and put some clear gloss on my lips. Julie and I walked into the club. The atmosphere was different. There weren't too many people, but it was still early. I spotted Tyler right away. He was behind the bar. I looked around but didn't see Brett or Alex. Julie and I walked up to the bar, and Tyler smiled at us. "Ladies, what will be your pleasure this evening?" God, the way he said that, I could have ordered an orgasm, and it wouldn't have been in a shot glass.

Julie smiled, "Hi, Tyler, we're celebrating tonight. Aubrey here is now part of the work force; we'd like two champagnes please."

"Congratulations!" His smile could bring you to your knees. "Two champagnes coming up." He turned to go get our drinks.

Julie looked around. I knew who she was looking for. A smile grew across her face, and then it dropped instantly. "Why don't we go get a table, Aubrey?" She was pointing to an area to our right.

I looked to the left, where her eyes had just been. I saw Brett sitting at a table and across from him was Alex and

Leah. As soon as I spotted them, she looked at me and gave me a sarcastic grin. I felt a little angry and slightly jealous—no very jealous and very pissed. I wasn't going to show emotion in front of her or Alex. *Once a player always a player, right?*

I had an idea. "Hey, Julie, do you have Mark's number?"

Julie just looked at me; she knew that I'd seen Alex. "Yeah, I have it, why?"

"Text him and tell him to meet us here to celebrate." I knew it was the immature thing to do, but I didn't care.

Julie just looked at me. She knew I would protect myself by getting mad rather than cry. "Do you think that's a good idea?"

"It's the best idea I've had all week." It really wasn't, but I was in the two-can-play-at-this-game frame of mind.

Fifteen minutes later, Mark came over to our table with a beer. "Hi, ladies, thanks for the text, Julie; I was around the corner when I got it." He raised his beer to me. "Congrats co-worker."

We all smiled and clinked our glasses with Mark's bottle. I noticed that Tyler wasn't at the bar anymore and that he'd been replaced with Brett. Julie got up and went over to say hello. I couldn't believe she'd waited this long. I knew it was for my benefit. Brett must have sensed her. He looked over and smiled at her. I was happy for her.

Brett leaned over the bar and gave Julie a kiss. I saw them talking but didn't know what about. Then Julie nodded in the direction of our table, and Brett looked over. His eyebrows furrowed together as he looked at me and then Mark. *Good.*

"So are you excited to start working?" Mark had no clue what was going on around us, and I wasn't going to point anything out.

Mark got me out of my daze. "Yes, I am. It's going to be so nice to finally put my brain and education to good use." I was smiling now. Mark was really good company. I thought he could be a friend. He told me about the people in the office. Someone named Lisa in accounting wore clothes too small for her and thought she was the next Miss USA. Andrea in advertising made a play for all the new hires. He winked at me and I laughed. He told me about his girlfriend, Jessica. I didn't know he had a girlfriend. I suddenly felt horrible for asking him to come out tonight. I didn't want Jessica to be upset.

"Mark, I hope Jessica doesn't mind your being out with us tonight."

"No worries, I told her. She doesn't mind; she has class tonight. She's studying for her Master's. She's almost done actually."

How nice would that be to have that kind of trust? "She sounds great, Mark. I hope to meet her someday."

He smiled and nodded. He continued giving me the 411 on the office staff. He was hilarious. I was in tears with laughter. And suddenly, there he was; I could smell him before I could see him. I looked up and saw Alex. Was he glaring at me?

"Are you going to introduce me to your friend, Aubrey?" The sarcastic way he said "friend" almost made me laugh, but the tone in his voice begged me to do otherwise.

I swallowed hard. *Was he mad? What right did he have to be mad at me?* I smiled. "Alex, this is my friend, Mark. Mark, this is my friend, Alex." I made sure to stress "friend" when I introduced Alex. He nodded and they shook hands. I hope he noticed that I referred to him just as my friend.

Alex spoke to me. "So have you two known each other long?" Mark looked at me. Knowing he could sense something was off, he excused himself and walked over towards the bar.

I looked at that gorgeous face that I'd dreamed about. "No, we just met today, actually."

"You seem very comfortable with him." Alex glanced toward Mark at the bar.

The nerve of him really! "How's Leah?" I looked around at the bar where Julie, Brett, and now Mark were . . . Hmm, no Tyler. "I don't see Tyler. Maybe he's now the lucky recipient of her affections." I couldn't keep the sarcastic tone out of my voice. He looked at me as if he just realized that I'd seen him with her. I swear the color on his face changed, not to mention his expression. "Look, Alex, not that I owe you an explanation or that you deserve one, but Mark works for Walker-Stone. He has a girlfriend and is very happy with her. We're just friends." I couldn't do this anymore. I got up to leave.

He didn't let me get far. He held my elbow. "Aubrey, there is nothing going on with Leah. Sometimes it's easier to just ignore her advances I wasn't acknowledging them. She was just sitting next to me."

"Whatever, Alex, I honestly don't care." That was a blatant lie. Of course I cared. I pulled my arm away and walked toward my friends to tell them I was leaving. Julie saw my expression when I approached them and could totally sense that I was going to lose it in one form or another.

She walked up to me. "What's wrong?"

"I need to get out of here." I was going to burst. I hated feeling this way. I looked at Brett sitting behind Julie. "Good-bye, Brett." Turning toward Mark, I said, "Thanks for coming out tonight, Mark. Next time, bring Jessica." I smiled the best I could and walked away.

Mark jogged over to me. "Wait, do you need a ride?"

"Thanks, Mark, but stay and have fun." I knew that Alex was behind me, but I didn't care. I felt nothing but confusion and hurt. It wasn't supposed to be like this. It was supposed to be research. He was supposed to be research. Why did I feel this way?

"No, really, I was just leaving, and Julie told me she drove here."

"Okay, if you're sure, that would be great."

Alex spoke up. "I'll take her home."

I looked at Alex. "No, thank you. You should stay here and service your customers." I made sure to sarcastically emphasize the word "service."

I turned away from him and looked at Mark. "Ready?"

Chapter 8

THERE'D BEEN NO WORD FROM Alex. *So much for my research. Oh well.* I had nothing to add to my journal about him. I didn't think his dismissing my feelings toward Leah was a romantic gesture, nor was not contacting me at all. Julie was going strong with Brett. I didn't bother to ask her about Alex, and she didn't volunteer any information. She knew me well enough to know that if I didn't ask she shouldn't tell. *Maybe I'll ask Mark what he thinks is romantic or see if Brett does anything like that for Julie.* I couldn't deny that my heart felt broken. To say that I was disappointed would have been the understatement of the year . . . no, the century!

I'd been at Walker-Stone two weeks now, and I'd settled into my job and drowned myself in work. Brian was pleased with our new clients marketing requests and then told Julie that there was another marketing event for The White Orchid. Julie and I just looked at each other. I wasn't sure how I felt. On one hand, I was excited, but on the other, I was apprehensive. What if he acted distant with me? Did I misinterpret everything? I doubted everything: his feelings for me and mine for him. Was there even an "us"?

Brian was going through the papers on his desk and handed some to Julie. "Julie, you're the lead on this account. I want you to meet with Mr. Logan at ten tomorrow morning, see what he has in mind, and have him review the updated contract terms. Aubrey, you're to accompany Julie. I want you to see our marketing approach firsthand, and this is one of our largest accounts. Mr. Logan asked for you by name; apparently, he's heard of you. He spends a lot of money on marketing, so we give him the red carpet treatment." I looked at Julie and then to Mark, who took notes.

Back at my desk, I put my head in my hands. I hadn't stopped thinking about Alex, and I couldn't let my personal life interfere with my new job. I was also thinking about my writing. I kept repeating the word "research" over and over in my head. I decided to text Alex.

> ***Me:*** *3:45 p.m.—Hey, Alex.*

Well, that said a lot. I was a dumb ass. Could I have written less? I suppose I could have omitted his name. I suck at this relationship stuff. My phone dinged.

> ***Alex:*** *3:51 p.m.—Surprised to hear from you. Can we talk?*

He wants to talk? Where has he been? I really missed him. I shouldn't, but I did.

> ***Me:*** *3:52 p.m.—I guess so.*

I was waiting for another text, but instead, my phone rang. I looked and saw that it was Alex.

"Hi." My heartbeat raced.

"Aubrey, it's really good to hear your voice. I wanted to know if you were busy after work today. May I come and pick you up and take you to dinner?"

I really wanted to go with him. I realized that I missed him. "Sure, I guess that would be okay. Thank you." *Could he hear my smile over the phone?* I didn't want to sound overly anxious or excited about it.

"I'll see you at five. I'll pick you up outside."

"Okay, see you then."

I went to Julie's desk to tell her I didn't need a ride home—that Alex had called and we were going to dinner.

"How did that come up?"

"I texted him." Julie raised her eyebrows and just looked at me. "I know. I know. I just couldn't help it. I miss him, Jules. I also still need to compile more research." Yup, that was going to be my excuse.

Julie offered some advice. "I know that Alex's reputation has made you skeptical. Hell, it made me skeptical. I didn't want to mention it before because I wasn't sure how you felt about him, but the expression on your face tells me he is more than research." I instinctively nodded. "I think you should know that I haven't seen him with anyone at the club, not the way I used to. I still say he may be the real deal. Think about ditching the book and just enjoy him. Tell him about it. Just ask for his insight."

"I don't know. I'll think about it. You're right, though. I do have feelings for him, but right now, they aren't very trusting. I believe what you said and what Brett told you, but from what I've seen, I just don't know." Saying that out loud broke my heart.

"Hopefully, you'll get some answers tonight."

"Yeah, maybe, who knows? I need to finish up some work before I leave."

Back at my desk, I felt as though the last hour of my

day had just dragged on. Julie had already left to go meet Brett. I packed up my laptop and files and headed outside.

My heart stopped when I saw Alex leaning up against his car. He smiled as soon as he saw me, and my heart sped up. There was no denying it to myself. Book or no book, romance or not, I was falling for him. How did the saying go? "You had me at hello?" Well, he had me with a smile.

My legs trembled as I walked up to him. He opened the passenger side door, took my laptop bag, put it in the back, and before I could get in, he hugged me. He whispered "I'm sorry' in my ear. I smiled, but I wasn't exactly sure what he was sorry for.

I sat in the passenger seat and watched him walk around the front of the car. He was amazing. His walk was effortless, and his looks were stunning. I noticed he had a different look in his eyes. I wasn't sure what it was, but it was almost as if he were afraid of something. He slid into his seat and turned to look at me. He took my breath away. His dark hair seemed longer, and his blue eyes were deeper, but they didn't have the spark I was used to seeing.

"I am really sorry." He grabbed my hand and kissed it.

"What are you sorry for?" All of a sudden, I was full of fear. Did he do something with Leah or another woman? If so, did I have a right to be upset about that? No, plain and simple, I didn't, but I knew I would be upset if that was it.

"I feel like I let you down. I should have texted or called you before you texted me today. I was confused. I knew you were mad about Leah, but I'm not used to anyone really caring about what I do or who I do it with."

"I'm sorry too. I really had no right to be upset. It's not as if you're my boyfriend. We just hung out. That's all." I shrugged my shoulders. I knew that wasn't the truth. That wasn't it, at least not for me. I found that I cared for Alex a lot. I was scared.

He pulled out into traffic and got on the highway. The car was really quiet. It was as if we were strangers or afraid to say anything for fear that we would offend the other. *What do I do? Should I start the conversation?* Then I thought about my research. I looked over, and he had a pensive look on his face. "Penny for your thoughts?"

He glanced over, and then his eyes went back on the road. "I want to get to know you, Aubrey. Will you give me that chance, give us that chance? I know I'll fuck up along the way, and I hope you'll have patience with me. In my line of work, obstacles are always there."

"Obstacles such as late nights and women?" I didn't notice that we pulled up in front of a restaurant named *Bisous.* I smiled when I saw the name of the restaurant. I didn't speak French, but I knew "*bisous*" meant kisses, thanks to my mom's emails.

Alex came around and opened my door and held his hand out. I took it, feeling that same tingle I felt the first time he touched me. He pulled me to him and held me. I felt my eyes start to well up with tears. He released me and put his hands on my cheeks, tilting my head up so our eyes met. "Yes, Aubrey, obstacles such as late nights and women. I need you to know that I don't want any other woman but you. I feel something with you that I've never felt before. It scares me, but I need you to know what I'm feeling. I want you and just you."

A tear slid down my cheek, which he wiped away with the pad of his thumb. Could he be any better? I was melting on the spot. "Alex, do you know what '*bisous*' means?"

Smiling, he said, "Yes, do you?"

"I do." With my face still in his hands, I looked from his eyes to his lips. He grinned and brought his lips to mine. My hands rested on his biceps. His tongue ran across the seam of my lips. I opened up as an invitation, which he accepted. We kissed as if we were all alone, not realizing we were standing on a public sidewalk.

I gently pulled away and brought my hands to his cheeks. Looking into his eyes, which were now sparkling, I said, "I want you too, Alex." That was the scary truth. I wanted this man more than I wanted anything in my life. My heart raced when I was with him and hurt when I wasn't.

He took my hand, interlacing our fingers, and walked me into the restaurant. We were greeted by an older gentleman with a heavy accent, who must have been born in France. Thankfully, he spoke English.

I asked Alex if he spoke French. "As a matter of fact, yes, I do. I studied it in high school and college, where I studied abroad in Paris for a semester. You said your parents were in Paris, right?" I nodded. "Do you speak French?"

"No, unfortunately, I don't. My parents took some courses before they started traveling abroad, and they would talk to each other. I picked up some words here and there, but that's it."

The waiter brought us the wine list and handed it to Alex, who selected the wine and ordered an appetizer for us. I was thinking how happy I was that we had a waiter and not a waitress. I didn't realize I was smiling about that fact until Alex called me on it. "What's the smile for? The cheese tray I just ordered?"

"No, although I do love a good cheese tray." I couldn't help but laugh. "If you really want to know, I was happy we had a male and not a female server."

He narrowed his eyes and looked at me. "Oh? Why?"

Was he serious? I exhaled and started twisting my fingers in my lap. "Really, Alex, do you not see how women react to you? The way they look at you when you walk into a room?"

He shrugged. "Not really. How do they react?" He was grinning. He totally knew.

"They look at you as if you could be their next and last meal, as if they want to rip your clothes off and run their fingers and lips all over your body." *There—blunt enough?*

His eyes went wide and then dark—sexy dark. "I only care how you react. What's your reaction? Do you want to rip my clothes off and run your fingers and lips all over me?"

I leaned over the table to get closer to him and crooked my finger to draw him closer. He leaned in and I whispered, "Yes, but I want more. I want your fingers and lips all over my body too. I want you to want to rip off my clothes. I want to be the woman who does it to you and for you to be the man that does it to me, but that will take some time. I'm not easy." I smiled, leaned back in my seat, and took a sip of water. I lifted my menu and started to peruse it as if I'd never said anything to him.

He sat there stunned. He definitely hadn't expected that. I was mentally patting myself on the back. *Let's see what his reaction to that will be.* I wanted him to know that I did want him but that I wasn't like the other women who just spread their legs for him. Would his reaction be a Neanderthal one or a romantic one? I knew which one I wanted—romance. I wanted my hero.

"Well, that was not the answer I expected." He sipped

his water.

I set the menu down on the table. "What did you expect?"

"I don't know, but that wasn't it." He was smiling, but had a serious look about him. "I do want to be the one who does those things to you; I want that more than you know. I'm glad to hear that you aren't easy. I think I already knew that, and that's why I am drawn to you. I want to date you—just you—and for you to just date me. I haven't been with anyone since I met you and really have no desire to. I just want to know you: what makes you happy and sad, what turns you on, and what turns you off. I want you to be the one I talk to about my day, and I want to hear about yours."

He put his hand out as a gesture for me to bring mine to his, which I did. "So will you date me? Will you be mine?"

He was rubbing my fingers with his thumb. I opened my mouth to answer when our wine and appetizer arrived. Once the waiter served us and Alex agreed on the wine, he asked for our order. I had no idea; my mind was a blank slate. All I could think about was Alex and me dating and my being his. What would that be like for me to be his and for him to be mine? He wants to know me—Aubrey. *How did this happen? This never happens to me . . . ever.*

The waiter brought me out of my thoughts when he cleared his throat. I ordered the Chicken Provencal, and Alex ordered a Filet Mignon. The waiter nodded and left us.

Alex looked nervous. "So what do you think? Will you date me? Can I call you mine?

I stared at him. I looked for any sign of insincerity; there wasn't any. "I think, yes, I'd like to date you too. I want to be yours and for you to be mine. I want to hear about your day, and I want to tell you about mine. I want to know what makes you happy and what makes you sad." I looked away and then back at him. "I want to be the one to make you happy."

Chapter 9

WE ARRIVED AT MY APARTMENT, and I invited him in. We sat on the sofa and Alex brought my hand to his lips. "How has work been?"

Maybe this was his way of getting to know me. "Actually, it's been good. I have a meeting tomorrow, but I'm nervous about it." I really wasn't nervous since the meeting was with him.

"Why are you nervous? I'm sure you're really good at your job. Who is the meeting with? Maybe I know them."

I was trying not to smile, but I'm a horrible liar, and my smile is a definite tell. I could never get away with anything with my parents or teachers. I couldn't keep a straight face, so I lowered my head so he couldn't see my mouth. I shrugged and spoke softly, "Well, this meeting is with a man, and he happens to be good-looking; I mean extremely good-looking, like totally hot, and his body is . . . Well, let's just say I hope I can concentrate."

I looked up, and his eyes were narrowing. "So you have a meeting tomorrow with an extremely good-looking man, and you're nervous because he's good-looking? Are you attracted to him? Is that what you're trying to tell me?"

Oh, this was too good. "Yes, that's what I'm saying.

When I see him, I want to rip off his clothes and run my lips all over his body." I looked up and bit my lip to try to prevent my smile, but it was too late; he was totally on to me.

He threw me down on the couch and straddled me. His fingers were all over me, and he started tickling me. We both laughed. "You are so going to get it for that. You had me thinking I was going to have to follow you to the meeting." I was laughing so hard I thought I was going to pee my pants. I was kicking my legs.

"Alex, please, I call uncle!" I had tears in my eyes from laughing. He stopped tickling me, and we were both breathing hard. I just realized that I was under him. My hands were on his muscular chest, and his strong arms were supporting himself at my sides. He dropped his head and kissed me. He bent at his elbows and lowered himself and rolled us until we were on our sides, facing each other.

He moved my hair away from my eyes with his fingers. I closed my eyes, trying to memorize the feeling—the grazing of his fingertips and the strands of my hair gliding across my face—I didn't want to forget any of it. When I opened my eyes, they met his. He lowered his head and kissed my forehead then my cheeks, moving down to my neck. I was getting goose bumps.

"You are so beautiful, Aubrey."

I could feel myself blush; I wasn't used to getting compliments. I didn't know what to say. If I said, "Thank you," it was as if I agreed, but I didn't, so I just smiled.

He began to kiss me. I lowered my eyes and felt every one of his touches. He started at my eyelids and trailed kisses all around my face. He ran his knuckles down my cheeks, and I felt my eyes flutter open. He slid his hand in my hair and brought my lips to his. Our tongues twirled together and I was lost in his touch, in his kiss, and in him. His lips on mine made my heart jump. I wondered if he could feel it. He made the clichéd butterflies flutter in my stomach. I almost moved my hand there to make sure I was okay. I wanted to pinch myself to make sure this was really happening, but if it was a dream, I didn't want it to end.

It was weird how comfortable I felt. Alex's position shifted, and he was lying on his back with my head on his chest. He was running his fingers up and down my spine. He spoke softly in my ear, "My father's company is hosting a fundraiser Saturday night. Will you go with me?"

I propped myself up. "Of course I'll go. What's the fundraiser supporting?" My head returned to his chest.

"Education to prevent drinking and driving." I heard his heart beat faster.

I put my hand over his heart and just lay there. I knew this affected him because of his Mom and sister and their deaths at the hand of a drunk driver.

"I would be honored to be your date." He kissed the top of my head and thanked me. We rested together. We were content just lying there; it was wonderful.

I heard beeping and could not imagine what it was. I moved my head and realized I wasn't lying on my pillow. I was still with Alex. We'd fallen asleep. I needed to get up. The beeping was the alarm in my bedroom. When I moved, so did Alex. I felt bad because I knew he could sleep in and it was only six in the morning. I slipped out of his arms and went to my room. I went into the bathroom and looked in the mirror. That was a mistake; I looked horrid!

I quickly jumped in the shower and started to get ready for work. I decided to wear a black shift dress and simple heels. I knew I was going to see Alex later at our meeting, so I took extra time to make sure I looked good. I walked into the living room, and Alex was still sleeping. Instead of waking him, I decided to write in my journal.

> ***Entry 4—Alex—The Romantic . . . My romantic boyfriend***
>
> *An amazing and totally romantic man, he asked me to date him and only him. I am so happy. We went to a wonderful restaurant, talked, came home, talked, and laughed. He is still chivalrous and just makes me melt. We're going to go to his dad's fundraiser on Saturday night. I can't wait to meet his dad. I am curious because they don't sound close at all. My guess is that he is going because of the cause and not the host. We have a meeting today. I am curious to see if he will act differently. Will romance enter the workplace? Is it bad that his workplace has seen more debauchery than romance?*

Just as I was closing my journal, Alex strolled in. I nervously threw the journal in my side table drawer and stood. I felt so guilty, but at this point my research was over. I was falling for Alex Logan, and my journal turned into my diary. I didn't want to forget anything that he did for me or that we did together. How could I have fallen so fast?

He looked amazing, even for just waking up and sleeping on the couch. "Good morning, beautiful." He came in and kissed my lips softly. It was so weird having him in my room. Although we were both fully clothed, I felt naked and fully exposed.

"Good morning, yourself, I hope you slept okay. Sorry you had to wake so early."

"I slept perfectly. I liked having you in my arms all night." He smiled and started walking to the bathroom.

Sheer perfection—that's what he was. "Alex, for the fundraiser on Saturday night, is it a black tie affair?"

He stopped and turned back to me. "Yes, it is. I hope that's okay. Also, Walker-Stone has purchased a table for some of its employees, but I want you with me at my table, not with them."

"Black tie is fine. It'll give me an excuse to go shopping, and I wouldn't want to be with anyone but you." I was smiling and headed into the kitchen as he continued into the bathroom.

I was starting to make some coffee when I heard, "Women and their shopping." Alex came up behind me and put his arms around my waist so my back was to his front. I leaned my head back so it was resting on his shoulder. I was really falling for him. My breathing altered and my heart raced. I was getting scared. I turned in his arms to look at him.

He kissed my forehead. "I am starting to know that look, Aubrey. What's wrong?"

"Nothing's wrong and that scares me. I'm not used to this." I motioned my hand between us.

"Just go with it, Aubrey. I feel it too and honestly never thought I'd like this feeling, but I do."

"Well, how do I argue with that? I have to go to work. Do you want to hang out here?" I was silently hoping he said no. I didn't want him finding my journal—not that he would snoop—but it still made me nervous.

"No, I'll head out with you. I should go get ready for

work too. I have a meeting with a hot marketing chick this morning." He laughed and smacked my ass.

"Yes, Julie is pretty hot." I smiled up at him.

"Well, I don't know about Julie, but I know that you are. I look forward to seeing you later." He leaned down and kissed me. Our tongues twisted together, and I heard a moan escape my throat. I really wanted him. I was so scared and excited at the same time that I hoped I wasn't confusing one emotion with another.

We broke apart smiling. He dragged his thumb under my lip to wipe away some moisture that was there. It was a sweet and sensual gesture. Was I falling in love with him? Is this what love felt like? It had to be too soon. He grabbed my hand, walked me out, and hailed a cab for me.

Chapter 10

I ARRIVED AT WORK EARLY. I had time to get some work done before we had to leave to go to the club for our meeting. I walked into the break room to get some coffee, and Mark was sitting at a table having coffee and staring at his phone. He didn't look right.

"Mark? Are you okay?"

He looked up at me, and he was either very tired or upset over something. "No, yes, I don't know. Jessica told me that she wants to take a break so she can concentrate on her studies. The University has a study-abroad program in London, and she's going. She didn't even talk to me about it. She just said she was going and wanted a break."

I was shocked. I hated situations like this. I never knew what to say or do. "Mark, I don't know what to say." Well, at least that was honest.

"What can you say, ya know? I didn't get to say anything to her. I would have been fine with her going. I'd never want to hold her back; I just didn't realize that she didn't need me to move forward."

I sat down at the table with him. "Why don't we go out later? I'll ask Julie to join us. It will be low key—nothing fancy—maybe grab some pizza and beer."

"Thanks, Aubrey. That would be nice. I don't know what to do with myself. I don't know if I'm pissed off or just in shock. No, scratch that. I'm pissed off because she shocked the hell out of me. It's too bad I really love her."

I looked at this man, who had the entire package, and my heart ached for him. All I could do was nod and be understanding. We left and went to our desks. I stared at my computer and thought about Alex and me. *Would this happen to us? Was something going to come along where he was going to want a break? Was someone else going to come along and pull him away from me? Could I hang on to a guy like him?* The thought of not having him around depressed me. What was worse was that I'd only known him a couple of weeks and I'd totally fallen for him. My head spun.

Julie came bursting into my office with a wide smile on her face. "Morning, *chica!*"

Her smile is generally infectious, but I couldn't get out of my own thoughts or how bad I felt for Mark. "Morning, Julie."

"What the hell is wrong with you? I figured you would be psyched that you'll be seeing Alex in an hour."

She didn't know I'd just left him. "I am, but I just talked to Mark."

Julie cut me off. "Yeah, I just saw him, and he looks like shit. Is he sick?"

"No, he isn't sick, unless a broken heart is an illness."

"Shit. Jessica? What happened?" Julie looked concerned and sad as if she knew what was coming next.

"Jessica is going to London to study and decided to end things with Mark. Well, she called it a break. The only thing that broke was his heart. I feel awful for him, Julie. I thought we could all go out tonight for pizza and beer.

What do you think? Can you come?"

"Definitely, that is an awesome idea. Want to see if Alex and Brett want to come?"

Did I? "No, I don't think it would be right to bring our happy relationships to dinner while he is nursing a broken heart. If you ask Brett and I don't ask Alex, the you know what will hit the fan."

Julie nodded. "Okay, the three of us it is. Get your stuff together; we need to be at the club in thirty minutes. I'll meet you in the lobby in ten."

I collected my files, sent Mark an email telling him we were on for tonight, and headed to the lobby.

We arrived at the club. I had an odd feeling when we walked in, because it was completely empty, except for a couple of women vacuuming. We heard the sound of bottles, so we went towards the bar where we spotted Tyler, who looked as if he were conducting inventory.

He looked over and saw us. "Hi, ladies, Alex is in his office. Julie, you know where it is, right?"

"Hi, Tyler, yes, thank you. We'll head on up."

Julie and I walked through the club, and I noticed the vases on the tables in the VIP area were empty. Did he replace the orchids every day? That had to be expensive. I didn't even know offices were up here. We approached a door and Julie knocked. "Come in." That voice, it really made me feel as if my knees were going to buckle.

Julie opened the door and I followed her in. Alex stood up and walked around his desk. He looked fabulous. He was wearing black dress pants and a light blue dress shirt with no tie and the sleeves rolled up revealing his muscular forearms. I had to touch the corner of my lips. It felt as if I were drooling. Thankfully, I wasn't.

He shook Julie's hand and then looked at me as though he didn't know what to do. How weird! Why did he just shake Julie's hand? I guess it was the professional thing to do, so I stuck my hand out. I had no clue what to do. He took my hand, but instead of shaking it, he brought it to his lips and kissed my knuckles. Mental note to self—*he is romantic toward me in a business meeting.*

"Have a seat, ladies. Would you like something to drink?" His voice was beyond sexy.

Julie and I spoke at the same time. "No, thank you." We looked at each other and smiled. I love her.

"Alex, Brian said that you wanted a new marketing strategy. Was there something wrong with the current one?" Julie looked concerned and sounded extremely professional.

"No, Julie, I've loved everything that you've done. We want to expand a portion of the club and add a wine room. That's where I need Walker-Stone to step in and create a promotion for us. We have some time because Brett and I will be traveling to different vineyards in Europe to explore the culture and regions of the wines we want to profile."

He's leaving? They're leaving? I felt the blood drain from my face. I immediately thought of Mark. Is this what he felt like? This sucks. What the hell is with Europe today? What a shitty way to tell us! Julie and I looked at each other and then back to Alex. Julie cleared her throat. "What would you like from us, Alex?" Her tone was a little clipped and the professionalism was starting to dissipate. I felt as if I was going to cry, and Julie didn't look much better, which didn't help me because she was the strong one.

Alex looked confused. He looked at Julie and then at me, and his expression went from confused to concern. "Let me rephrase what I just said." Just then Brett walked in, and Julie looked as if she wanted to slap him.

"Hey, gang, are we all on the same page? It's great, right?" Brett was beyond happy. He was practically bouncing on his feet. Was he excited to be leaving Julie?

"Brett, have a seat. I was just trying to explain to the ladies what we need to have happen. Let me try this again." Alex cleared his throat. "Julie and Aubrey, Brett and I would like you to accompany us to Europe. We'll be gone about two weeks. I've already spoken to Brian, he has cleared your schedules, and I've assured him the new contracts will be signed. You have them for me, right, Julie?"

What the hell? Julie and I sat there with our mouths open. It finally registered to Julie. "Yes, the contracts are right here." She handed them to Alex. "I really appreciate this opportunity, Alex." She sounded thrilled.

Alex smiled. "You can dispense with the formalities and the business acumen for now and go hug Brett. Alex laughed and then turned to me. "Aubrey, are you okay? You do want to come with us, don't you?"

"Yes, of course. I'm just a little surprised; that's all. What about the club? Who's going to take care of it?" The thought of going away with Alex made me delirious.

"Tyler will be in charge. Most of my staff has been with me for years. This place could really run itself." He came around to the front of his desk where I was sitting. I stood up, he put his arms around my waist, and I reached my hands to his shoulders. "I was dying to tell you yesterday and then again this morning. That's why I couldn't wait to leave this morning. I thought I would slip and tell you."

"Alex, you are an amazing man." I reached up and kissed him. I wanted him so badly I could hear my heartbeat in my ears and feel it between my legs. We rested our foreheads together, and our breathing became ragged. God, I really wanted him. We finally separated, but he held on to my hand.

"Okay, now that we have all hugged, kissed, and agreed, why don't we go out to dinner tonight and discuss our travel plans? We'll leave on Monday. You both have passports, right?"

Monday? No way, that only gave us a couple of days to get everything together. We nodded. "Great, so dinner at let's say six?"

I shifted in my seat; he wasn't going to like this. "We have dinner plans. Can we go to lunch since we're already here and it's almost lunchtime?" I could feel Julie's eyes on me. Had she forgotten about Mark?

Alex looked at me. Yup, I was right; he looked confused. "Uh, sure, lunch is fine." He sounded disappointed.

I felt as though I needed to explain, "We're going out to dinner with Mark, and before you get any ideas, we're taking him out because his girlfriend left him to go study in Europe and he is upset. We're friends, nothing more."

Alex nodded. He kissed me on my temple and said, "You're a good person. Lunch it is."

"You're a great man, Alex. Thank you for understanding. You have to know that I don't think of Mark as any more than a friend. He's really hurting right now. I'd ask you to come to dinner, but I don't want to show off how happy I am when he is so sad."

"You're that happy, huh?" He had a glorious smile, the kind you would see in toothpaste commercial.

I took his hands in mine. "I am beyond happy. What do you think about coming over later tonight? Do you have to work all night?" I looked into his navy eyes and ran my tongue over my lower lip in anticipation of his answer. His eyes were following it.

"I think I can come over." He winked and his chest rose. I could tell his was as affected as I was.

"Good, I look forward to it. Now, I'm starving. How about that lunch?"

Brett and Julie were getting friendly in the corner of the office, so Alex not so gently bumped into Brett on the way out of his office to get his attention. Julie laughed and Brett punched him in the arm.

We went to a classic 1950s-style diner around the corner from the club. We all ordered as soon as we sat down. We had a lot to discuss and didn't want to waste time.

Alex started telling us about our upcoming trip. "So, this is the plan. Our flight leaves from here to Tuscany, Italy, on Monday morning at eleven. Then we'll tour the wine country of Northern Italy until Thursday. We'll then board a plane and go to Sicily to discover the wines of the Southern region. We'll leave Sicily on Monday and travel to France then fly out that Saturday to come home."

Holy crap, we are going to France! My parents are in Paris. If I'm there and don't see them, my mom will freak out. Was I ready to introduce Alex to them? I suppose I could say he is a client. I wonder if he remembers that my parents are there. We are spending most of our time there. He looked at me and must have noticed my expression. Julie decided to chime in, "Aubrey, we should go see your parents."

Thanks, Julie. "Uh, sure . . . Okay, we can do that . . . I mean . . . if we have time." Shit really? My heart started to race. I was prone to having anxiety attacks. I hoped I wasn't about to have one, because that would be totally embarrassing.

Alex grabbed my hand. "Would you like to do that? Brett and I don't have to come. We can hang back and you and Julie can visit."

I shook my head. "No, I want you to meet my parents and for them to meet you, unless that would be weird for you; then we don't have to. I'll leave it up to you." Yup, here it comes. I am officially rambling and feel as if my chest were going to explode or get crushed. "Can you excuse me, please?" I stood up to go to the restroom, but not before I bumped into the table and almost knocked over my chair. I rushed across the diner and hurried into the ladies' room. I looked in the mirror and noticed I looked pale and splotchy. Great, Alex probably thinks I am a total freak. I wet a paper towel and blotted my face. I ran my hands under cold water and held them on the back of my neck to try to calm down.

He must have followed me, because he was waiting for me when I came out. He looked pale as well and very concerned.

"Are you okay? You don't have to introduce me as your boyfriend if you don't want to."

"I would like nothing more than to introduce you as my boyfriend. I wasn't sure how you felt about it." And that was the God's honest truth.

He moved toward me, reached his hand out, and held my chin between his thumb and forefinger, tipping my head up so our eyes could meet. "I'd love nothing more." He placed a gentle kiss on my lips. "Come on. Let's get back to the table." As we walked through the diner, I noticed the women appreciating my boyfriend. That was something I needed to get used to.

Julie was talking on the phone. "Yes, sir, that's correct . . . Yes, I have them . . . We'll be back in about an hour. Oh, okay . . . Thank you . . . Yes, I'll tell her." She looked up at me. "Thank you, Brian." She tossed her cell in her purse. We were all looking at her. She looked around the table and then at me. "That was Brian."

We all laughed.

"Yes, I gathered that much." I rolled my eyes and smirked as to say, "Really, Julie?"

Julie just looked at me with this mischievous look in her eyes. "He said after we drop off the contracts we can have the rest of the week off to prepare for our trip." She was bouncing up and down. "This totally rocks, Aubrey. We're going shopping."

I remembered I needed to buy a gown for Saturday night, and I could definitely use some new items for the trip. I thought a trip to a lingerie store would be in order. Then I had a thought. "Alex, where are we staying when we're in Europe?"

He looked at Brett, who looked at Julie, who looked at me. "I rented a villa in Tuscany and Sicily, and we're staying at a hotel in France."

Okay, that wasn't what I really meant. I really was wondering what the sleeping arrangements were. I looked over at Julie, who had an I-am-going-to-have-so-much-sex-on-this-trip look in her eyes, and I totally knew that she would be sharing a room with Brett. I was sure they'd had sex from the comments that she'd made about him and the way they were so familiar with each other. I must have had the opposite look on my face.

Alex whispered in my ear, "Aubrey, you can have your own room if you'd like. This is a business trip, and I don't want you to feel uncomfortable."

Oh, yeah, I was uncomfortable, not with the sleeping

arrangements but with this conversation. I needed to change it. Brett was looking at Julie as if she was wearing a French maid's outfit and at me as if I were wearing a nun's habit. I had to change the subject, but thankfully, our food arrived, so the crisis was avoided. The guys and Julie were talking about the marketing plan, and I had thoughts of sex in my head. I really wanted him. What if he didn't want me? I was really hoping that something would happen tonight. Should I initiate it? I had a hundred thoughts running through my head.

"So what do you think, Aubrey?" I faintly heard my name. I looked up and everyone was looking at me.

"I'm sorry, what?"

Alex laughed, "Did you hear anything that we said?"

Can I just die right now, please? "No, I'm sorry. I didn't. I was thinking of everything I need to do before we leave."

"Well, why don't you girls take off? Brett and I will pay the check and see you girls later."

I slid out of the booth and Alex followed me. He walked in front of me and turned around so I would have to stop. "Are you okay?"

"Yes, Alex, I am. Sorry, I'm just distracted. I have a lot on my mind right now."

"I hope I'm part of that." He smiled at me.

I was breathing heavier. "You're most of it." Julie walked up to us and grabbed my arm to pull me away from Alex. "I'll see you later." I blew him a kiss since I was halfway out the door. He smiled and went back to Brett.

Chapter 11

DINNER WITH MARK AND JULIE was nice. I really hoped that we took his mind off Jessica, even if only for an hour or two. I felt a connection to Mark. Even though I had only known him for two weeks or so, I was comfortable around him. He was easy to talk to and a genuinely nice guy. I was really angry with Jessica, and I didn't even know her. I never understood how someone could just walk away or in her case fly away without a second thought. I wish I knew someone to set him up with.

Julie and I felt horrible about talking about our impending trip to Europe. We weren't going to say anything, but since Mark was in the meeting with Brian, he asked us how it went. He seemed happy for us, but I know as soon as he heard "Europe" he thought of Jessica. I told him we would bring some wine back for him and get together with him when we got back.

I was out later than I thought I would be, and I needed to put my purchases from my shopping excursion with Julie away. I think I spent everything that I had made so far at Walker-Stone. I bought some lingerie, sundresses, comfy shoes for the trip, and some lingerie for tonight, just in case. I also found a gorgeous one-shouldered, sapphire-blue, chiffon gown for the benefit. According to Julie and the salesperson, it brought out my eyes. I guess that was a good thing. I looked at the clock, and it was getting late. I wondered when Alex would be over.

I decided to change into my new pink lacey cheeky thong and bra. I didn't know if he would see it, but it made me feel pretty and actually gave me a little confidence knowing that I had something sexy on. I shaved my legs for the second time that day and was thankful that I'd gotten my lady parts waxed while I was out. I put on a cotton sundress that had a pattern of white and pink flowers, orchids to be exact. That was intentional. I put my hair up in a messy pony tail with loose curls around my face, a little blush on my cheeks, clear lip gloss on my lips, and put on my nude peep-toe pumps to finish my ensemble. Now all I needed was Alex.

I put on some soft music, lit a few candles, and grabbed my journal.

Entry 5—Alex—I've fallen

Today Alex surprised Julie and me. He told us he was taking us to Europe for business. I really am falling for him. I trust him, which is weird for me. Do I tell him? Do I wait for him to tell me? What do I do? I think I'll write a book entitled My First Love, and it will be all about Alex and my feelings for him. Even if this doesn't work out, which would completely depress me, he is my first love. My heart is racing just writing that line. Can you imagine when I write a book? I hope it has a happy ending. Oooh, my buzzer is ringing. My first love may be here!

Until tomorrow . . .

I tried to collect myself. I pushed the intercom button. "Yes."

"Hey, beautiful, it's me."

My heart raced just hearing his voice. I buzzed him in and took a quick peek in the mirror.

He knocked on my door, and when I opened it, his mouth fell open. "Wow, Aubrey. You look amazing! Let me look at you."

I backed up and twirled around for him. He grabbed my hand and pulled me into him to dance. The music was on, and it was a slow, soft song. The vocalist sang of lovers who were far away from each other and who would look at the ocean in hopes that the waves would carry their voices to the other side. My hands were on the back of his neck, and his hands were laced on the small of my back. I tipped my head back to look at him.

He looked back at me. "Please tell me you did not have this dress on when you met Mark for dinner."

"Nope, this dress and what's under it is just for you." I felt so unabashed. Yes, that was unabashed for me. Some women may have answered the door in just the cheeky thong.

He tilted his head and gave me the most incredible smile. "What's under the dress?" He moved his eyebrows up and down. He was so cute.

Yup, here come my nerves. Can I do this? I took his hand and brought him over to the couch. "Would you like a drink? Wine?"

He leaned into the cushion of the couch. "Sure, that would be great."

I went into the kitchen and asked, "Is white okay?" I

was afraid that if I had red wine I'd spill it.

"White wine is fine, but I'd rather have you."

I thought I was going to spill the wine all over. He really is an amazing man. I was glad I was getting to know him and that Julie assured me that he didn't seem like a player anymore. I was laughing inside thinking about the tame-the-player entry in my journal. I wondered if he would laugh about that. I hoped that someday, when we were old and gray, we would laugh about it. Old and gray? Where did that come from? I shook my head to get those thoughts out of it.

I brought our wine to the living room. It dawned on me that the wine I was serving wasn't even close to what we would be having on our trip. I handed him his glass, and he looked at me from head to toe. His expression changed. It wasn't a lustful look or even a happy one. He looked sad. Had I done something?

"Alex, is everything okay?" Holy crap, what happened from the kitchen to here?

"Everything is fine. I just noticed the flowers on your dress."

Oh, no, did he not like that I chose a dress with orchids on it?

"My mom and sister would have loved you, Aubrey. I wish they were here." He set his wine glass on the coffee table and took mine and did the same. He took my hands in his and pulled me onto his lap. His arms were now around my waist, and his forehead was on my shoulder.

"If they were like you, I'm sure I would have loved them too. I'm sorry if I made you sad tonight. It wasn't my intention. I did think of you when I saw this dress. It reminded me of the flowers you'd given me. I saw it and it made me smile, just like when I see you."

He had a pensive look on his face, as if he were thinking about what I'd said. What did I say? I started thinking about it. *Oh no! I said that if they were like him I would love them. Did he not want me to say that? Did I say that I loved him? I guess he could think that. Oh my God it was too soon. Do I love him?* I tried to stand up and get out of this funky conversation. As soon as I moved, he held me tighter. I just looked at him with no expression. I shifted on his lap a little; I was feeling really uncomfortable.

"Aubrey, did I hear what I thought I heard?"

"I don't know. What do you think you heard?" I could tell he didn't want to tell me, and I didn't know if I wanted to tell him. I would probably scare him off. *Shit. This is why I suck at this.* I thought if we stopped talking it would be for the best.

I straddled him as we sat on the couch. I put my hands around the back of his head and pulled him to me. Our mouths crushed together. His tongue . . . Man oh man, his tongue . . . The way it perused my mouth I could only imagine what it would do in other areas. I couldn't get enough.

He pulled away, breathing heavily. "Aubrey, I want you. I haven't wanted anyone as much as I do you." His mouth was on mine again.

I looked into his gorgeous eyes. "I want you too, Alex."

With that, he stood up. My legs were now wrapped around his waist, and my head rested on his shoulder. He carried me down the hall and paused. "My bedroom's on the left." I could feel his smile on the top of my head.

He set me down so I was standing in my bedroom. He reached around to my back and unzipped my dress. It slid down my body and pooled at my feet, exposing my new pink lacey lingerie. He looked at me, making me feel so wanton. I was shocked that I didn't feel embarrassed or self-conscious.

He laid me down on my bed and just hovered over me. Supported by his gloriously muscular arms, he looked into my eyes. "Are you sure, Aubrey?"

"Alex, I have never been surer of anything or anyone . . . ever." That was his green light, and boy did he go. He slid the straps of my bra down, exposing my breasts, which were aching to be touched.

He kissed my collarbone and up my neck. "You're beautiful, Aubrey. I'll never hurt you." He continued his kissing trail behind my ear, which made me flinch.

God, was he real? His hands gently cupped my breasts, his lips now on mine. His kiss was so gentle. He moved his hands to the sides of my head, threading his fingers through my hair, making my breasts miss his touch.

"Alex." I couldn't catch my breath; he felt so good; this felt so right. "I'll never hurt you, either." It was at that point I decided I would rather live romance than just write about it.

We kissed as if we couldn't get enough of each other, our tongues exploring each other's mouths. He pulled his head away and trailed kisses down my neck, finding the spot that sent chills through me. I giggled, tipped my head down, and brought my shoulder up because it tickled.

He laughed. "Did I find a sensitive spot?" He trailed more kisses down my chest, kissing each breast, down my stomach to the top of my panties. He pulled back and rolled off me. His index finger traced the top of my panties and down my sides, grazing the outside of my thighs, to the inside of my legs. I instinctively spread my legs for him.

I looked down at him, and he was smiling. "I am going to find every sensitive spot on your body. I am going to do things to you that no man has ever done."

At that, I tensed up and closed my legs slightly. No one had ever done what he already had. *Does he think that I've had all the experience that he has? Should I not be doing this with him? Am I just like everyone else? Does he say these things to everyone?* My mind was racing. I sat up and slightly pulled away from him, totally breaking the moment.

"Aubrey? What's wrong?" He was looking at me with those dark blue eyes.

What's wrong? I was a freak and couldn't handle when a man spoke to me this way because no one ever had, and I didn't trust men. *What do I do now?* I wanted him, but I wanted him to know there had only been one other man and in no way did he do what Alex was doing.

I closed my eyes and hung my head a little. "Alex, you're right. You were touching me as no one ever has before, because no one has touched me like this." Is this not the time for this conversation? I totally suck at this. "I'm not a virgin, but I've only been with one other man, and he was in it for the sex and that's it. We were together once, my one and only time. I'm not as experienced as you are." I felt like an ass for making him sound as if he'd been with hundreds of women. Had he? I didn't think I wanted to know. My chest was starting to hurt, and my breathing was altered, not a great time for an anxiety attack. I had to tamp that down.

He moved his body up the bed so our heads were side my side, his propped up in his hand and mine on my pillow. "Look at me, Aubrey." I turned my head; I could feel my eyes misting over. "I'm glad I'm the only man who has touched you like this." He took his finger and ran it down my side and back up again. "I want to be the man who makes you feel this." He kissed the sensitive spot on my neck, making me smile. "I want my hand to be the only one feeling you like this." He moved his hand to my breast and then in between my legs. "I want to be the only man kissing you like this." His lips kissed my forehead, eyelids, the corner of my mouth, and then my lips. "Can I be that man, Aubrey?"

Could he? I really wanted him to be. "Yes." That's all I could say.

He smiled, stood, and took his shirt off. Still on the bed, I sat up on my knees. I ran my eyes and hands down the sides of his chest, down the amazing "V" leading into his shorts. I unfastened them and pulled them off him. Standing in front of me was the most gorgeous man I'd ever laid eyes on. I took in his size through his black boxer shorts and could that see his erection wanted to burst out of the waistband. I looked up at him through my eyelashes, licked my lips, and brought my upper one between my teeth.

I moved my hand to the outside of his shorts and ran it up and down his length. I peeked up and he was smiling. I decided to take this a step further. I was nervous, but I did it anyway. I took off his boxers. He was amazing, delicious. I needed to taste him.

I licked my lips and took him in my mouth. I heard him groan, which made me want him more. His hand tangled in my hair, moving my head back and forth, guiding me. He was starting to thrust in and out of my mouth, which was working along with my hand gently caressing his balls. My speed accelerated as did his thrusting. We both moaned.

"Aubrey."

"Hmmm." I was totally lost to him.

"Aubrey . . . honey."

"Hmmm."

He yanked me up and tossed me on the bed. With my legs between his, he reached over to his shorts and grabbed a condom out of the pocket.

I looked up at him. "So I was a foregone conclusion?" I giggled.

He tore the package open, and rolling it down his considerable length, said, "No, you are anything but a foregone conclusion. I was just hopeful."

He leaned down and kissed me with such passion that I thought I could orgasm right there on the spot. All my senses were on alert. He ripped off my thong and tossed it aside. I opened my eyes and noticed his were looking between my legs. He pushed my legs apart with his and rubbed me, first with one finger then two. His palm was doing things to me that I didn't know could be done.

"Alex . . . Oh my God . . . Alex . . ."

"You are so ready for me, Aubrey. I need to be inside you. I want to feel you wrapped around me." He started moving up my body so that our chests were touching.

"Yes, I need you to be inside me, please." I didn't want to wait anymore; I needed to belong to him. I spread my legs and wrapped them around his waist. He slowly entered me. I could feel every inch of him; I felt so full.

"Aubrey . . . Oh my God . . . You are so tight; you feel amazing."

He was rocking against me, sliding in and out of me, and kissing me. His tongue was mirroring his entire body's movements, making love with mine. We were moving as one. I arched my back and moaned.

"Alex, I am so close, please . . ." I couldn't catch my breath. My hands were rubbing his back, my nails now digging into his shoulders, holding on. I couldn't get enough of him. "Alex . . ."

He stopped moving and pulled out of me. I instantly missed him. He moved down my body and brought his head between my legs. His tongue and fingers worked simultaneously, driving me to the edge.

"Give it to me, Aubrey. Let go now; I want to do this for you."

I screamed out his name; I couldn't take it. My entire body was on fire; I had never felt anything so amazing in all my life. He crawled up my body with a look of satisfaction and pride on his gorgeous face. His smile said it all. I needed him back inside me. I reached down to his tight ass and urged him on top of me. He slid into me, making my head go back and roll to the side. Our chests slid against each other, and I felt myself start to tighten around him.

He pumped into me. "I'm there, sweetheart. You are amazing; you feel amazing." His mouth devoured mine between his words. "Come with me, babe. I want to do this with you." He thrust in and out, and his pace increased. I looked up, our eyes met, and he exploded inside me as I did around him. He rocked in and out until he was completely expelled. His arms lowered, and he lay on top of me. Our hearts beat together.

The feel of our sweat mixing together was intoxicating. He buried his head in the crook of my neck. He pulled out of me and rolled to his side. I immediately felt the loss. He rolled me until we faced each other.

"Aubrey, that was amazing." His kiss was tender against my lips. "You are an incredible woman. Thank you for letting me be the one to touch you." He kissed my eyelids. "Make love to you." He kissed my cheek. "Be with you." He kissed me again, this time taking my mouth as if it were giving him life. "I love having this mouth around me, on me, and screaming my name." He smiled wide.

I smiled up at him. I had no words. How could I not respond to that? I was so afraid I was going to tell him that I loved him. I didn't though. I knew I did, but I didn't want to say it then. I couldn't. Instead I hugged him and held him tight. I could feel our hearts beating against each other's.

I exhaled. "You're pretty incredible yourself." I leaned back and took in the sight of him. "Your body is breathtaking. I could look, touch, and appreciate it all day." I laughed a little, but was completely serious. I didn't want to lose this feeling. He looked at me as if he were embarrassed. No way did he not know how hot he was. "That can't be the first time you've heard that."

"No, it isn't." He kissed my nose. "It's the first time it's made me happy to hear it."

Our night ended with us just holding each other. Perfect.

Chapter 12

I HAVE TO ADMIT I didn't look too bad tonight. Alex was picking me up at six to go to the fundraiser. I made sure my makeup was just right, and I left my hair down so I wouldn't have to fuss with it if it started falling down had I put it in an up-do. I had time, so I thought I would write in my journal.

Entry 6—My Love

I made love to Alex last night. Yes, made love. We didn't have sex. We didn't fuck. It was soft, loving, and wonderful. I think I may have told him that I loved him in a roundabout kind of way before we went to bed, but I didn't say anything after that. Should I say something? Should I wait for him?

I truly love him and I am scared. What if he doesn't love me? He told me he wouldn't hurt me, and I believe him. I don't want him to say "I love you" just because I said it first. I want him to feel the same way. I've only known him a short time, and I've never believed in love at first sight, until now—until Alex.

I am scared. He scares me. He is too good to be true, but I want him to be true more than anything. I love him.

I am madly in love with Alex Logan. I hope my heart survives him.

Until tomorrow . . .

I put my journal in its place in my side table and went to the bathroom to fix my makeup. I got a little teary eyed when I was writing about Alex. I fixed my eyeliner and decided to wait for Alex in the lobby of my building. I opened the door to leave, and he was right there, ready to knock. We both jumped a little since I startled him and he me. We laughed.

I had my hand on my chest to catch my breath as my eyes took him in. He had a black three-piece tux on that had to be custom made for him. God, he was beautiful. "You are going to be turning heads tonight, Mr. Logan."

He smiled a beautiful model-white smile. "You better believe I will. When I walk in with you on my arm, heads definitely will turn. You are gorgeous, Aubrey." He leaned in and kissed me. His hands went around my waist, and he pulled me into him. Our kiss got heated, and I was sorry that we were dressed and had to leave. I could tell how he felt since his erection was pressing against my stomach. "I have something for you."

"I know. I can feel it." I smiled at him.

He laughed. "That's for later, but for now I want to give you this." He reached into his pocket and pulled out a long, slim, black velvet box.

He handed me the box. My hands were shaking. "What

is it?"

"I guess you'll have to open it." He winked.

Smiling, I raised the cover on the hinged box. My eyes immediately filled. It was a beautiful platinum bracelet with an orchid in the middle that was encrusted in white diamonds. "Alex . . ." I couldn't stop the tears that were streaming down my face. "It's beautiful."

"May I?"

I nodded, and he took the bracelet out of the box and put it on my right wrist.

I was studying it. "I love it. I love that you're sharing an orchid with me." I looked up at him.

He moved his thumb under my eye and across my cheek to wipe away my tear. I leaned into the palm of his hand. I looked into his eyes. I wanted to tell him so badly that I loved him. "I better go fix my face."

"Your face is perfect. Let's go. The car is downstairs."

He took my hand and entwined our fingers together. I looked down and wasn't sure which fingers were mine and which were his. He was the piece to my puzzle that I didn't even know was missing. He was part of my heart. I never wanted someone as much as I wanted him, and there would never be another that would make me feel like this.

We arrived at the fundraiser, and there was a red carpet outside. I was nervous. People were lined up to get in, and photographers were there. My hands twisted on my lap. "Don't be nervous, Aubrey."

I looked at him and then back out the window of the limo. "I'll try not to be, but there are so many people here. I know how important this is to you. I just don't want to trip and fall. I'm sure all the other women you've brought here were much more graceful."

"I've never brought a date to this event. It's too personal. No one mattered as much as you do. I want you here with me—only you."

I turned and looked at him. "I want to be here with you too." I wanted to tell him so badly, why wouldn't the words come out of my mouth? We stared at each other, both of us smiling. Then he put his hand on the back of my neck and pulled me in for a kiss. I didn't want the kiss to end. He had to know how I felt.

He pressed a button on the console next to him, which must have signaled the driver because he was opening my door seconds later. He helped me out of the limo, and Alex followed. He held my hand and we went in.

The ballroom was magnificent. It was decked out in black and gold. There was gold tulle draped on the ceiling and on the back of the chairs that were wrapped in white silk. There was a dance floor and a small stage for the band, which was playing background music. There was a table that had place cards on it with the guests' names and seating assignments. I wondered who we were sitting with.

We found our table, number two; it was placed near the stage and dance floor. The round tables sat about eight people, and the place settings were beautiful, which would easily accommodate a seven-course meal. In the center of each table was a floating candle with a white orchid in each one. Alex put our name cards down on the table in front of our seats.

"I have a couple more surprises for you tonight." He smiled, took my hand, and led me to the dance floor. He pulled me into him and started dancing with me. The band was playing "The Way You Look Tonight." I love that song.

There weren't any other couples dancing, but I didn't

care and neither did Alex. I looked around the room, wondering which man was his father. It seemed like a sea of tuxedos; just then, a man turned around and looked at us. I could tell by his smile that he was Jack Logan, since it matched Alex's. He looked at me and gave me a curious look.

I looked up into Alex's gorgeous navy eyes that were looking down into mine. "Did you tell your dad that you had a date tonight?"

"No, I haven't talked to my dad in a while. His assistant knows. Why?"

"Because there is an older version of you looking at us, and he doesn't look thrilled."

"It isn't you, Aubrey. That's just my dad. I'm not his favorite person. Let's finish this dance, and then I'll introduce you."

The song ended, and we walked over to his father. *Why wasn't he his favorite person?* He should be so proud of Alex. He owned a successful club, he was smart, and he was his son. I stopped walking. Alex turned around and looked at me. "What's wrong?"

"Why aren't you his favorite person?" I really hoped I wasn't overstepping.

Alex ran his hand through his hair. He pulled me over to our table, which was still empty, and he pulled out my chair for me. He sat and turned to face me; he took my hands in his. "Aubrey, when I was young, my dad was never around. He was always at work." I just looked at him. "I know what you're thinking. I work a lot too, but I'm not married with kids. Anyway, my mom did everything for my sister and me. She drove me to my baseball and lacrosse games and drove my sister, Ellie, to her dance recitals. The day they got in the accident that's where she was going. She was taking Ellie to her recital. My dad should have been driving the car, but he was out of town on business. It was a Saturday and his priority was work. He should have been with us. Who knows if the accident could have been avoided or if the timing would have been different, and . . ."

I put my hand on his left cheek. "Alex, you don't have to tell me this. I can see it's hard on you."

"No, I want you to know. I blamed my dad. We had a huge blowout. It was horrible. I felt as if I lost my entire family that day. Ever since then, for the past sixteen years, we've learned to co-exist, and that is about it. He wanted me to join his business, to fulfill his dream of leaving it to me as his legacy. I wanted nothing to do with it, so I opened the club, exactly the opposite of what he wanted me to do. His legacy should have been being a good father and husband, not being a rich businessman."

I nodded and tried to absorb everything. "You were twelve, Alex. Naturally, you'd be upset and look to blame someone. How are things now?"

"We talk occasionally. He knows that I want nothing to do with his business, but at the end of the day, he is my father, so let me introduce you."

We stood up, and Alex steered me in the direction of his father with his hand at the small of my back. We reached his dad, who was talking to an older couple. They turned and saw us. I looked up at Alex. He looked a little tense.

Alex kissed the woman on her cheek and extended his hand to the man. "Patrick, Nancy, I'd like you to meet my girlfriend, Aubrey Ryan. Aubrey, this is Patrick and Nancy McManus." We shook hands.

Nancy looked surprised. "It's very nice to meet you,

Aubrey. I didn't know Alex had a girlfriend." She leaned toward me. "He's going to break a lot of hearts tonight with that news."

I just smiled. I wasn't sure what that meant. My heart was the only one I was worried about breaking. His father walked up to Alex. "Son, it's good to see you. Who is this lovely young lady?"

"Hi, Dad, this is Aubrey Ryan, my girlfriend."

"Girlfriend? My boy is off the market?" He chuckled and extended his hand to me. "It's a pleasure, Aubrey."

"Hello, Mr. Logan, it's nice to meet you too." I started feeling self-conscious.

"Please call me Jack." He smiled and I reciprocated.

"The room looks nice, Dad. And it looks as if there's going to be a good turn out."

I glanced around the room. It was starting to fill up. There had to be 300 people here. I looked at the door and could have sworn I saw Julie. I wished she were there. Then I remembered that Walker-Stone had a table at the event, but that usually meant the executives would attend. *I could use someone on my side tonight.* I also hoped that Nancy and Patrick were not at our table. Nancy rubbed me the wrong way.

"We should probably go to our table now." Alex took my hand, and we said good-bye to Patrick and Nancy. His dad shook Alex's hand.

"We should get together soon, son. Bring Aubrey over, and we can have dinner one night."

Alex looked puzzled. "We'll see, Dad." And we walked away.

Walking to our table, we were stopped by a few more people. Alex introduced me as his girlfriend to everyone. I really liked the sound of it, but wasn't particularly pleased with the reactions I was getting, not to mention that most of the reactions were from older women. What was that about? I'd have to ask him later. I did notice plenty of women who eyed my man. I couldn't blame them really. He looked delectable, but he was mine. I held on to him tighter.

We went to our table, and I noticed that it was still empty. Alex's phone beeped. He must have received a text because he was typing back. I looked up to see Brett, Julie, and Mark walking toward us. I looked at Alex and he smiled. "Surprise!"

I leaned over and kissed him. Julie looked gorgeous. She had a floor-length black satin gown on, and her hair was up in a perfect twist. Brett and Mark looked amazing in their tuxedos. Julie sauntered up to me.

"How awesome is your boyfriend? He sent us an invitation and even sent a car to get us. How fantastic is that?" She kissed me on the cheek and then planted one on Alex's. "Thank you, Alex. This is amazing."

Brett shook Alex's hand and gave me a quick hug and kiss on the cheek. "Good to see you, man. Thanks for the invite and ride over. I thought Julie was going to pop something; she was so excited for this. Aubrey, you look beautiful. Take care of my man here."

I smiled. I looked at Mark, who looked a little uncomfortable. I turned toward him and gave him my best smile. "Hi, Mark, I'm so surprised that you're here."

"Hey, Aubrey, you look great." He turned to Alex and extended his hand. "It's nice seeing you again. Thank you for the invitation."

Alex shook his hand. "I'm glad you could make it." They took their seats at our table. I felt bad because there was an empty seat between Alex and Mark, where Jessica should have been.

I turned to Alex. "Thank you for inviting them."

He smiled he leaned in to whisper in my ear, "You know what, Aubrey?"

I looked at him and smiled. I could feel my cheeks blushing. "What?"

"I'm happy. You make me very happy."

His breath was so warm. I could feel it on my neck. His cologne was amazing. He smelled so good, but he always did. I leaned into his ear. "You make me happy too, Alex." He pulled me in for a kiss.

Brett cleared his throat. "Uh, guys, want to keep it PG before the old folks around here need to restart their pacemakers?" We all laughed.

There was a tap on the microphone, and Alex's dad was on the stage. "I would like to thank everyone for coming tonight. We are all here to support a very important cause that is near to my heart and my son's. He would like to say a few words. Alex."

I didn't know that he was going to be speaking tonight. Alex kissed me, stood, and walked over to the stage. I looked around the room and felt that all eyes were on me. I shifted in my chair and kept my eyes on my boyfriend.

Alex took the mic. "Thank you, Dad." He cleared his throat and looked out to the guests. "Education to prevent drunk driving affects all of us. Thirty-one percent of car accidents are related to drunk driving." He looked nervous and confident at the same time. I wanted to go and hug him. "Approximately 10,000 people died last year alone." He looked down as if he were gathering his thoughts. "As some of you know, I lost my mother Angela and sister Ellie at the hands of a drunk driver." He cleared his throat again. "Thanks to many causes against drunk driving and educating the public, the number of yearly fatalities has decreased. As my dad said, we want to thank you for coming this evening. This is a good cause and one that is very personal to me." He looked up at me, and I could tell he was starting to struggle. I nodded and smiled. He smiled back. "Ladies and gentleman, have a good time this evening, open your wallets, and donate for a wonderful cause. Life is too short not to make a difference, and through your generosity, we can save lives. Thank you."

Alex walked off the stage and everyone applauded. The band started playing as the wait staff brought out our salads. I stood when Alex reached our table. "That was really nice. Are you okay?" I worried about him and how difficult that had to be.

"Having you with me makes everything okay, even dealing with my dad. I hate public speaking, and he makes me do it every year. Every year, I say the same thing. I hate it. What I want to say is take care of your loved ones, be there when you need them, and put them first. I think my dad would get the message then that I don't want to speak about it in front of people. I love the cause and donate to it, but making me talk about it . . . Well, it pisses me off quite frankly.

I nodded and we sat down to start on our salads. The rest of the food made its way around, and it definitely was a seven-course meal. I was starting to wonder how much each plate cost. They had to make a lot of money tonight.

The food was fantastic as was the company. I didn't eat too much for fear that I would pop a seam in my dress. Our plates were cleared, and the band was starting to get people on the dance floor. Brett and Julie left the table first.

I felt bad for Mark. I was going to ask Alex if he would be upset if I danced with Mark, when I heard a familiar voice. I looked up and saw Valerie.

"Alex, that speech was lovely." I rolled my eyes and looked over at Mark, who was looking at Valerie. She was rubbing Alex's shoulder.

Mark then looked at me and I shrugged. "Valerie, you remember my girlfriend, Aubrey, and this is Mark."

"Yes, hello, Aubrey, I didn't realize you came with a title now." She looked toward Mark and nodded.

She was such a bitch to me, but on some level, she seemed nice. I idly wondered if she knew Leah.

Alex stood and held his hand out to me. "Dance with me." It wasn't a question, and I was more than happy to get away from Valerie.

I took Alex's hand and looked to Mark. "Excuse us." Mark smiled. I knew he was genuinely happy for me.

On the dance floor, I looked at Alex and then back to the table where Valerie was now sitting next to Mark.

Alex ran his fingers through my hair and looked into my eyes. "What's wrong?"

"Oh nothing, well, no, that's not true. I'm wondering if Valerie plans on going for Mark now or if she is going to continue coming on to you, even in my presence."

He twirled me and spun me around, making me laugh. "Aubrey, I don't care about Valerie that way. I want you, and if she wants to go after Mark, I have no problem with that."

"I guess I just don't want him getting hurt." What I really wanted to say was, if they get together, I wanted it to be because of Mark, not as an excuse to hang with us.

We danced another song and walked back to the table.

Mark was getting up to leave. "Thanks again, Alex, this was very nice."

Shaking hands with Mark, Alex said, "I'm glad you could make it. I'll have my driver take you home."

"That's okay; I can grab a cab, but thanks."

I wondered what happened to Valerie, but I took it as a good sign that she was gone if she was into Mark for the wrong reasons. I hugged Mark good-bye and told him I would see him when I came back from my trip.

Alex pulled me into his arms. "Want to get out of here?" He smiled, and I could feel myself throb between my legs.

I looked at his beautiful eyes. "Most definitely."

Chapter 13

WE SAID OUR GOOD-BYES TO Jack and some other guests. We spotted Julie and Brett looking as if they were going to start dirty dancing at any minute. Julie caught my eye, and I nodded toward the door. She smiled and whispered in Brett's ear, and they left with us.

The leather seats of the limo were a welcome feeling. The event was nice, but draining. I knew it took a toll on Alex. The relationship with his father was definitely strained and so were the looks I was getting from women of all ages. Julie must have picked up on it too since she blurted out, "Boy, Aubrey, you were not a favorite among the ladies tonight."

The three of us looked at her. Brett grabbed her hand, and I looked at Alex then back to Julie. "I picked up on that too. Alex, what is the deal with that Nancy woman? She did not look pleased at all to hear that I was your girlfriend."

Alex looked at Brett with a worried look, and Brett shrugged his shoulders. "Your man is popular, Aubrey. All the moms in town want him with their daughters. You just took one of New York's most eligible bachelors off the market."

My mouth fell open a little. I knew that women liked him and I knew why, but to hear he was considered one of New York's most eligible bachelors? I had no idea. I guess if I had gotten out more and took my head out of my books, I would have known this. All I could say was "oh." I was so eloquent.

Alex picked up my hand and kissed the back of it. "I could care less what anyone thinks or who they want me to be with. I know what I think and who I want to be with." He smiled that panty-wetting smile of his. I rested my head on his shoulder.

The car came to a stop; I looked out the window and noticed we were at the guys' apartment building. I looked back at Alex.

He winked. "I thought we could spend tonight at my place."

I smiled and the driver opened the door. We all got out and headed toward the elevator. Julie and Brett were laughing about some guy who was drunk at the bar, telling bad jokes. I was so happy for Julie. She was totally falling or had fallen for Brett. We got in the elevator, and Alex invited Julie and Brett up for a night cap. Part of me didn't want them to come, but I really needed to spend time with my best friend. I looked at Julie with pleading eyes; she answered for them and said, "Yes."

We walked into Alex's apartment. It was gorgeous, really not what I expected. It was spotless, and I thought he must have a cleaning person. The palette of the apartment was gray, black, and white. It was crisp and contemporary. There was a picture of a white orchid hanging in the dining room. He had a black leather couch in the middle of the living area with glass coffee and side tables. There were travel books on the coffee table and a little statue of the Eiffel Tower on his mantle, which reminded me about our impending trip. His kitchen was off to the left. It was large for an apartment, but then again the apartment wasn't like any apartment I had ever seen. I thought Brett's was large, but compared to Alex's, it didn't seem that big anymore. I lazily wondered what his bedroom looked like, but thought I would stow that thought for a while.

Alex poured Julie and me a glass of wine and grabbed beers for himself and Brett. Brett and Alex were sitting on the couch when Brett noticed one of the brochures for the winery we'd be visiting in Tuscany asked Alex about it. This opened a window of opportunity for me because I needed to talk to Julie. We excused ourselves, and I pulled Julie toward the sliding glass door leading to the balcony. I told the guys I wanted to see the view, and what a view it was. I could see Central Park, and the skyline was adorning it.

I closed the door behind us. Julie looked at me curiously. "What's up? You look as if you're going to burst."

"I'm just so happy, Jules. I really am. I had no idea I could find this with Alex; I really think he could be the one! I just wanted to share that with you." I thought my cheeks were going to explode from my wide smile.

She grabbed me and hugged me. I almost spilled my wine. "I'm so happy for you guys! It's really soon though, are you sure?"

Way to burst my bubble of bliss! "Yes, I'm sure. I didn't expect it at all. When this started, I had one intention and that was to write my book, but that doesn't even matter anymore. I don't see romance the same way anymore. All the sweet things Alex does are romantic: a kiss on my cheek, his smile, and the way he looks at me. He is romance; he is my romantic hero. I don't need to write about a fictional one; I have a real one in him."

Julie had a giddy look in her eyes. "Wow, you got it bad! Did you tell him about the book? He'd probably laugh about it."

"No, and I am not going to. I don't know if he'd laugh about it. He's been let down before by someone who loved him. I can't do it again." I was thinking about his father. "I thought about it, but what good would it do, especially if writing is the furthest thing from my mind right now."

Julie looked down and grabbed my arm, looking at the wrist with the bracelet on it. "Um . . . What's this?"

"It's gorgeous, right? Alex gave it to me tonight."

"It's beautiful, Aubrey." She was examining it and turning my arm in all directions. "Let's get back to our men. All this happy talk is making me want to get into Brett's pants." We both laughed and walked into the living room.

"There they are." Brett stood and grabbed Julie and kissed her hard. "Ready, babe?"

Julie and Brett left. Alex swept me into his arms, carrying me. He carried me down a hallway leading to his bedroom. He walked in, put me down, and I looked around the room. It was gorgeous. He had a beautiful king-size bed made of dark wood that looked inviting.

"I've wanted to get you in here all night." He kissed me, and our tongues were twisting with each other's. I loved the way he tasted, and I could smell the orchids that I noticed in a vase on our way in and wondered if he bought them assuming I'd see them. He reached around my back and unzipped my gown; it fell to the floor and landed around my feet. I stepped back and out of my gown, standing in my royal blue corset and garter set. Since I was still wearing my high heels, I felt amazing. He stood back and looked at me. "Aubrey, you are breathtaking."

"I want you, Alex. I want you so much. I've been fantasizing about getting you out of this tux. May I?"

He was moving his hands up and down my arms. He smiled and put his hands out to the side. "Be my guest."

Biting my top lip, I dragged my tongue over it, my eyes never leaving his. I took his jacket off and tossed it, untied his bow tie, removed his cufflinks, and slowly unbuttoned his shirt, which not only frustrated him but me as well. I didn't want to rush this. I opened his shirt, and the sight of his abs made my mouth water. Deciding to tease him a little more, I put my right hand on his chest, ran it down to his waist band, and back up to his broad shoulders. I brought my hand around to his chest and then his back, leaving a trail of kisses where my hand had just been. I closed my eyes and could feel every muscle. When I opened my eyes, I noticed a tattoo on his back near his left shoulder. It was an orchid with angel wings. Each wing had a name in it: Angela in one and Ellie in the other. I kissed his tattoo and he shivered. He must have realized what I had just seen. I couldn't believe I hadn't noticed it last night.

I continued my pleasure circle until I was standing in front of him. I glanced at him and went to my knees. "Aubrey . . ." His breath was ragged; I loved it.

"No talking, Alex." I unbuckled his belt and unbuttoned his pants, pulling them down along with his boxers. He sprung free. I couldn't help but smile. I gripped him and moved my hand up and down his length. I licked the tip and around the ridge of its crown. I was running my fingertips up and down, teasing, and I could feel him stiffen as I continued my exploration. I took him in my mouth, my tongue now where my hand was. I really wanted to do this for him and for me too.

Alex's hands were now threaded through my hair, and he was holding me to him. He was moaning, which was giving me the encouragement to continue my ravishment. He tasted so good. I was moving quicker now, licking and sucking him as if he were going to disappear. I held his ass in my hands and what a fine ass it was! God, I loved this man with everything I had.

"Aubrey . . . If you don't want me to . . . Mmmm . . . Oh . . . I'm going to . . . Aubrey . . ."

I moaned and sucked harder. My tongue was moving on its own up and down his vein. He gripped my hair and I felt him explode. His salty warmth slid down my throat and on my tongue; it was amazing. I sat back on my heels and just looked at him as if he could go again. He helped me up and put his arms around my waist. I glanced up, and the look on his face was one I had never seen before.

"That was . . . I don't know what that was . . . fantastic, amazing, the best . . . Aubrey . . ." Alex exhaled, ran his fingers across my forehead, and brought his knuckles down my cheek.

"I am glad you enjoyed that." I couldn't help but sound prideful. "I'll assume by your reaction that it was good for my first time doing that." I glanced up at him and licked my lips.

"You've never done that before?"

I shook my head. "Nope, I never wanted to. I never wanted anyone the way I want you."

Alex was smiling, and his eyes were full of lust and

hunger. "I'm glad that I'm the one you want, and speaking of wanting, you are way over dressed. I love what you're wearing, but I'd rather look at your naked body." He kissed my shoulder. His hands went to my back and unfastened my corset. It fell away to the floor. His mouth went to my right breast while his hand was squeezing and pulling on my left nipple. I felt myself get hot between my legs. He alternated between each breast, and I didn't even notice he was walking me toward the bed until my legs hit it, making me sit on the edge. Alex knelt down and removed my shoes one at a time. He unhooked my stockings and rolled them down, sending goose bumps up and down my legs. He picked up my foot and licked the instep and ran his tongue up my right leg. He pulled my thong down and tossed it next to my gown. "Lie back, Aubrey."

My back was on the bed, and my ass was hanging half off of it. He put my right leg on his left shoulder. He brought his mouth closer to my center and blew lightly on me; I could feel my juices releasing just from that move. I moaned and he lifted my left leg, bringing it up on his other shoulder. His thumbs spread me open, and they were gently rubbing me. I was feeling totally exposed. No one had ever done this to me or made me feel as if they wanted to. Garrett was a wham-bam-thank-you-ma'am kind of guy. Alex most certainly wasn't, so I was unsure what to expect. "You're so amazing, Aubrey."

"Mmm hmm" was all I could say. I knew I was ready. I could feel myself throbbing as if I were calling him into me.

He ran his tongue from the bottom of my slit to the top and around my clit. He started rubbing his thumbs on the outside of my entrance. He slid one in then pulled it out and replaced it with his tongue. My hand went into his hair. He was thrusting his tongue in and out while his thumb was rubbing me. My hips moved in unison with him, and the building pressure felt incredible.

"Alex, I'm going to . . ." I didn't have the words. I was literally panting. This felt better than any experience I'd ever had. I could feel my body respond to everything he did.

"Give it to me, Aubrey; I want to taste every bit of you."

That did it. I exploded and yelled his name, and my legs vibrated on his shoulders. My eyes were closed and I saw spots. I opened my eyes, and Alex was moving us both onto the bed until our heads were on the pillows. He rolled toward me and kissed me. I could taste myself on his lips. I wasn't sure if I liked the taste, but I did like that we were mixed together. He moved the comforter and sheets, until we were under them.

His hand was running through my hair, and he was staring at me. I wanted him so badly. I needed to make love to this man. "Make love to me." My request was out there, waiting for him to comply.

He kissed me and said he needed to go grab a condom. I didn't want him to. I wanted to feel him. "Alex, it's okay. I'm on the pill, and I've only been with one other man, and we used protection."

"I've always used protection, Aubrey. I've never considered being with someone without it . . . until now, until you."

"Well then, I guess we're all set." I smiled and kissed him.

He rolled me on my back and looked at me as he entered me. I was so slick and he was so hard that we fused perfectly. He rocked back and forth. The feeling was amazing and something I'd never forget.

"Aubrey, you feel as if you were meant for me. I can feel every inch of you around me. You feel so perfect."

He was thrusting faster, licking from my neck down to the swell of my breasts and back up my neck to my sensitive spot, making me flinch. He chuckled and caressed my breasts with his tongue. He teased, kissed, and licked every inch of me. I felt the buildup that was happening in my core and pulsed around him.

"Aubrey, I'm going to come. My God, Aubrey, are you ready?"

"Yes, Alex, now please." We both came together, and with our bodies slammed together, we both cried out. My fingers grabbed his ass and moved up until my arms were tight around his neck. Our sweat was slick, and we were both breathing heavily. I let go and rested against the pillow. He lowered himself so he was on top of me and kissed me. He held my head between his hands.

In my head, I was thinking, "I love you, Alex." I just couldn't say it out loud.

I needed to get up. I was afraid of what I would say. "I'll be right back." I headed toward the bathroom."

"Don't take too long." I looked back at him. His hands were clasped behind his head, and he looked as though he'd just conquered the world. I couldn't help but be mesmerized by his chest, arms, and face. He definitely had the total package.

I got cleaned up and wiped the eyeliner and mascara off from underneath my eyes. As I looked in the mirror, I couldn't believe all of this was happening to me. If I hadn't wanted to write a romance novel and hadn't confided in Julie, I never would have gone to the Speed Dating event and thus never would have met Alex. It's so funny how things turn out. I went back into the bedroom, and Alex was still in the same position. I just laughed at the shit-eating grin on his face. He looked edible.

I climbed on the bed and cuddled up next to him. I propped my head on my hand and started making circles on his magnificent chest with my fingers. "What's that look for?"

He took my hand and kissed my knuckles and then each finger one by one. "I was just thinking how lucky I am that you came into my life." He looked at the bracelet on my arm and exhaled. His eyes became sad. "I wish you could have met my mom. She would be so happy that I found you." His fingers were softly trailing up and down my arm.

"I would've loved to have known her too. Want to tell me about her?"

He kissed my bracelet and held my hand to his chest. "My mom was the best. I played lacrosse when I was younger, and I was very good. I was playing on the Junior Varsity team when I was in the seventh grade. She came to all my games, never missed one. She was everything to me. She was about five foot five, had dark hair and brown eyes, and had a beautiful smile. Everyone used to say we had the same smile."

He looked up to the ceiling, as if he were looking into heaven, remembering her smile.

"She was wonderful and a very giving person. She helped watch the neighbor kids when their parents worked since my mom was home because my dad didn't want her working. It was too bad because she was a talented interior designer, but my dad didn't like the way it looked if my mom worked." Alex shook his head.

"He should have been proud of my mom; I was. All my friends called her Mom and thought I was the luckiest kid around. My sister, Ellie, was five years older than I was. I always thought she was lucky because she spent more time with Mom. She even got to be with her when she died." A tear ran down his cheek.

I rolled on top of him and kissed his tear away. "She sounds like she was wonderful, Alex. I think she was lucky to have a son like you, just as I'm lucky to have you." I laid my head on his heart, and we held each other, the beat beneath my ear lulling me to sleep.

Chapter 14

I WAS HOME, MAKING SURE I had all my things packed for the trip. Alex, Julie, and Brett were expected to pick me up within the hour. I was so excited. I'd had a great weekend with Alex. We spent Sunday together going over what we needed for the trip, and Alex made sure to tell me that he was going to take me shopping while we were in Europe. I couldn't imagine shopping in Italy and Paris. I hadn't written in my journal in a couple of days, so I figured now would be a good time.

Entry 7—Alex—My Everything

Saturday night Alex took me to a fundraiser supporting Education against Drunk Drivers, and he gave a speech that I knew was difficult for him. I wish I could have held his hand while he spoke, but I am sure that would have turned some heads. Speaking of heads, boy did they turn! I knew Alex was a good catch, but I never thought he was considered the one to catch. To me, he was Alex, my Alex. He is my world now, and I would give up anything for him, just as I am giving up the notion of writing my romance novel about a man and the romantic things he does or doesn't do. Alex is everything romantic: his smile, the way he looks at me, his touches, just everything. I think I would die if I didn't have his touches. I fell fast for Alex, and his wanting me is extraordinary.

I met his dad, and I feel bad for the way they are with each other. I can tell they are both hurting in different ways, but some are the same too. They both lost what sounds like two wonderful women; Alex resents his dad for it and misses his mom and sister terribly. I am sure that his dad feels horrible too. It's sad because they lost each other during this time, and it should have brought them together. Families are funny that way. Alex will be meeting my parents next week. That should be interesting.

Until I return!!

I closed my journal and tossed it in my drawer. My parents were beyond excited that I was coming to Paris and bringing friends with me. I hadn't told my mom that Alex was my boyfriend because when I'd told her we were visiting, I wasn't sure what we were to each other. I knew my mom, and if I'd told her I loved Alex, I would have gotten the third degree and Alex would have gotten worse than that. I suppose when we got there she would find out, but maybe by seeing us together, she'd be more accepting of the idea instead of me just springing it on her.

I looked at the clock and figured Alex should be at my place soon. I knew Brett and Julie were already with him. I went through my carry-on bag for the hundredth time, verifying I had my ID, passport, cell-phone charger with a European adapter, and my parents' info. I also had my laptop and some other things for work.

I was going crazy waiting in my apartment, so I decided to head down to the lobby to wait for them there. I took the elevator down, and as soon as the door opened, I saw Julie. "We're going to Europe today!" She was yelling and jumping up and down.

All I could do was laugh. I love Julie; she's the best. "How awesome is this, Jules? We get to be together and with our men. If you'd told me a month ago that his would be happening, I wouldn't have believed you. Where are the guys?"

"They're in the car. They told me to come get you. I think they wanted me out of there because I was bouncing around the car like a lunatic. But, come on, we are going to Europe!" She grabbed both my hands in hers and started swinging me around in a circle as if we were kids.

"Okay, okay! Let's get to the car so we can get to Europe." I wheeled my bag and Julie took my carry-on.

We arrived at the airport, and Alex had purchased us first-class tickets. I was so surprised. I'd never flown first class before. The plane was great. The seats reclined all the way to look like a bed. It was as if we had our own room with a TV monitor, charging station, really nice pillows, and blankets. The seats were lined up one in front of the other. Alex was behind me rather than next to me. I was a little sad because I wanted to hold his hand during the flight and cuddle with him. But, who was I to complain? This was awesome.

We sat down and buckled up per our flight attendants' instructions, Alex knocked on the back of my seat. I unbuckled and propped myself up so I could see him. He was so gorgeous. "As soon as that fasten seatbelt light is off, I'm coming up there. Be ready. This is an overnight flight." He winked and I couldn't help but smile. I was so happy.

I sat back down and clicked my seat belt. I was staring at the seatbelt light, willing it to turn off, and we weren't even in the air yet. I grabbed the magazine that was provided and started glancing at the movies that were going to be shown on this flight. I had seen most of them, so I figured I'd just listen to music and read.

We were in the air and were being served dinner, which I had never received on a plane. The flight attendant brought me my tray, and there was a white orchid in a vase. I looked up at her and she smiled; then she looked at Alex and winked. My smile broadened knowing he'd done this. He was the ultimate romantic boyfriend.

The dinner was actually good, which surprised me since I'd heard horror stories about airplane food. I had a glass of wine too, it was awesome. I took the flower out of the vase and held it when my tray was removed. I turned to thank Alex, and he was sitting in his seat with his left leg bent over his right and his chin propped up in his hand. He had the most genuine smile. He definitely looked pleased with himself, but there was something else: contentment.

"Thank you for the flower. I love it." I had it in my hand, so I lowered my nose to it and inhaled. "This scent . . . I love that it reminds me of you." I smiled and turned back into my seat. I put my headphones back on, closed my eyes, and held the flower to my cheek.

The sky was darkening; it was getting late. I reclined my seat and looked up to see the fasten seat belt sign turn off. I smiled. I covered myself with the blanket and settled into what I now considered my bed for the night. I heard Alex talking to the flight attendant. I couldn't hear what they were saying, but she had a huge smile on her face when she walked by me.

I smelled him before I saw him. I needed to ask what cologne he wore, or maybe it was just the scent of my orchid. I rolled to my side, and he slid in next to me. We were facing each other. "Hey, babe," he whispered.

God, he was sexy as hell. "Hey, what are you doing?"

"Kissing my girl and then going to sleep."

"I don't know that the flight attendant would approve."

He was kissing me on my neck and around my ear. "She lives in the city, so I offered her unlimited VIP access to the club if she ignores us. I told her I didn't want to get her in trouble, but if she could do what she could, it would be appreciated."

He looked proud of himself that he was able to work this out. He covered himself with the blanket and held my hand until we started our descent. Sadly, he had to return to his seat, but we'd been lucky to lie next to each other all night.

Chapter 15

THE SUN WAS SHINING, AND the city of Tuscany was amazing. This had to be one of the most beautiful places I had ever seen. The landscape of rolling hills and bricked streets was just amazing. Everything about it was fantastic, even the people; they were all so nice and friendly. It was different from New York. There weren't horns blowing, and people weren't racing around, not caring about who was in their way.

It was calm, almost serene. Alex was holding my hand and Brett was holding Julie's as we walked into the villa that Alex had rented. I couldn't believe how gorgeous it was. The marble foyer was grand, but not over the top. There was a country-style kitchen and an expansive living area with couches and occasional chairs. The home was decorated in rich earth tones; it was welcoming and warm. Julie loved the villa as well. "Dude, this place rocks! Thank you so much for bringing us here! Look. You can see the sea and there is a pool; it's unbelievable, Alex!"

Alex laughed. "I'm glad you like it and that you and Aubrey could join us. Your marketing strategies are the key for us being successful; we need you both here for this."

Julie realized she'd just called him "Dude." "Um, yes,

of course, Alex, I didn't mean to imply that we were on a vacation." She stepped into her professional persona. "We'll work very hard to make sure that this venture is a success. That's our primary goal and objective. We're here for you and your business, sir."

What the hell had just happened to her? Was it jet lag? All the three of us could do was stare at her. Brett had his head tilted to the side like a dog when you call its name. I think if he could have made his ears move he would have. I stood there with my mouth slightly opened. Alex had one arm across his chest and the other hand propping up his chin. He looked the most serious, and he was the first one to laugh. Brett and I followed.

"Geez, Julie, lighten up!" Alex was laughing. "I know this is technically a business trip, but we're all friends, and I want us all to have a good time while we're here. Although, if you could refrain from calling me "dude" in front of potential business associates, that would be great. He shoved her shoulder.

We spent the next few days visiting wineries in Northern and Southern Italy. Between the wine and the food, I was sure I gained ten pounds. Alex and Brett made great contacts with some of the wineries, and Julie was busy taking photos and gathering the necessary information she would need to come up with a great marketing plan. I was helping Julie. My experience really wasn't needed until Julie wrote all the copy for the plan. When we were leaving Sicily and on our way to Paris, I was a nervous wreck. I could only imagine what my parents were going to think. I told them I was coming on business, but I knew that when I introduced Alex as my boyfriend it would be a surprise to them. Hell, it was a surprise for me.

We checked in to the hotel where Alex had rented us a suite. The hotel was amazing. The lobby was incredible, adorned with copper and beautiful columns. The staircase was curved and expansive. I imagined a bride coming down the staircase while the train of her white gown followed behind her. We took this grand staircase to our suite; all the while I was imagining me in that flowing gown. I looked over at Alex, so self-assured and amazing; yeah, I could definitely picture it.

Alex unlocked the door to our room, and before I could look around, he lifted me up. My legs instinctively wrapped around him, and he grabbed me and pushed me up against the door. I could feel the panels of the door on my back. I instinctively reached for the doorknob for support, but he whispered that he had me. Boy, did he have me! I tightened my legs around him, and my elbows rested on his shoulders, my fingers in his hair.

"I need you, Aubrey, right now." He feverishly kissed me; his tongue darted in and out of my mouth then down my neck, sucking my pulse. I felt his arousal press between my legs. His hands kneaded my breasts; I was going to lose it.

"Ahhh . . . Alex . . . I'm . . . going . . . to . . . ahhh. I want to feel you, Alex." I lifted his shirt off, and he followed suit with mine.

He pulled down the cups of my bra, freeing my breasts, which welcomed the cool air. Our chests rubbed together while my hands explored his back. He had me pinned so tightly against the door that I thought I could go through it. His thighs held me up so that I hardly needed to hang on.

I moved my hands to his pants; I needed them off. He sensed my need for him. He gripped me around the waist and carried me to the bedroom. He tossed me on the bed, stepped back, and looked at me. I was lying there in just my jeans and my bra, which was only half on; my eyes were fixed on him.

His gaze became animalistic. "Strip for me."

My heart pounded at his voice and command. "What?"

"I said, 'Strip for me.'"

I stood up next to the bed. Alex leaned against the wall a few feet away. He had his arms crossed, and his eyes were full of lust. I focused on him. I wasn't sure I could do this, but I wasn't going to let him down.

I stared into his eyes. I licked my lips and ran my hand down my stomach until I reached the button on my jeans. I slowly unbuttoned them, turned around, bent over, and lowered them. I heard him take in a breath, and I knew I was affecting him. My ass was in the air, and my hair was grazing the floor. I took the opportunity to look around my leg and glance at him as I stepped out of my jeans. He looked as if he were in a trance. Good. This was working. I reached for my panties and lowered them next. I stood and turned to him. I slowly walked toward him, unhooking my bra in the process. I lowered the straps with my fingertips, one arm at a time. I held on to the strap with my index finger and extended my arm. I dropped the bra to the ground, and it landed at his feet. His eyes followed it all the way down. I stood there naked. His eyes roamed my body. "You're beautiful."

He quickly removed his jeans and boxers. He picked me up, and I found myself pinned to the wall that he had just leaned on. My left leg was supported by his right arm. He thrust two fingers inside me. I bucked up against him. I needed him.

"Take me to bed."

He spun me around, and before I knew it, I felt the cool sheets against my back. He flipped us over and moved me on top of him. His hands were kneading my breasts, and I was rubbing my sex up and down his stiff length, coating him. He felt amazing; I felt . . . Alex.

I took his arms by the wrists and held them down on the mattress. I positioned myself so his erection was pushing into me. I took him all the way in and felt completely full. I lay on him, chest to chest, and kissed his jawline, feeling his light scruff on my lips. I kissed the corner of his mouth and he smiled. I straightened my arms to look at him. I couldn't get over the beauty this man possessed. He had a light tan from all the outdoor winery tours we'd enjoyed, and he was sporting a five o'clock shadow, which looked beyond sexy.

I straightened myself and sat up on him. I threw my head back and started to raise and lower my hips. I rode him until I could feel myself tighten around him. I knew I was reaching my peak. I moved faster with determination.

He put his thumb on my clit and rubbed it. "Massage your breasts, Aubrey."

I did. It felt good and odd at the same time. I'd never touched myself, well, not when I wasn't alone, so I stopped.

"I said, 'Massage your breasts, Aubrey.'"

Again I complied; it did something to both of us. His hands went to my hips, and his fingers gripped my ass. He was making me go faster, and he was thrusting into me. "Alex . . . I . . ."

"You feel so good, babe. Come for me . . . now."

We both exploded. I could feel his heat, and I was clenching and shaking around him. I felt sated and exhausted. I collapsed on him. He held my face in his hand, holding my hair back. "The things that you do to me, babe, and the way you make me feel are incredible; you're incredible."

I honestly didn't ever think I'd ever get sick of hearing those words. He thought I was incredible. Why couldn't I just say it? I love you, Alex. See, I could think it, but I couldn't get the words out.

I kissed his lips. I didn't want this feeling to end, but I eased him out of me and got out of bed. I grabbed his hand and tugged it toward me. "Let's shower; we're meeting my parents soon, unless you've changed your mind."

In a way, I hoped he had. My mother could be difficult, and that was putting it mildly.

"Never, I want to meet them and thank them for you."

"Are you real?"

He was pulling me toward the bathroom. "Come shower with me, and I'll show you how real I am."

I followed him into the shower where we made love again.

Chapter 16

WE WERE MEETING MY PARENTS at a small intimate restaurant that our concierge had told us had delectable French cuisine. The owner was an American, which was good because some of the menus I looked at were rather scary to me, but this one looked great.

My parents were already there when we arrived. My mom saw me and waved so I would see her. I kept hoping that she would keep her cool once she met Alex and Brett. Both were wonderful male specimens, and a woman would have to be blind not to notice. They knew Julie, so that helped me relax. She knew how to handle my mom better than I did on most days.

We walked up to their table, and my mom pulled me into a hug. "It's so great to see you, honey." Then Dad hugged me while I was still hugging Mom. She looked over my shoulder. "Hi, Julie, sweetheart, you look beautiful." She really did. She had on a blue-and-white striped maxi dress, and her hair was perfectly cascading over her shoulders.

"Hi, Mr. and Mrs. Ryan, it's great to see you."

"Oh, Julie, please call us Tom and Jill." Julie just smiled.

I grabbed Alex's hand and brought him closer to my

parents. "Mom and Dad, I'd like you to meet," I took a deep breath, "Alex Logan . . . my boyfriend; Alex, these are my parents, Tom and Jill."

Alex shook both of their hands. "It's a pleasure to meet you. Thank you for letting us join you for lunch."

Mom looked at Alex with wide eyes and then to me. "It's our pleasure. We were unaware that Aubrey had a boyfriend. I thought you were all business associates."

Oh boy, here we go. I pulled Brett into the picture. "This is Brett; he works with Alex and also happens to be Julie's boyfriend." If I had to go through a ration of shit, I thought I'd bring Julie along with me. They shook hands and we all sat down.

Mom started on her maternal inquisition. "So Alex, Aubrey told me she was coming to Paris to go to some vineyards. What type of business do you own?"

"I own a night club in Manhattan called The White Orchid, and we're expanding to include a wine room. That's why we're in Europe. Julie and Aubrey are heading up the marketing efforts."

I saw my mom's nose turn up.

"A night club, hmm." She leaned over to my dad and in a snotty tone said, "Tom, he owns a night club."

"Yes, I heard him, Jill." My dad took a sip of what I assumed was a Manhattan.

I just smiled at Dad and squeezed Alex's hand. He squeezed mine back, turned to me, and smiled. I shrugged my shoulders.

The waiter came to our table and handed Alex the wine list. "Would everyone care for some wine?"

I nodded and said that sounded great and looked at the others at the table. Luckily, we were all in agreement, so

Alex ordered two bottles, a Chardonnay and Bordeaux.

I was really hoping my mom would get off her high horse and stop thinking Alex owned a seedy club. But of course, I had no such luck and neither did Alex. "So this club you have, it must keep you busy and your hours must be . . . long," she glanced at me, "and difficult."

Alex sipped his water. "Yes, it does keep me busy, but between Brett, our other partner, and me, it isn't too bad."

"I can't imagine that it's very profitable. Is that why you want to expand to try to make more income? In today's economy, you need to be careful how you spend your money."

I wished I could crawl under the table right then. I repeated, "Please be done, please be done," over and over in my head. No such luck.

The ridicule continued. "And I can imagine all types of women must come in and out of there." She actually used finger quotes when she said "types."

"Mother!" Oh my God, really? If Alex wanted to stay with me after this, it would be a miracle.

"Jill!" My father was trying to intervene, but to no avail. She had to continue her interrogation.

"I've heard the name Logan before." She looked deep in thought and sipped her wine until the apparent light bulb went bright. "Are you related to Jack Logan of Logan Industries?"

Alex fidgeted in his chair. I glanced over at Julie and Brett, who were pretending to peruse their menus. I was willing Julie to save me, but she looked nervous. She never looks nervous.

"Actually, Jack Logan is my father. Logan Industries is his company."

My father nodded in acknowledgement. My mother couldn't leave it alone; she had to keep going. "So your father owns one of the most successful companies in New York, and his son owns a night club? What does your mother think of all this?"

That's it. I felt like throwing up. My lips thinned as I glared at my mother. "And Alex owns one of the most successful night clubs in Manhattan." Just then the waiter returned with the wine. Alex tasted the red and I tasted the white. Alex nodded to the waiter, signaling that it was good, and I did the same, except I swallowed my taste like a shot. The waiter poured the wine after asking who wanted red and white. He stepped away from the table since he could tell we weren't ready to order.

Alex swallowed a sip of wine and looked at my mom. "Actually, my mom passed away, so I honestly don't know what she would think. I hope that she would have been proud of my decisions, but I guess I'll never know." He was trying, but he was starting to get defensive, not that I could blame him.

My mom paled. I looked at Alex as he glanced at me. He looked completely on edge, not a look I was used to seeing on Alex. "I'm proud of you, Alex." I kissed him on the cheek. He visibly relaxed and smiled.

My dad cleared his throat. The tension was so thick that a knife would have no hope of slicing through it; you would need a chain saw. He put his hand on my mother's. "We're sorry for your loss, Alex. So where have you kids been so far?" I was so thankful for my dad.

Julie chimed in. "We went to Tuscany and Sicily before coming here. We stayed in the most fantastic villas that Alex rented for us—just total red carpet treatment all the way. We even flew first class."

All of those things didn't matter to me, but Julie knew they would matter to my mom. At this point, I didn't care what or how my mom felt. I was so embarrassed by the way she was treating Alex. I wouldn't have been surprised if he left me right then and there.

The waiter came and we placed our orders. I didn't even want to eat; my appetite was completely gone. I wanted to leave; that was all I wanted to do: leave and be alone with Alex and do some damage control. My head just spun; I was praying not to have an anxiety attack.

Brett and my dad were talking about baseball and how my dad misses going to games back in New York. Julie chimed in with her two cents every once in a while. My mom looked at me and then to Alex, who was looking into his wine glass as if he had a lot on his mind and he was waiting for the wine to speak to him. He probably did have a lot running though his head; the main thing probably was how to get the hell out of here. "Will you excuse us, please?" I stood and held my hand out to Alex. He took it and I led him out of the restaurant.

We stood on the cobblestone street, and I turned to look at him. "Alex, I am so sorry my mom is acting this way. I am completely mortified. I don't know what has gotten into her." I hugged him and rested my cheek on his heart. It had such a steady and calming beat. "Please know that I am very proud of you. I don't care about the expensive lifestyle. I would live in a shack if it meant I could be with you. Please tell me you know that."

"I know that, Aubrey. Don't worry, okay? Everything will be fine with your mom. This is just new to me. I've never had to deal with a girl's parents before."

We walked back into the restaurant. My mom looked a little calmer. I was wondering if it was Julie or my dad who told her to chill, most likely my dad. Julie was out of sorts herself.

"Alex, I'm sorry for the way I acted earlier. I'm sure your club is very nice. I love my daughter, and I just want her to be happy." My mom sounded sincere. Maybe this lunch could be salvaged.

"Well, we agree on that. I care for your daughter . . . very much." He lifted my hand and kissed it.

My mom and I both smiled, and the conversation turned for the better. We had our lunch, and the waiter brought out dessert and coffee. I lifted my coffee cup, and the sun streaming in the restaurant windows caught the sparkle of the diamonds on my bracelet.

"Aubrey, honey, this bracelet is exquisite. I've never seen anything like it." She reached for my arm to get a closer look. Mom was closely examining it when she realized the diamond-encrusted flower was an orchid. She gently released my arm and looked in my eyes, which were wide with wonder at what her reaction would be. "It's beautiful."

"Alex bought it for me. I love it." I leaned over and kissed him.

"So an orchid on the bracelet and your club is called The White Orchid?" My mom needed to let this all go.

"Yes, that's an orchid, and, yes, my club is named The White Orchid. It was my mom's favorite flower. It's how I keep her close to me."

My mom nodded. "Well, it is beautiful."

Thankfully, the waiter brought the check and my dad reached for it, but Alex intercepted it. He slid his black American Express card in the folder without looking at the tab and handed it back to the waiter.

My parents thanked him, and I couldn't have been more thrilled that this was over. We stood and said our good-byes, and I told my mom that we were going to be too busy with work to see them again before we left. My mom was disappointed but said she understood.

We got back to the hotel and headed to the bar. "Alex, I'm so sorry. You didn't deserve that today. I feel horrible. Sometimes I don't know what gets into my mother." I looked over at Julie with pleading eyes. Luckily, she caught my look and chimed in, "My mom would have asked how you were in bed." We all looked at her and laughed. Thankfully that broke the tension, and I started to relax—we all did.

We decided to brainstorm a little on the marketing side of the project since that was the reason for Julie and me being there, well, part of the reason. Julie asked if they knew what they were going to call the wine room. Brett and Alex blankly looked at each other. "I'll take that as a no." Julie continued, "You actually don't need one right now, but if you want to start promoting a few weeks prior to the opening, you'll need one before then and any logo and artwork that would accompany it."

Brett grabbed her at the back of her neck and pulled her in for a lip-searing kiss. When they broke apart, he said, "You are so sexy when you talk marketing."

Julie dropped her chin to her chest and rolled her head to the side. "How about we go back to the room and I can give you the best marketing presentation ever. I'll even look for a white board and a laser pointer."

Brett gave Julie a sexy smirk, and I was sure that was the last we would see of them again until the morning. That was fine with me because it meant I'd get Alex all to myself for the rest of the day and night.

Our last day in France was productive and exhausting. Alex and Brett made great connections and we learned a lot about wines, different regions where the grapes grow, and proper food pairings. It was really interesting. I didn't think it would have been; I just was looking forward to tasting the different wines. I always ordered the same type of wine, chardonnay. I had no idea what country it originated in and honestly could care less. Now I knew and I found it interesting. I wasn't sure if it was because I had visited the most romantic settings I had ever seen or if it was Alex.

He made every tasting sexy. I was watching him at our last tasting, same as the others. I don't know if it was the fact that this was our last day or because my feelings for him were beyond what I could ever dream of them being. He would close his eyes and inhale the wine's aroma then swirl the wine around in the glass. It was mesmerizing, and apparently, it showed if the wine had "legs," which was a good thing if it did. He would take a gentle sip of the wine and let it rest on his tongue; I was just staring at this point, wishing I was resting on his tongue. He swallowed the wine and nodded and glanced at me with the most seductive look I had ever seen, which ended with him winking at me and me getting wet. Holy hell, I needed him in a bad way . . . a very bad way. My breathing altered, and I knew that Alex noticed the rise and fall of my chest.

He quickly asked the woman at the winery for the labels of the wine that he liked, and he did so in French, which was the sexiest thing ever. Alex or Brett would always ask for the wine bottle's label if they liked the wine. Apparently, all the information that was needed in regards to the specifications of the wine could be located on the label, so that was the easiest way to ensure they had what they needed. Plus, Julie wanted to incorporate the labels in her marketing plan. Alex thanked the woman and grabbed my hand, and we hurried back to the hotel.

We practically fell into our room. Alex grabbed me and pinned me against the door. When I brought my left leg up around his hip, he lifted up my right one and I linked my ankles together around his waist. My arms were stretched above my head. He leaned into me and lifted my shirt over my head. His trim waist and broad chest made my mouth water. I couldn't wait to get his shirt off him. I could stare at him all day and not tire of it. I really loved this man.

His hips were pressed against mine, and I could feel his arousal. He was frantically kissing my neck down to the swell of my breasts. My nipples hardened, and I would have sworn they were pulsing. He lowered the cups of my bra and swirled his tongue on, kissed, and sucked on my breasts. I couldn't help arching my back; I needed more. I moaned his name and he grunted some words that were incomprehensible, but still sounded sexy as hell.

"Alex." He brought his lips to that delicate spot on my neck, making me flinch and giggle. He licked his way up my neck, around my ear and sucked on my earlobe, giving it a light nibble. My legs instinctively squeezed around him. I felt as if I were ready to shatter in a million pieces. "I need you, Alex." My voice was all breathy. I felt as if he could knock the wind out of me with his sexy look, his cologne, and most definitely his searing touch.

He lowered his mouth to mine, kissing me with determined passion. "You need me? Do you, Aubrey? Do you really need me?"

I couldn't think. I needed him more than I needed the requirements to survive; he was my necessity. "Yes, Alex, I need you . . . now." I kissed him. "I will need you tomorrow and always." I hadn't ever spoken truer words. I couldn't imagine my life without him, not that I had him. I pushed that thought aside.

He pulled away from me and I whimpered. He looked into my eyes and carried me into the bedroom. He laid me on the bed and kissed me. The kisses were different than the ones I'd just experienced while pinned against the door. These kisses were gentle and unhurried. We discarded the rest of our clothes. Alex was propped up above me. He looked down at me. "I want to give you now, tomorrow, and always, Aubrey. I have never wanted anything as much as I want to give you that. I need you too; you have no idea how much."

We made love and it was beautiful. It was gentle, sensual, and perfect. He finished and was lying on top of me when I felt tears fall down the sides of my face, running into my ears. I didn't know why but my heart felt as if it were going to pound out of my chest. It was a different feeling than the anxiety attacks I was used to. It was full of love for a man that I never thought could be possible.

Alex lifted himself and looked at me. His eyes went from love to concern to confusion. "What's wrong? Did I hurt you?"

My eyes closed, and when I looked up at him, I wiped my tears. I wondered how to explain this, when I didn't understand it myself. "I don't know. I am so happy. I really am. I'm filled with such true emotions for you." I closed my eyes and more tears fell. I whispered. "It scares me."

"You're scared of me?" He rolled off me and pulled me to my side so we were facing each other. I put my hands under my head and just looked at him.

"I'm not scared of you, well, not you directly. I'm scared that this is too good to be true, that someone more beautiful and more exciting could come along and . . . that you'll leave me." My head was spinning. I was totally ruining this, but this was what I was feeling. "My heart is breaking at the thought." I immediately thought I should tell him my original intention when we met. Maybe he would laugh about it. I knew it didn't matter; I just wanted to be honest with him. "Alex, when we first met," I swallowed hard, "I wasn't looking for love. I was looking for—"

"I don't think anyone knows when that one special person will come along. I saw you and knew immediately I needed to have you. I was lucky you continued to talk to me after what Julie told you and the other interruption." I knew immediately he was referring to Leah. I looked away from him. He put his palm on my cheek to turn my head and make me face him. "I told you I will never intentionally hurt you. Never. I'm not that guy anymore. I don't want the extracurricular club life. I want to run a successful business, and I want you by my side when I do it. That's it; that's all I desire."

We continued to look at each other. I was getting lost in his blue eyes. I ran my fingertips along his hairline and kissed him. Instead of making love, we held each other. It was a wonderful and melancholy feeling at the same time. I'd always had that feeling that when something seems too good to be true it probably is. I always wait for the proverbial shoe to drop and drop hard, especially on my heart.

Chapter 17

I WAS BACK IN MY humble apartment, daydreaming of Alex and the amazing time we had together. I didn't want to forget anything, so I wrote it down.

Entry 8—My romance, my love, the shoe . . .

I spent two weeks in Europe with Alex, Julie, and Brett. We toured Italy and France, enjoying the most amazing wines and scenery. Our alone time was spent having mind-blowing sex and sharing kisses that would make ice ignite. I can't believe the man Alex turned out to be. I trust him, I love him, and I hope he loves me.

We saw my parents and it was terrible. Well, my mom was terrible. She is a money lover and I'm not. I am a lover of romance and love. To me, money is secondary. I was a wreck, waiting for her to completely embarrass me in front of Alex. I didn't have to wait long, but Alex was a trooper.

I tried to tell him about my book and what my intention was in going out that first night, but he stopped me, and we made love instead of talking. I really need to tell him. He really can't get mad. If you think about it, it is really funny. Yes, I thought he was a player, and, yes, I thought he was going to use me, and, yes, I thought I could use him, but he stole my heart; well he didn't steal it – I gave it.

Alex is romance personified. Just the way he looks at me and talks to me has taught me what romance is. It isn't the flowers, gifts, or dinners out. It's in his eyes and his words. I love him, plain and simple.

We'd been home for three weeks, and although it was great to be home, I missed the beauty of Europe. Julie had been busy with Brett, and Alex had been super busy at the club. On top of the normal work he had to do, he'd been working on the addition of the wine room. We still saw each other every day. We would have dinner together, and he would come over after work, which would turn into mind-blowing sex, and then we'd have breakfast and then make love in the shower. It was a wonderful daily routine.

Mark and I were getting closer at work too. Julie was slammed with work, so most of her lunches were working lunches. Mark turned into my lunch mate, and thankfully, Alex was fine with it. He knew that I would never cheat on him and that Mark and I were just friends. He would tell me that Mark was lucky to have me, and I told Alex that I was lucky to have him.

Mark was really funny, and I was glad to see him smile; he had a really beautiful smile. Sadly, that smile had been rare since Jessica had left. He'd only heard from her once, and when he did, she told Mark that she was subletting her apartment and that he needed to move out within two months. To say that Mark was shocked was an understatement. We were at lunch when he got the news, and he was devastated.

"Aubrey, what the fuck am I supposed to do? We're in New York City. I can't afford an apartment on my own. How am I going to find a roommate? I don't know why she's being like this. One minute she loves me, and the next I'm homeless thanks to her. What the fuck!" He dropped his head in his hands and was rubbing his hands through his hair.

I felt horrible for Mark. I thought if Jessica had been here, I would have slapped her. "Hey, doesn't Walker-Stone have an apartment they reserve for when important clients come to New York?"

"Yeah, they do, why? What are you thinking?"

"I'm thinking if no one is scheduled to use it soon, that you should talk to Brian and ask him if you can use it. Brian is a cool guy, and I bet he'd let you use it."

Mark just stared at me. I wasn't sure if that was a good or bad thing. "Do you honestly think that if I go to one of the owners of one of the most prestigious marketing firms in New York and ask to stay at the company's apartment he is going to let me? Not to mention that I have to let my boss into my personal shit. Yeah, I don't know."

"You won't know until you ask." I didn't understand why this was so difficult. Mark needed a place to stay, Walker-Stone had one, but he wouldn't ask; this had to be a case of male pride. He reminded me of Alex.

"Why don't I call Alex and Julie and maybe we can all go out tonight. It'll get your mind off things. We can go to the club, and you can check out the wine room that he plans to open." I looked at him with hope and airiness.

Mark just looked at me. "You know what? Yeah, let's do that. Why should I sit around being pissed off when

Jessica is obviously okay?" He stood up to leave and I did as well. "Set it up and let me know. I'll be there. Meanwhile, I need to go scour the Internet for apartments."

He kissed the top of my head, and we both walked out and went back to work. I called Alex to ask him if we could all get together tonight. It was Thursday, and the club wouldn't be too busy.

"Hi, babe." Seriously, his voice could just make me rip off my clothes.

"Hi, handsome, how is your day going?"

"You know, busy, but it's good. What's up? Is everything okay?"

"Yes, everything is fine. Well, everything is fine with me; Mark on the other hand, not so much."

"Oh?"

"Yeah, Jessica has been pretty harsh with him. Not only did she leave him but she told him he needs to get out of her apartment because she's decided to sublet it. He isn't in a good place right now. His girlfriend dumped him, and his impending homelessness has him completely stressed out, so I thought that we could all hang at the club tonight. I was going to call Julie too. I know you and Brett have to work, but at least we'd all be together. Maybe Mark will find someone to have fun with. What do you think?" I felt as if I were rambling.

He chuckled. "I think you had me at 'all hang out at the club tonight.'"

"Good, I was hoping you'd say that."

"Why don't you guys come right after work? I'll order dinner, and we can eat in my office and then head down to the club."

"That sounds awesome. Thanks, Alex."

I told Mark and Julie, and they were both up for it. We all left work a little early, which Brian was fine with, and went home to get ready. We decided to meet at the club at six.

I took a quick shower. I wanted to look fresh for Alex. As the hot water was running over me, I thought about how lucky I was to have him. He was really a great man, and I would never do to him what Jessica did to Mark, especially when it was unprovoked. I just didn't understand how a person could do that to someone they claimed to once love.

I got out and toweled off. I left my hair down and put some loose curls in it, letting it drape over my shoulders. My makeup was light. I hoped to be dancing with Alex tonight, and I didn't need makeup dripping off my face. I put on my navy short skirt, a white top, and my navy peep-toe pumps. I didn't want to look as if I was on the prowl, but I didn't want to look like a frump either.

I made it to the club at five fifty-five, and it was pretty busy. I'd forgotten it was ladies' night. I spotted Julie and Mark at the bar, talking to Brett and Tyler. Walking over to them, I looked around to see who was there. Since it was happy hour with drink specials for the women, the ratio of men to women seemed even. Naturally, Leah and her entourage were there, and she was hanging on some guy who looked as if he just wanted to get out of there and be done with her. I rolled my eyes and went to my friends.

"Hi, guys. Where's my man?"

Brett smiled. He was such a doll, and I was so happy for Julie. "He is in his office setting up dinner. We were told to wait for you."

"Well, I'm here now, so let's go up."

When we arrived at the office, Brett went in first and

stopped so fast that we all ran into each other. It was like a train crash with all the cars ramming into the one in front of them. Julie smacked his shoulder. "Dude, keep walking. I almost broke a heel."

We were all laughing, well, until I looked at Brett's face; then I wasn't laughing anymore. Something wasn't right. Was it Alex? "What's the deal, Brett?"

"Um, why don't we give Alex a minute to finish up his meeting?"

I thought he was setting up dinner; now he was in a meeting? I was confused, so I pushed by everyone to go in, and my heart sank. There was Valerie in Alex's arms. He didn't even notice us. It didn't look like a friendly embrace. Her head was on his chest, and his right hand was stroking her hair, while his left was on the small of her back. I stood there paralyzed. I wanted to leave, but I wanted to stay. I didn't want to say anything, yet I wanted to scream. My chest started to hurt, and my breathing was getting ragged. I just stood there and watched. She eventually pulled away and kissed his chest as he kissed the top of her head. That did it for me. I thought I was going to have an anxiety attack.

I was standing just inside the doorway, and everyone else was behind me. I knew they could see over me, so they'd just witnessed what I had. I was so embarrassed, but I needed to find out what was going on. I cleared my throat and also tried to calm my staggered breathing.

Alex and Valerie split apart, and she looked as if she'd been crying. Did she want him and he'd told her no? Was that why she was crying?

Valerie was wiping her eyes. She looked at me and gave me a shy smile; it seemed forced. I turned to my friends, who were still partly in the hallway. Brett smiled at Valerie,

Julie scowled, and Mark walked away with her. What the hell was that about? Where was Mark going?

Alex came up to me and pulled me into a hug, well, a half hug, because my arms felt as if they each weighed a hundred pounds. I didn't hug him back. He whispered in my ear, "It's not what it looks like."

"I suppose that's a good thing, since it looked pretty bad. What's going on?" Alex didn't look that great either.

"Valerie came to tell me that Anthony suffered a mild heart attack and was in the hospital. She was on her way back there when she stopped in to tell me what happened." I looked up and our eyes met. "Valerie came to tell me and was upset. I was consoling her. That's it. That's what you saw."

I felt a little hideous because I'd thought the worst. "Is he going to be okay?" I knew that Alex really liked Anthony, and I would have hated it if he'd lost him.

"Yes, actually, he'll probably be going home tomorrow."

He looked at Brett. Julie and Mark were back. "Hey, sorry about that; come in and let's eat. I'm sure it's getting cold."

I looked over at the table. There were boxes of Chinese food almost covering the entire table. We all sat down and I looked at Alex. "How many people did you plan on having here for dinner? Did you order the entire menu?" We all laughed.

Alex popped a dumpling in his mouth and shrugged his shoulder. After swallowing, he said, "I didn't know what everyone liked, so I got a variety."

We finished dinner, cleaned up, and were going to head down to the club. I held Alex back and told everyone else we would meet them down there. I needed to get something off my chest.

"I'm really sorry if I jumped to the wrong conclusion earlier. I feel horrible for Anthony and Valerie. Are you okay?"

He held me. "I'm fine; I just got spooked when Val told me. That's all. You really don't need to worry about me wanting someone else. It's just you, okay?"

I nodded and we left hand in hand down to the club. The music was picking up as was the size of the crowd. We went to the bar where Tyler was serving drinks. He looked at me. "Cocktail, Aubrey?"

"Yes, please. I'll have a Chardonnay."

Alex was by my side, and his hand was rubbing the small of my back. I closed my eyes and wondered if we would always be close like this. I really hoped so, but it scared me. "Dance with me?" His voice reverberated through me.

I smiled, no beamed. "I would love to."

Alex led me to the dance floor, pulled me into his arms, and started moving back and forth slowly. Although the song was fast, we were moving to our own beat. My head rested on his chest, and his cheek was on the top of my head. He was moving me in a way that made me want to get the hell out of there and move with him alone somewhere. I didn't notice anyone on the dance floor. I was in my own bliss bubble and wanted to stay there with Alex forever.

Forever lasted only a few minutes longer since Alex's back was bumped and we were shoved a little. Alex turned us around to see who it was, and it was the bitch and her entourage. They were dancing in a circle, and the way they were dancing, all they needed was a stripper pole. Leah noticed Alex and looked at him up and down and then licked her lips. Alex wasn't fazed by her gesture. Instead, he moved us to the opposite side of the floor.

We weren't dancing anymore. We were just standing in each other's arms. I was so comfortable, felt so secure and protected. We left the club and went back to my place. Alex didn't stay over because we both had early days, and we knew we were going to see each other at our meeting tomorrow.

I was back at work the next day when my office phone rang. "Aubrey Ryan."

"Hey."

"Hi, Alex, is everything okay?"

"Can you come downstairs? I'm in the lobby"

He didn't sound right. "Sure, I'll be right down." I didn't bother waiting for the elevator. I tried to catch my breath since I took the stairs at high speed. I opened the door and there he was. God, he was beyond gorgeous. I think he gets better looking as time goes on. He was leaning against the wall, right leg bent with his foot resting on the wall. He was wearing black suit pants and an ice blue shirt with one button undone at the neck. His hands were in his pockets, and he was looking down. I felt as if I could burst just at the sight of him. I wiped my hands on my skirt and started walking toward him. He must have heard my heels clicking on the marble floor because he looked up. The air from my lungs was completely gone. I stopped and just stared. I didn't want to attempt another step. I felt as if I were going to fall over. He pushed off the wall and started walking toward me.

Our eyes were glued to each other. I was idly wondering

what expression I was wearing. He was getting closer, and I felt the buttons on my blouse tighten as my breathing got deeper. I looked down and felt his fingers on my chin, lifting me up to look at him. No words were spoken. He took me in his arms and hugged me. My right cheek was resting on his heart. I could feel and hear it beat. It was strong and steady just like Alex.

He grabbed my hand and led me out to the sidewalk. He grabbed my face between his hands and thoroughly kissed me. I couldn't get enough of him. I felt as if I hadn't kissed him in months, and it hadn't even been a day. It scared me how much I needed this man. My chest was tightening at the thought, but I tried to push that aside. He broke apart from me and stepped back resting his head on mine.

"Is everything okay, Alex? Did something happen? Is Anthony okay?

"Everything is fine; I just wanted a minute with you before our meeting. I woke up and thought of holding you, and since I didn't want to grab you in the meeting and I didn't want to wait until afterwards, I thought I would do it here. Why? Did you think something was wrong?"

I shrugged. "I guess I'm always waiting for the proverbial shoe to drop. That's all."

"There will be no shoe dropping today."

He kissed me and didn't care that we weren't alone. New Yorkers really don't care what is going on; they just walk around you.

"We need to go into the meeting. You can tell me about the shoe issue during the dinner that I have planned for us tonight. We can talk more then."

I nodded and smiled. We took the elevator up to my office. We passed Mark on the way into the conference room. He looked at us and smiled. Alex stopped and offered his hand to Mark and said that it was good to see him again. Mark nodded and led us into the conference room where Brian was sitting at the end of the table and Julie was preparing the ad board. She looked at us and smiled.

The meeting went well. Brian and Alex were pleased with our work, and we were moving forward toward launching the marketing blast for The White Orchid's wine room.

"Alex, do you have a name for the wine room yet? I'd like to start looking into logos and create my marketing material around it." Julie was the ultimate professional. She had just told me that morning that if a name wasn't given to her soon, she was going make one up herself. Of course she wouldn't do that, but it was holding up the marketing plan.

"Actually, I have selected a name." He looked at me and grinned. I felt myself flush, and then I peeked over at Brian, who had a questioning look on his face. "I'm calling it *Amoureux*."

Brian looked at him and said, "And that means?"

"Lover." It flew right out of my mouth. Alex had called me that in Paris. I could feel my face getting hotter. Brian gave me a curious look. I shrugged. "I picked up a little French while I was in Paris." Julie and Alex laughed. I shot them a look that said thanks a lot guys! Geez, could I be more embarrassed?

Julie finally chimed in, "That's brilliant, Alex. I love it, and I can totally work with that. The marketing strategy for *Amoureux* is going to rock!"

The meeting adjourned, and we all walked out of the conference room. Alex walked me to my desk. We had planned on going out to dinner together, but since I had work to finish, I would be meeting him there. He hugged me and told me he'd send a car to pick me up at six. I thanked him and admired the view as he walked away.

Chapter 18

I ARRIVED AT THE RESTAURANT in Little Italy and joined Alex who was seated at a quiet table. He held my hand across the table and just smiled at me. I couldn't be happier that we'd gotten past the Valerie misunderstanding, which I'd totally blown out of proportion.

"I hope you're hungry, because I ordered for us." He had a devilish look about him, but I just smiled. I wondered what he had ordered, but I was sure it was going to be delicious. I also didn't care because my focus was on Alex and making him understand me a little better: my overreactions, anxiety issues, and my fears.

"I am hungry, and I look forward to spending my time with you tonight." Before I could finish my thought, the waiter came with our wine. The label looked familiar to me, and it dawned on me that it was one of the wines we had in Italy.

Alex picked up his glass, motioning for me to do the same, and said, "To us, to understanding and exploring new adventures and each other." He winked.

We tapped our glasses together. I needed to get my thoughts off my chest. "I know that what I saw with Valerie was innocent and I blew it out of proportion. It's a typical move on my part. As I mentioned earlier, I have a knack of forcing the shoe to drop. I guess it's a way of protecting myself."

"Yes, tell me about this 'shoe' of yours." He finger quoted the word shoe.

"As you know, I'm not good in the relationship department. Aside from you, I've only had one other boyfriend, Garrett. Something always goes wrong, in everything, not just relationships. So to prevent the apprehension of when that 'shoe' will drop, I try to force the issue. This way I am in control of my heart breaking. I don't know if I could take it if I lost what we have. I only dealt with that feeling for a few minutes, but it felt like days."

"Aubrey, I told you I would never intentionally hurt you. I don't feel and have never felt for anyone the way I feel for you. Besides, I think Valerie has a thing for Mark."

"Wait, are you telling me that Valerie likes Mark?" He shrugged.

"By the way, I hooked him up with an apartment in the building next to the club. It isn't anything fancy, but the landlord owed me a favor, so I collected.

"Well, you have been busy. Thank you for doing that. What other little secrets are you keeping?" I was joking, but he got serious.

"I don't keep secrets, Aubrey."

No secrets . . . I need to tell him about my journal. "Alex, I want you to know something . . ." The waiter came and brought us our meals. I looked at the beautiful plates and realized he'd recreated our dinner in Italy. *How do I tell him about why I wanted to get together with him? He has to know that I'm not using him and that my intentions are honest. It really isn't even important anymore.* I decided that it was a non-issue.

"What do you want to tell me?" His eyes were looking at me with hope and anticipation.

I swallowed and felt as if I were going to speak for the first time. "I love you, Alex."

He looked shocked. Shit! I shouldn't have said it. Telling him that I was contemplating using him might have gone over better. I looked down at the napkin that I was twisting in my lap.

Softly but confidently, he said, "I love you too."

My head shot up. I couldn't help but smile at him. He smiled back and what a smile my man had. He was just beautiful. I could look at him forever and never tire at the sight of him.

"Aubrey, I haven't heard those three words since my mom passed away. I mean my dad would tell me, but I didn't believe him. I was more of a disappointment to him. I am so glad it's you who said those words to me."

I was shifting in my chair. I wanted to get out of there and make love to my man. I needed him to possess me in every way possible. I lifted my napkin, gently ran it over my mouth, and placed it on the table. Alex looked at me and signaled for the waiter to bring us our check and to-go boxes. Obviously Alex had the same idea I did; we needed to get out of there; we'd eat later.

We were almost running into his apartment. Our lips felt bound together in a searing kiss. I couldn't let go of him. I didn't want to . . . ever. We tore each other's clothes off in the living room, and he scooped me up and carried me to the couch. He lay down holding himself above me. I ran my hands up and down his abs and traced the beautiful V in his hips with my fingertips. I looked up at him in awe. I couldn't believe this was happening to me. This amazingly gorgeous man loved me. He lowered himself, and I felt his erection press against me. I needed him intimately, emotionally, and mentally. I had never felt the need for anyone as I did for Alex. He moved so he was half on me and half on the couch. He ran his finger down my neck, around the outline of my breasts, over my nipple, and down the center of my stomach to the top of my sex. He ran his finger up and down my slit. I couldn't help the moan that escaped me. I bucked my hips toward his hand. I looked over at him. He was watching his hand.

As he slid one finger in, I reached down to him. I grabbed his erection in my hand and started moving in the same rhythm that he was moving in and out of me. He slid in another finger, then another. "Oh Alex, please, I need to feel you; I want you."

He removed his fingers and rolled us so I was on top of him. "Take me, Aubrey. I'm yours."

Could there be anything better than hearing that? I didn't think so. I slid him inside me and started rocking and moving him in and out. I leaned back grabbing his thighs for support. He pinched my nipples, and I was on the verge of climaxing. I loved this man. I felt tears stab my eyes. He rubbed the top of my thighs with his thumbs, and I started to shatter. "I'm coming, Alex!" I was rocking at a furious pace. "Come with me; I need to feel you with me." He flipped me over and started thrusting into me. I exploded in a sweet spasm and so did he. I could feel his muscles tense and his cock throb inside of me. He felt amazing. We were amazing.

Chapter 19

ALEX AND I HAD SPENT the next two weeks with Brett and Julie, preparing for the private opening of *Amoureux*. The marketing blitz that Julie prepared was brilliant. *Amoureux* would be opening to the public the following weekend. The guest list for the private opening that night was short. It consisted of close friends and Alex's Dad. I was so proud of Alex and Brett. They worked so hard on this. When we arrived at the club, we headed down to the wine room, where Tyler was making the final preparations for the tastings. He was working with the caterers to make sure the right foods were paired with the appropriate wine, according to Brett and Alex's specifications.

I was with Julie in *Amoureux* when Alex and Brett walked in. Julie and I looked at them in awe. I didn't think I would ever tire of looking at him. Alex and Brett both had on black suits. Alex wore a gray shirt and a black tie, while Brett wore a white shirt and a burgundy tie. They looked edible. Julie and I smiled in appreciation of our men. Brett went to Julie, and Alex strutted over to me.

"You look beyond handsome this evening, Mr. Logan." He beamed that glorious smile at me, and I swear I felt it between my legs. I crossed them in anticipation of what was to come . . . literally.

"You are gorgeous, my love." He spun me around. I had on a black strapless cocktail dress and my black Jimmy Choo high-heel pumps.

I blushed. "Thank you. Are you excited for tonight?"

"I'm very happy that this day is here. I would be lying if I said I wasn't nervous." I knew he was thinking about his dad. The infamous business tycoon who wasn't fond of his son owning a nightclub was going to attend the opening.

"It's awesome, Alex, no worries tonight. Everyone will love it and what you guys have accomplished. I know I do. I love you."

"I love you more than I did yesterday." He kissed me, and it felt as if it went on forever, which was perfectly fine with me. Brett interrupted us and told us the guests were arriving.

I looked around the room. It was stunning. The décor was soft burgundy and cream with high tasting tables, soft padded stools, and wooden wine racks. The lighting was dim and was complemented by the votive candles on the tables. It was pure romance.

Brett and Julie were positioned at the door, while Alex and I stayed in the center of the room, explaining what was being offered and welcoming everyone. Brian was the first to enter the room with his wife, followed by Mark and Valerie; I guess Alex had been right about them. Mark kissed me on the cheek and shook Alex's hand. "Thanks for hooking me up with that apartment. I move in, in a few weeks." He was happy and I was happy for him.

I really didn't dislike Valerie; I disliked the way she'd

acted around Alex the first time I met her. She kissed Alex hello and gave me a quick hug. I smiled at her "How's your dad?

She laughed. "He's cranky and ornery because he had to rest at home, so I guess he's getting back to normal. We both smiled and nodded at her. I could tell that Alex was both pleased and relieved to hear that. Mark and Valerie made their way to the caterers to start their first tasting.

Alex looked toward the entrance and my eyes followed. Jack Logan was standing there with a woman. She looked as if she were my age. Oh, this was not good. I looked over at Alex, and he was grinding his jaw. I put my hand on his forearm. He grabbed my hand, and we walked toward his father. "Son," Jack said and stuck his hand out. Alex took it, but his arm looked as if it weighed a hundred pounds the way he lifted it to meet his dad's hand. He dropped it and grabbed mine.

Jack looked at me as if he'd never met me before. "Dad, you remember my girlfriend, Aubrey."

I extended my hand. "Hi, Mr. Logan." He shook my hand and smiled. I hated the vibe I got from him. Alex squeezed my hand.

"Son, this is Darla." Alex just looked at him. "Darla, my son, Alex."

She handed him her hand palm down as if to say, "Here you go; you may kiss it." She licked her bottom lip before biting it. Alex took her hand and shook it. *Ha-ha, no kisses for you, Darla!* My insides were doing the happy dance.

"Have fun and please enjoy the wine." Alex spoke to them like strangers.

As we walked away, I took Alex's hand in mine. I couldn't help but ask, "Who is Darla?"

He shrugged. "I think she works in his office. I'm not sure why he brought her here. I didn't realize he was dating."

I could tell that put him off balance. No sooner had we removed ourselves from the uncomfortable feeling brought about by Jack and Darla than we were being greeted by Leah. Tyler had obviously invited her, since she was on his arm.

I had Alex's hand in a death grip and was sure that he would have a bruise or a broken bone or two. Alex glared at Tyler. They exchanged looks; although, Tyler obviously was oblivious to the fury that Alex's eyes displayed. Tyler had to know that she was a thorn in my side. Leah, on the other hand, looked pleased with herself.

She kissed Alex on the cheek. "Hey, baby, this place is nice." *Nice? Nice?* This room was gorgeous. She was such trash. She looked at me. "Did you decorate this?" I could feel my eyes glaring at her.

"No, but she was the inspiration for the name."

I smiled and looked up at him. He winked at me.

"Yeah, what does *Amoureux* mean and what language is that?"

"It's French and it means lover." He looked at me and kissed me on my temple.

Leah rolled her eyes and made a sour face.

Okay, my glare was gone, and I was rejoicing at her discomfort. Tyler and Leah walked away, and I let out a breath. I just couldn't stand her. Alex excused himself just before Valerie came up to me and said, "She is vile." I was shocked, so I laughed. "What's so funny?" Valerie looked confused.

"We have something else in common. I can't stand her

either."

"What else do we have in common?" She looked confused as if I were setting her up for something.

"Alex and Mark—I think we can agree they are both wonderful men." Valerie nodded in agreement.

I scanned the room, looking for Alex. He was standing a table with Mark, and they were both looking at Valerie and me. I think our men were waiting for us to break out into a cat fight; instead, we walked over to them and hugged them.

The rest of the night went off without a hitch. Everyone enjoyed themselves, and pride was radiating off Brett and Alex. The guests cleared and Alex grabbed me. We were hip to hip. His body swayed leading me into a dance. I faintly heard the music that was being piped into the room. "I want you to always be my dance partner, Aubrey." He spun me then dipped me. My head was almost to the floor. He lifted me up and my head spun. I always felt that way with Alex. He made my mind and body feel and do things that I never thought possible.

"I'm going to take you home now, to my home, where we'll continue this dance."

The look in his eyes told me what dance we would be continuing, and I couldn't wait to get there.

I felt comfortable in his apartment even though it was vast. He took his suit coat off and placed it over the arm of the sofa. He pulled me into him, and as he said he was going to do, he continued the dance. "I love dancing with you, holding you, feeling you against me. I love moving with you to our own beat. We don't need music; follow my heartbeat, Aubrey."

My head rested on his chest, and I did just what he said.

We moved together, our legs intertwined, rocking back and forth. His hand was holding mine, strong enough to make me feel possessed, but light enough that if I were made of glass I wouldn't break. "I'm really happy, Alex. You make me happy. I just wanted you to know that."

He stopped moving and I looked up at him. His eyes . . . God, his eyes were amazing. They told a story, but they were difficult to read. He took my hand in his and led me to the bedroom. He turned me around and unzipped my dress. It fell to the floor, revealing my black lace panties and strapless bra. He kissed my shoulder then my neck, making my shoulder rise and my head tilt. He whispered, "Ahh, my favorite spot." I nodded. He'd rendered me speechless at this point. He let his hands run down my spine and unclasped my bra. His hands moved to my front. He put his hands on my waist and started moving our hips back and forth. Sliding his hands to my breasts, he gently caressed them, sending a shockwave to my core. He rested one hand on my collarbone and the other on my hip. My head rested on his chest. He leaned down and kissed my cheek.

I turned in his arms and pressed my hips against his. I brought my fingers to his tie and loosened it until it was open. I continued unbuttoning his shirt and removing his cufflinks, which I slid into the pocket of his pants. I removed his shirt and just looked at his chest. It was an amazing chest supported by amazing abs; he really was fantastic. I leaned in and kissed his heart while unfastening his pants. He kicked them aside.

"I love your heart, Alex. You may cover and guard it with muscles and walls, but you have a wonderful, gentle, and caring heart." I trailed kisses from his heart to the base of his neck. "Thank you for choosing me to share your heart with."

He laid me on the bed and kissed me. It wasn't hurried; it wasn't aggressive; it was loving and romantic. Everything I had ever dreamed of or fantasized about was here lying next to me. We made love, but it was different from the other times. It was as if he poured his soul into me.

He held me in his arms, my back to his front, and rested his cheek on mine. "I feel so safe with you, Alex. It's something so new to me, and I'm so afraid. I don't want to lose this. Please, promise me we won't lose this."

"I never want to lose you either. I loved having you by my side tonight; I love having you by my side every day. You are an amazing woman, my woman. I love and trust you with my life."

"I love and trust you too. I know I didn't at first and it's difficult, but I guess since I have a boyfriend like you, I have to accept the fact that women will want my man. I'll kick their asses if they touch you, you know."

He laughed, "I bet you will. You don't have to worry about that. I don't want anyone else to touch me, and I don't want to touch anyone else. Only you, Aubrey."

I was running my fingers along his arm that was draped across my hips. "Your mom would have been proud of you tonight."

He exhaled. "I would like to think so. I wish your parents had been there. They could have seen what you and Julie did. Your work is amazing. Have you always wanted to be an editor?"

"No, I wanted to be a writer." I immediately tensed up. I really need to tell him about the journal. There wasn't anything wrong with it since it was now about us and my love for him.

"I was never good at writing. I envied those who were

eloquent with a pen. I was lucky I passed English." We both laughed. "It's late. Let's get some sleep." He kissed my cheek. "I love you."

"I love you too."

Chapter 20

WE SPENT THE NEXT WEEKS together. When Alex wasn't at the club, he was with me. I would go to his place, or he would come to mine. *Amoureux* was a hit. It was all the rage and brought more people to the club, which was both good and bad because many patrons had to wait. They weren't always happy about that.

Alex came over after a busy Friday night at the club. He was exhausted and I was tired too. I needed to get up early and help Mark move into his new apartment. The alarm buzzed at six. I quietly rolled out of bed and took a shower. I was going to be gone most of the day, and by the time I got back, Alex would be at the club. I didn't want to wake him, so I left him a note.

> *Good morning,*
>
> *I am heading out to help Mark move. I hope you slept well. You looked so peaceful sleeping I didn't want to wake you. I know that you will have another long night tonight.* ☺
>
> *Call me when you get up.*
>
> *I love you,*
>
> *Aubrey XOXO*

I left the note on the bedside table and tossed the pen in the drawer. I left and went to help Mark.

Mark's new place was nice. He had taken a few days off and painted it. A cleaning person had come in and cleaned it. That was my gift to him, considering I didn't want to be the one doing it; it was totally worth it. We unpacked boxes as they came in, organizing everything. Thankfully he was a guy, so there wasn't too much in terms of knick knacks and general hoarding-type items. Valerie walked in with Chinese food for dinner. We were so busy that I didn't realize I hadn't eaten lunch. I'd been glad Mark had a coffee and croissant waiting for me when I got here this morning. What time was it? I grabbed my phone and noticed it was shortly after six. I noticed I didn't have any calls from Alex. *He must be busy. I'll call him on my way home.* I finished eating with Mark and Valerie and decided it was time to head home. Every bone in my body ached, and I couldn't wait to take a shower. I hugged Mark and Valerie good-bye and dragged my ass home.

I tried calling Alex, but it went straight to voice mail. I thought maybe his battery had died. I was sure he'd call me when he could. When I got home, I went straight to my bathroom, and peeled off my clothes, which felt as if they were painted on me. I felt gross. I let the hot water run over me. I thought about the last few months of my life and how it had changed. I had a burst of energy and decided that I would get dressed and head over to the club. I got out of the shower, toweled off, and threw a robe on. I dried my hair and went to get dressed. I walked in my room and felt my heart drop to the floor. Lying on my bed was my journal opened to the first page. There was a note resting on it.

I needed a pen to write my loving girlfriend back, and to my surprise, look what I found. I hope you have enough material to write your book. A friend mentioned that she overheard you and Julie talking about using me for a book, but I thought she was jealous and trying to cause trouble. I guess she was telling the truth. At least someone was.

Good-bye, Aubrey.

Alex

My eyes immediately filled with tears. *He has to know this was a long time ago.* I looked at the page he read. It was about using the player. *Didn't he continue reading? And who was this "friend" who overheard Julie and me?* It had to be Leah or one of her friends. Maybe it was that first night at the club when we were in the ladies' room? I had no idea. My head spun. *Is this why I haven't heard from him?* I had to go to him and explain.

I threw on a pair of jeans and a t-shirt and my flats. I ran out of my apartment and took a cab to the club. I sent a quick text to Julie, telling her what happened. When I got there, a line had already formed outside. There was some pushing and shoving going on, and while the bouncers were handling that, I snuck in without waiting. *Who knows if Alex told them not to let me in?* The club was jumping, people were dancing, and the beat of the music mirrored that of my heart, strong and fast. I made a beeline toward the bar. I wasn't sure where Alex was going to be, so I thought I would ask Tyler since he was normally bartending.

My heart stopped. Alex was at the bar with empty shot glasses in front of him. Was he drunk? He never drank to excess because of his mom. I walked toward him, wanting to explain everything. There were people everywhere. I made it through the crowd and stood about four feet away from him. He looked at me just as Leah was walking by trailing her fingers across his shoulders. He grabbed her arm and pulled her into him and kissed her; no, he devoured her. My chest tightened, my heart raced, and I couldn't breathe or move. I stood there and stared. I stared at this train wreck that was my life. Alex broke the kiss and looked at me. "How's that for a player? Go write about that in your book because WE ARE DONE!"

I turned and ran out of the club. I think I passed Julie on the way. I wasn't sure. I couldn't think; I needed air; I needed to get out. I was trying to break through the crowd to get outside. I wanted to go home, I wanted to cry, and I wanted Alex. The hysterics came in full force. I pushed my way out the door and into mayhem. There was a fight or something going on, and I was shoved so hard that I fell and smacked my head on the sidewalk, or was I in the street? I heard voices, was that Brett's voice? All I heard was, "Oh my God, it's Aubrey! Someone call 911!"

I tried to open my eyes; I couldn't. All I heard were voices. I heard Julie. "Aubrey, wake up. Open your eyes for me." Her voice was gentle, and then it changed. "You asshole, you should have read the entire journal. You should have talked to her. She loves you! Look what you did to her!"

Then there was his voice. "Aubrey, open your eyes, honey." I couldn't. I tried, but I couldn't. I wished I could because all I could see were Alex and Leah. Sirens. I heard sirens. I saw . . . blackness.

When I woke up, I heard beeping. My head hurt and my arms hurt. I tried to move, but it hurt. I heard muffled voices. Where was I? I tried to think about what happened and where I was. "Aubrey, honey, can you hear me? It's Mom. Your dad and I are here. Can you hear me?" It felt as if I was blinking, but I couldn't see anything. I nodded. *Man, my head is killing me.* I tried to raise my hand up. My arm hurt, but I managed to touch my head and felt gauze.

"Water. I need some water." My throat was killing me. I felt a straw against my lips and took a sip.

"Aubrey, I am so glad you are awake. We've been so scared."

"Julie?"

"Yes, I'm here, Aubrey."

A voice I didn't know spoke. "I see the patient is awake. I'm Dr. Griffin. How are you feeling, Aubrey?" I felt my eyelids being held by his thumbs, so I knew my eyes were open, but I couldn't see.

"My head hurts. I can't see anything. Why can't I see anything?! Oh my God! Am I blind? I'm blind! Everything is black! I'm going to be blind?" I burst into hysterics. "I'm going to be sick; I'm going to throw up! Mom? Julie? Is anyone here?" Pure panic set in. I was screaming their names. Were they here?

I heard an unfamiliar voice telling me she was going to sit me up. I felt hands on my arms, and I felt the back of the bed moving to a sitting position. "I'm Nurse Michelle, and I'm holding a basin in front of you. If you need to be sick, I'll help you."

"Get everyone out of here. I don't want anyone else in here. Nurse, I'm going to be . . ." I vomited and prayed I expelled in some type of container and not all over myself. I dry heaved. I felt a wet cloth across my forehead and then across my mouth. "I'm so sorry." I couldn't stop crying.

"Nurse Michelle, are you still here?"

"Yes, I'm right here. I know this is frightening, but I need you to try to calm down. Your blood pressure is accelerating." I heard the beeping of the machine becoming more rapid. I took deep breaths and heard footsteps. "Aubrey, Dr. Griffin is here now; he's been taking care of you."

An odd and older voice spoke to me. "Aubrey, I know you're scared and confused. I don't know what you remember from the night of your accident, but you've been in a coma, which is normal for a head trauma. Your CAT scan shows that you have what is called *commotio retinae*. Your loss of vision could be temporary or unfortunately permanent. Only time will tell with this type of injury. Do you see any flashes of light or shadows?"

"No, nothing, I don't see a thing!" *What do I remember? What do I remember?* Closing my eyes and trying to think back, I remembered running . . . the club . . . Alex . . . Leah . . . kissing? He kissed Leah and his hands were on her. I remembered her smiling. Everything was so fuzzy. I felt as if I were seeing a dream, not my actual life.

Dr. Griffin let go of my wrist; he must have been feeling my pulse. "Would you like anything before I leave? Some water maybe? You may not think so right now, but you're a lucky girl."

Yeah, I'm lucky all right. "Yes, please, I'd like some water. I have a friend here; her name is Julie. Can you please ask her to come in?"

"I'll get her for you. Your parents and boyfriend are here too."

My boyfriend . . . not anymore he isn't. My heart broke at that thought, but as far as I was concerned, Alex Logan was not my boyfriend. He wasn't even a friend. He was probably here out of guilt, or maybe he thought I would sue him since it happened in front of his precious club. "Thank you, just send Julie in please." I knew my parents would be upset, but I needed to speak to Julie first.

I heard the door open and close and then open. Was this going to be my life? Just sounds? How would I work? I needed my eyes to work. I couldn't stop the tears. Somehow I was hoping my tears would wash away all the bad that had happened to me.

"Hey, girlfriend." She sounded so sad.

"Julie, what am I going to do?" My crying returned in full force and my body shook; my chest ached. I could feel her arms around me. I hugged her and realized I had an IV in my arm because it tugged a little. Julie released me, and I rested back on my bed pillow.

"I am so sorry this happened to you." I could hear her crying and sniffling.

"Julie, please tell me what happened. I need to know everything." I made sure to stress the word "everything."

"I really don't think now is a good time."

"Yes, it's the only time. I need to know."

"Tell me what you remember, and I'll do my best to fill in the blanks."

I brought my fingers to my temple and felt a bandage. "I remember being in the club. Alex . . . Oh my God, Alex was making out with Leah! Why? Why was he with her? He had his hands on her! Why?" I realized it wasn't a dream; it had actually happened!

"He found your journal and only read the beginning part where you said you wanted to find and use a man for romance. He didn't read any of your entries. Apparently, Leah and friends told him that you were using him the first night you met; they heard us talking in the bathroom. He told me he didn't believe them, but then he read your journal. He was drunk and grabbed Leah to hurt you like you hurt him. That's what he told me anyway."

It finally dawned on me that because of Leah and her bitches he knew all along. Was it all bullshit? *Holy fuck! I am an idiot.* He'd seemed so genuine. I couldn't deal with this. My tears came back full force.

"Hurt me? He wanted to intentionally hurt me? He promised." I was trying to remember. "I ran out of the club. I remember leaving. I don't remember anything after that."

"According to the statements that were given, you ran into a few people who were arguing and you were pushed. You fell and hit the back of your head on the curb. Brett had just arrived at the club, saw you on the ground, ran into the club after calling 911, and rushed to find me and Alex."

"As if Alex would care . . . I lost everything—my sight, my work, the only man I've ever loved—it's all gone. Why didn't he talk to me? Why was his first instinct to hurt me and not believe my feelings were real? Were his feelings real or was he playing me?"

"I don't think he was playing you, and I don't think you do either, but you can ask him. He's been here since Saturday night."

"What day is it?"

"It's Thursday. You've been here for five days. Do you want me to get Alex?"

Did I? No, unfortunately, in my blackness all I could see was him and Leah. My last visual memory was my so-called boyfriend making out with Leah. "No, I don't want to see him, ever. Tell him to leave and not to come back."

Saying those words tore at my heart. I couldn't feel anything anymore. I felt dead inside. There was a knock on the door, and I heard it open.

"Sweetheart, can we come in?"

Julie let go of my hand. "It's your mom and dad. I'll let you guys talk."

I wiped my tears. "Thanks, Jules; go home to Brett and relax, and please pass my message along."

"Okay, I'll be back tomorrow." She kissed the back of my hand and left.

"How are you feeling, sweetheart?" My mom's voice was shaky.

"I feel horrible. I don't know what I'm going to do next." I felt exhausted.

"Aubrey, we spoke to Dr. Griffin, and he's going to send you for another scan. If it looks stable, in a week or so, you'll be able to travel. We'd like to bring you back to Paris with us. We can take care of you there, and you won't have to worry about being on your own. It's just until you get better; then you can decide what to do, okay?"

I couldn't think about this right now. "I'll think about it, Mom. Thank you and you too Dad. Dad's here too, right?"

"Yes, honey, I'm right here." My dad touched my shoulder.

I love my dad. I love both my parents, but my mom could be trying. "I'm sorry you had to rush all the way over here."

Dad grabbed my hand. "We wouldn't want to be anywhere else. Think about what your mother said. It's late and visiting hours are over. I want you to rest. We'll be back in the morning." They kissed my head, and I assumed they left because I heard the door open and close.

Chapter 21

THERE WAS SOMEONE IN THE room; I heard breathing.

"Nurse Michelle?"

"No, it's me." He sounded exhausted, or was he just feeling guilty?

"Get out, Alex. Please, just leave." I felt the tears escape my eyes and trickle into my ears. I could smell him and feel his warmth; he must have been standing next to me. "I asked you to leave. I want you out of here."

"I am so sorry, Aubrey. This is my fault."

"No, I don't blame you. I blame myself for not telling you about my journal, but most of all for trusting that you loved me, that we were real. I tried to tell you about my journal a couple of times, but something always stopped me. It didn't matter; it was a non-issue. You should have kept reading or called me to talk, but instead, you decided to hurt me by being with the one person I detest the most. You believed what she told you all those weeks ago, and you purposely hurt me. You promised you would never do that; you promised me." My tears came out like a waterfall, I felt air escaping my lungs, and my chest hurt. Maybe I was actually feeling my broken heart.

"You knew that I was insecure and scared, but what I

saw . . . The last visual I will ever have is your mouth and hands on Leah. I don't even have to close my eyes to see it. It's all I see in my blackness." I turned my head away from where I thought he was. "Please, just go." My chest was bouncing up and down in my hysteria, and I could hear the beeping increase on the machine next to my bed. I tried to slow down and catch my breath. I didn't want anyone rushing in there and telling me I had to stay in the hospital longer than necessary.

"I'm sorry. You have no idea how sorry I am. I do love you, only you; it will always be you. What I did was wrong. I know that now. Julie made sure that I knew that. I can't change what happened, but let me help you, please. I'll hire the best doctors, and we'll get help for the apartment; let me take care of y—"

"No. I'm moving to Paris." Wow, I hadn't realized I'd made that decision. "I'll be leaving as soon as I get the all clear. We are over, Alex. What we had, whatever it was, is done. I'm done. Now, please, I am begging you to just go and don't come back." I was doing my best to hold it together; it wasn't working very well.

I felt his thumb wipe a tear off my cheek and then felt his lips where the tear was. "I will always love you. You can put thousands of miles and an ocean in between us, and I will still love you. You are my soul. I fucked up. I won't say good-bye to you, Aubrey. I will never say good-bye to you." He inhaled, and I could tell he was upset. Was he crying? Did I care? Nope.

I heard the door close. I broke down in sobs. I loved him so much it made my heart hurt more than my head. I remembered the note that he left me. He'd already said good-bye.

A couple of days later, after being discharged with a

"take care of yourself" and a walking stick, I was back in my apartment. I was using the walking stick to try to navigate. I didn't want any help. Julie was over, and she was packing for me. She was going to Paris with me to ensure that I arrived safely, because I was an invalid now. At least that's how I felt.

My parents had gone back the day before to prepare for my arrival. Apparently, they were installing ramps and doing whatever else was needed to have a blind person, excuse me, a visually impaired person around. I was really trying not to be bitter, but I thought of how my life was going to be. I had an education that I could no longer use, a job I could no longer perform, and I was constantly banging into things. Okay, yes, I was feeling sorry for myself.

Days had passed and they'd been all the same: dark. The doctor said the swelling had gone down enough for me to travel. He was concerned about me finding a doctor in Paris, but my mom assured him that she had everything lined up, including doctors, braille instructors, even a driver to take me places.

"Thanks for your help, Julie. I couldn't do this without you. I will though, someday. I want to be able to be on my own and to live my new life. I need to learn how to cope with this. Going forward, my attitude will be thankful. And I am, Jules. I am thankful that I am alive and for you and my family."

"It'll work out, I promise. I'll always be here for you." The buzzer rang. "I ordered Chinese food; that must be it. Have a seat on the couch and I'll get the door."

I loved that she didn't try to help me to my own couch. I found it just fine and sat down. I reached for the coffee table and pulled it toward the couch so we would be closer to the food.

The door opened, but Julie didn't say anything. I heard whispering and a kiss sound. "Let me guess. Brett is here to see you off. Hi, Brett."

"You caught me, Aubrey! I couldn't let my girl leave me without a proper good-bye kiss." They were so lucky. They never had any barriers or lies between them.

"I'd leave and give you privacy, but you could be naked right now and I wouldn't know." I laughed. No one else was laughing. "Okay, guys, lighten up. I'm trying to get out of my self-imposed pity party, so you could have laughed at that. Help me find some type of humor in this. I can't live the life I have now without humor."

"I agree. Hi, Aubrey, how are you doing?"

"What are you doing here, Alex?" I would have known that voice anywhere. I didn't need my eyes to know it was him.

I heard him exhale as if he were frustrated. "Please don't be mad. I just wanted to tell you to have a safe trip and to give you something. I'll put it on the coffee table."

I shouted at him and I knew I was loud. I wanted to make sure that he heard me. I think I wanted myself to hear it too. "I don't want anything from you; please, take it back." I started feeling around the coffee table in front of me to find the gift. My hand felt a box about the size of a ream of paper, but it was much lighter. Picking it up in my right hand, I held it out. "Take it. I don't want it. I don't want anything from you except for you to leave. As a matter of fact . . ." I reached down to my wrist and grabbed my bracelet. I couldn't release the clasp, so I tore it off. "Take this too." I threw it in the direction of his voice, and my hand slammed into his chest. He put his hand on mine. "Take it!" I pulled my hand away and out from under his.

I was willing myself not to cry. I needed to stay strong. If he saw me upset, he'd know he could still get to me.

"I'm not going to take my gift back." I heard it plop on the table. "If you don't want it, get rid of it yourself." Was he getting mad? What the fuck? *He was mad at me?*

"Fine, I will." I stood up to go into my room and banged my leg on the table, forgetting that I pulled it closer to the couch. "Shit!" I reached down to rub my shin. That hurt like hell. I guess that was a sign of things to come: my banging into things.

"Let me help you." Alex grabbed my elbow. Julie must have left the room with Brett or I would have heard her and she would've been at my side.

I pulled my arm out of his grasp. "No! Don't touch me! Never touch me again. Get out! Just get out!" My voice was elevated to the point where Julie started yelling. I could hardly hear her over my own voice.

"What's wrong? What's going on out here?"

"Get him out, Julie, please." I was gasping for air. "Brett can stay, but Alex needs to leave." The buzzer rang. It was the Chinese food. "I'm going to bed. I've lost my appetite. Good night, Brett. Julie, I'll talk to you in the morning." I walked slowly to my bedroom, moving my walking stick side to side, and closed the door.

I flopped on my bed and shoved my head in my pillow and screamed. I didn't blame him. That wasn't why I as upset. It was the image that I couldn't scrub from my brain and the fact that he'd broken me and had set out to hurt me . . . with her. It didn't even matter that it was her. I tried to picture other things, the good times we shared or shopping with Julie, but every time I did that, I realized that I would never do or see those things the same way again. I couldn't see what I was shopping for or watch a movie. I just wanted to sleep and get as far away from Alex as possible. Truth be told, I missed him and I really missed us. I loved him more than anything. I just couldn't forgive him right now or maybe ever. I wanted to expel him from my brain.

Chapter 22

JULIE AND I ARRIVED AT Charles de Gaulle Airport where my parents picked us up to bring us to their chateau. It was so odd being back in Paris. I started remembering the places Alex took me, the food we enjoyed, and the walks we took. I guess coming here wasn't going to rid me of the memory of Alex. I needed to move on, not remember what once was. As we walked through the terminal, I could hear the footsteps of many and realized this was my life now: surrounded by people, but still alone—in the dark and alone.

My parents' chateau seemed vast; I could hear Julie's voice almost echo. I didn't get the usual tour of the upstairs. I was shown where my room was on the first level and the adjoining bathroom. It was easy to maneuver with my walking stick. My mom had arranged the furniture in such a manner that there weren't any obstacles in the way.

Julie unpacked and came down to my room. I was tired and lay on my bed just thinking. "Aubrey, I have something for you, and before you get mad at me, let me explain what it is."

"Why would I get mad? You make me sound as if I turned into an ogre."

"Well, it isn't from me. Alex gave me the gift he bought you. He wanted me to bring it with me and pass it off as my gift to you, but I don't want to lie to you. He took the bracelet, but not this. He insisted."

I sat up and I felt the bed dip where Julie sat down next to me. "Fine, what is it?" I knew I sounded ungrateful.

"It's a braille tablet. You can listen to music, make calls, and download books in braille and audio versions. He actually downloaded some for you already, and there is an unlimited credit account assigned to you, so you can get whatever you want."

I was stunned. I didn't even know there was such a thing as a braille tablet. Julie took my hand and placed the tablet in it. I held it with my left hand and felt it with my right hand. "Thank you."

"It's pretty cool, right?" Julie was trying to sound upbeat.

"Yeah, it's cool." For as cool as a braille tablet could be, it was cool. "I apparently start braille lessons next week."

"That's awesome. Think of it as learning a different language. I hope your teacher is from America!"

Julie and I burst out laughing. "Could you imagine if the teacher only spoke French? I'd be totally screwed." We were laughing so hard that my eyes were tearing. It felt so good to laugh. "I'm going to miss you, Julie. Promise to visit me, okay?" Julie hugged me and promised we would keep in touch. We also made a pact that if I didn't ask about Alex she wouldn't mention him.

The next couple of weeks were very different for me. Julie went back to the States, and I was on my second week of braille lessons. My teacher was great, very patient. She was an older woman from London. I had class with her for two hours a day, so I was catching on quickly and was making good use of the tablet.

My parents finally allowed me to venture out on my own as long as I took the driver they hired with me. His name was Frank. I asked him to take me to a coffee shop with Wi-Fi and we ended up at a quiet café. The smell of coffee and pastries was overwhelming. I could gain ten pounds by just inhaling. Frank walked me in and described the layout for me; the ordering counter was at ten o'clock, the restrooms were at six o'clock, the door was at three o'clock, and I was sitting at eight o'clock. He tried using North, South, East, and West, but that didn't work for me. So he utilized the clock method. It seemed simple enough.

Frank brought me my coffee and told me that he would be outside and to take my time. He was going to be in the car reading. He was a man after my own heart; although, I doubt he was reading romance novels. The thought of it made me laugh. My dad told me that Frank was a former military man, so he was probably reading a historical novel.

I pulled my tablet out of my tote bag. My headphones were already attached, and my braille teacher had taught me how to navigate the home page to open books and start the audio feature. I was inserting my headphones when I felt as if someone were watching me. I'd felt it before, but this time it was different. I heard footsteps to my right, and then they stopped.

A man cleared his throat. "*Puis-je vous joindre?*"

Holy hell! That sounded sexy. Too bad I had no idea what he said. "I'm sorry. I don't speak French."

"Ah, an American. Yes?"

He had a super thick accent, which made the English language sound amazing. "Yes, I'm from the United States.

What did you say before?"

"I asked if I could join you."

"Oh. Um . . ." Yeah, that was eloquent. Who was this guy? I assumed that if anyone who remotely looked like a serial killer walked in here Frank would have been in here in a flash. I didn't know what to say, so for fear of being known as a rude American, I said, "Sure."

The stranger sat down and apparently was eating something because the aroma that was coming from his side of the table smelled delectable. "Pardon my manners. My name is Chance, and you are a very beautiful woman."

That was a different introduction. Was I beautiful? I wasn't even sure what I was wearing since my mom picked out my outfit. "My name is Aubrey Ryan. It's nice to meet you, Chance."

"Are you hungry? I can get you a croissant or a different type of pastry."

"No, thank you. I'm happy with my coffee, but I appreciate it." God, his voice was so soft, and his accent almost made me swoon.

"What do you have there?"

Where? Was he pointing to something? Then it dawned on me that he didn't know I was blind. "I'm sorry. I'm visually impaired. Were you pointing to something?"

"Oh, I am sorry. Yes, the black little computer. What does it do?"

Hmm, it's black. I didn't know that. "It's a braille tablet. It works like a normal tablet, except it has raised characters so I can read it with my fingers."

"That is interesting. I have never seen anything like it. I mean I have seen tablets before, but nothing like that. Where did you get it?"

This guy was full of questions. "A friend of mine gave it to me." I smiled at the memory of Alex. Then that fateful image of Alex and Leah popped in my head, and I dropped my head a little.

"This friend is a boyfriend, yes? You are too beautiful to be single."

There it was again, that word: beautiful. I felt tears and shook my head to try to contain them. "It's from an ex-boyfriend." A tear slipped. I quickly tried to wipe it away. I prayed he didn't notice.

"I'm sorry. I didn't mean to bring up an unhappy time for you. I just went through a break-up not too long ago, so I understand."

He had noticed. "I'm not unhappy, not really. I wouldn't be good for him. I don't think I was ever good enough for him, and now that I'm blind, he would feel obligated to take care of me. I don't want to be anyone's obligation. " I hated that I felt that way and worse that I just blurted that out. I shook my head. "Anyway, how is it that you speak English so well?" I needed to get off the subject of my ex.

"I bought Rosetta Stone." He laughed. "I kid you. I spent time in America after I graduated school."

"Well, your English is very good. I studied English in college. It was my major, so I can assure you that your translations are up to par."

"Up to par? Like golf?"

I laughed and realized I hadn't done that lately. "Something like that. I might have to teach you some American idioms."

"I look forward to it. Well, I should be going. I will be back tomorrow at the same time if you would like to join me." I heard his chair back up. "I would like it if you did. It was nice meeting you."

"You too. Bye."

I stayed a little while longer and listened to my audio book. I wasn't really concentrating. I was thinking about Chance and what a nice surprise that was. I hadn't spent any time with a guy since Alex. Chance was nice. I felt comfortable with him, and his accent was amazing. I realized that I had no idea what he looked like. Was he older than I was? Younger? This no sight thing was a bitch! The things we take for granted. Like my reading . . . I missed reading the words.

I went outside, and Frank met me at the door. It was such a weird feeling being dependent on someone. I was going to ask Frank if he noticed any creepy guys walk into the café, but he would either think I was nuts or he would be accompanying me every time I went there. I didn't want that, so I kept my question to myself.

He drove me home, and I was greeted by my doting mother. "You're just in time for dinner. Did you have a good time at the café?"

I knew that she would be worried and probably called Frank a hundred times to check on me. "Yes, Mom, it was very nice. Frank helped me get around, and I listened to a book while having coffee. It was relaxing. I almost felt like a normal person." I didn't bother telling her about Chance. She would have grilled me.

"Honey, you are normal. You just have a hurdle to get over. And you never know; your sight may return. We're going to see Dr. Beaumont tomorrow. Let's see what he has to say."

Dr. Beaumont was apparently the top-rated ophthalmologist in Paris, and my mom was thoroughly excited that she was able to secure an appointment with him for me. "Okay, Mom, we'll see what he says." I knew my mom held out hope that I would regain my vision. It wasn't that I'd lost all hope, but I didn't want to get too excited. The last time I'd gotten excited about something it all went to hell, and I couldn't endure that let down again.

We had dinner, and I decided to relax with my parents in the sunroom. They would normally be watching a movie before bed, but as soon as I walked in, the television went off. "Please don't do that. There is no need to change your routine for me. I like listening to the television." It went back on.

"I'm not going to stay up too much longer anyway. I have a braille lesson at eight in the morning and then my doctor's appointment after that." I loved my tablet and wanted to finish listening to the book I had started earlier that day before I was pleasantly interrupted by Chance.

Chapter 23

HE WANTED TO MEET AGAIN at the café. I'd told him I could probably go there after my doctor's appointment. *Did I want to see him again?* I realized I did. It was nice and comforting to sit with someone who didn't treat me with kid gloves. I didn't have to worry about any romantic feelings since my heart was completely shattered and still devoted to someone else: a man who I would never have or see again. I wondered what he was doing or, worse yet, who he was with. I thought about emailing Julie, but I wasn't sure if I really wanted to know. *I wish I didn't care about him, but I do.* My anger had subsided a tad, but I still had that clear picture of him locking lips with that tramp in my head. Ugh! Would that ever go away?

My braille teacher told me I was her star pupil and that I was catching on quickly. Apparently, having the tablet helped me to excel in braille letters. I was waiting for Frank to pick me up to take me to the doctor's office. I knew he had to get my mom first, so I had some time. I decided to audio text Julie.

> *9:16 a.m.—Hey, Jules! I just wanted to say I miss you! Say "hi" to Brett for me. Love you.*

I put my tablet away in my tote bag and heard my mom call out to me. Before I knew it, Frank was at my side. "Hello, Miss Aubrey, did you have a good lesson?"

"Hi, Frank, yes I did. Thank you." I was hoping to hear good news from the doctor too.

My mom walked me into Dr. Beaumont's office. It smelled clean and sterile. I didn't hear many voices in the room, so I assumed not a lot of people were there. We only waited a few minutes before we were called into the back. I was glad my mom came in the examination room with me. It's weird not knowing what is going on around you.

"Good morning, ladies. I am Dr. Beaumont." There was that thick French accent. His didn't sound as sexy as Chance's, but it was still pleasant. "I've looked over your chart that was sent to me from Dr. Griffin, and according to this, you have *commotio retinae*. Do you know what that means, Aubrey?"

"Not really. I mean Dr. Griffin explained it to me a little, but to be honest, I was so out of it that another explanation would be helpful."

"*Commotio retinae*. In layman's terms it means your retina suffered a concussion. I would like to do an MRI to determine whether there are changes in the retina since your last scan."

"Okay, will I ever regain my sight? Sometimes I see flashes of light, but they don't last long." I knew my mom would be surprised to hear that. I'd never mentioned it before because I was starting to accept my predicament, while she was still grieving for me.

"I cannot say either way. It has been known that people who have suffered a concussion to their retina have recovered their vision in days or weeks after the trauma occurred, but that does not mean that just because this happened to you over a month ago you won't regain your sight. The flashes of light that you see are a good sign; I just don't want to give you false hope. Why don't we schedule the MRI and go from there?"

"Okay. Thank you."

"My receptionist will schedule your appointment on your way out. Plan to see me two days after your MRI. In the meantime, if you have any questions or there are any changes to your vision, please call me."

We thanked him and made the appointment for the next Monday. I had the entire weekend to dwell on what they would or would not find. My mom and I headed to the car. "Why didn't you tell me you were seeing flashes of light?"

"I didn't want you to get excited if it didn't mean anything." I heard her exhale. "I promise from now on I'll tell you everything."

My mom patted my hand. "Let's go do some shopping and go to lunch. How does that sound?"

"Mom, what does my hair look like? I usually get it trimmed every six weeks, and it's been over two months."

"It looks good, but maybe it could use some shaping up. Would you like to go to a salon and then lunch? We can go shopping another day or after lunch if you want."

"How about we go to the salon and then lunch? After that, I think I want to go to that café that Frank brought me to yesterday. It was relaxing and I enjoyed being there." Not to mention I was hoping Chance would be there.

"Sounds lovely."

The salon took longer than expected since we didn't have an appointment, but it was worth the wait. At least I knew my hair looked good. I was keeping it in a ponytail most days because I couldn't style it, and I didn't want my mom to do it every day.

We ate *alfresco* at a bistro. It was a lovely day out; the air was crisp and refreshing. I loved it. The food in Paris was always delicious. I now knew why my mom thought she was gaining weight daily. "Thanks for everything, Mom. I know this isn't easy on you and Dad."

"Don't be silly. You don't have to thank me. I love you, honey, and I only want the best for you."

"Thanks, are you ready to go?"

"Yes, let me call Frank to bring the car around. I'll have him drop me off first and then take you to the café since the house is closer."

I walked into the café and tried to remember Frank's clock description. I walked to the counter and ordered my coffee. The barista told me she would bring it to me. It suddenly dawned on me that I didn't know if there were any available seats.

"Can you please tell me if there is an empty table I can sit at?"

"Yes, there is. Turn to your left and go five paces. There is an empty table that will be on your right."

I smiled at her and was appreciative that she described where I was to go rather than wanting to guide me there. Getting used to someone always assuming I needed help was going to send me off the deep end. I didn't want to be a burden. I appreciated the gesture, but I'd rather do it on my own. I sat down after thanking her. I felt good. It was nice to be able to feel a little sense of independence.

"*Bonjour, Belle. L'esprit si je peux m'asseoir?*" I laughed at the recognizable voice.

"Hi, Chance. I have no idea what you said aside from

hello, but it sounded so good it really doesn't matter. Have a seat."

"I said, 'Hello, beautiful, mind if I sit down?'"

"Oh." I blushed. "I really should learn how to speak French. You could have said that I was ugly or something like that, and it still would have sounded amazing."

"I would never lie to you, much less say you were ugly."

God, his accent! I could never get enough. It was weird how comfortable I was with him. "Thank you for the compliment."

"How was your doctor's appointment?"

Wow, he remembered. "It was good. Thank you. I have to get some tests done next week, but I'm not getting my hopes up."

"There is nothing wrong with hope is there? Without hope, what do we have? Life would be stagnant; we always need to hope for something. I hope that you regain your eyesight, but even if you do not, I hope that you find happiness." He stressed the word "hope" every time he said it. It was sweet.

"You're a good guy, Chance." I took a sip of my coffee. "How is it that you're available every afternoon? Don't you work?" I was hoping that I didn't sound rude.

"In France, we take as you would say 'breaks' in the afternoon, and I am on holiday. I am taking a break for a while. I had the time coming to me, so I took it. I am glad that I did, or I would not be here with you."

"Well, I'm glad you took it too. I miss my friends from back home. I would love to talk to my best friend. Her name is Julie. It's just very hard to connect with the time difference. When I wake up, she's still sleeping, and when she's home from work, I'm usually sleeping. Even if I woke up at four in the morning, she would be hard to reach because she would most likely be with her boyfriend, Brett, at the club. I lowered my head and started playing with my coffee cup. Just saying "club" brought the thought of Alex back. "We text each other, but it's not the same. Then there's Mark, but I would run into the same time challenges." I shrugged my shoulders. "It is what it is, right?"

"Ahh, Mark, the ex-boyfriend, yes?"

"No, Mark is not my ex-boyfriend; he is a close friend of mine. Alex is my ex-boyfriend." I exhaled and squirmed in my chair. I could feel tears threatening. I hated that even saying his name affected me so deeply.

"I am sorry; I did not mean to upset you."

"You didn't upset me, not really. It's just hard sometimes. That's all."

"Do you still have feelings for this man, Alex? Do you not want to meet other men to possibly make you happy again?"

Was he referring to himself?

"To be honest, I guess I'll always have feelings for him. He was and I guess will always be my one and only love. I don't want to meet men and pursue a relationship right now, but I do like hanging out with you. I would be a burden anyway, but if you can put up with my occasional mood swings, it would make me happy to be your friend."

"I would like to be your friend and spend time with you. How about tomorrow we go to the park and have a picnic? I will pack the basket myself and everything."

The waitress came to our table to ask if we wanted refills. I couldn't resist. "Excuse me, miss, can you please tell me if this gentleman sitting across from me looks like a kidnapper?"

Chance and I both laughed. I didn't expect her to respond, but she did. "No, he doesn't, but I would definitely let him kidnap me."

I think my mouth was hanging open.

Chance said, "*Merci,*" and she walked away.

"Did you just thank her for wanting to be your kidnapping victim?" I was shaking my head, grinning.

"Okay, what are you thinking? You shake your head and have that cute grin on your face. What does that mean?"

"Oh, I was just thinking that it is totally my luck that I apparently have this good-looking man with me and I can't see him. Can you describe yourself?"

"I guess I can. I am about six feet tall, I am twenty-nine years old, and apparently, I don't look like a kidnapper. So how about that picnic tomorrow? I can pick you up at your place."

"Well, that wasn't very descriptive."

"I'd rather wait for you to regain your vision and see for yourself. Now may I pick you up?"

I hoped I could see him someday. "No, that's okay. I'll meet you at the park. Just tell me the time and place. My parents hired a driver for me, so I can get to wherever I need to go." No way was I going to let him come and pick me up. My mom would have a field day. She would flip out if she knew I was meeting him for coffee. Knowing her, she would have Frank run a background check.

"As long as you can get there, I will meet you at the rotunda in *Parc Monceau* at noon. If your driver is from Paris, he will know where it is located."

I unfolded my walking stick and stood. "Thanks, Chance, I look forward to tomorrow."

"*Adieu, belle dame.*" He took my wrist and kissed my hand.

Man, he was sexy as hell, and I couldn't even see him or understand him sometimes. It almost made me wonder what it would be like to date again, not now, of course, but someday. I needed to make sure that I was not holding Chance back from meeting someone. It couldn't be much fun hanging out with a blind woman who doesn't speak your language, is still in love with her ex-boyfriend, and didn't trust that a man wouldn't hurt her again.

Frank brought me home and told me my parents were sitting on the back patio. I made my way outside. I loved the smells that surrounded the chateau: roses, wisteria and other flowers that I couldn't identify. It was autumn, and the air was crisp and clean. If I were to guess the temperature, I would say that it had to be in the high sixties. It was very pleasant out. It reminded me of New York, except there were no sirens and loud horns blaring at my parents' place.

"Hi, guys, I'm home." I wish I felt as if I were home. Where was home really? Some people say it is where you hang your hat or where your heart is. Well, for me that was two totally different places. My hat was hanging upstairs, but my heart was back in New York. I really tried not to think about it too much; it was too hard. I was happy that I had a new friend to talk to.

"How was your afternoon, dear? Did you have any more flashes?"

And that was exactly why I didn't want to tell my mom that I was having them to begin with. That would now be her daily question. I understood that she was concerned, but sometimes I didn't want to think about it, not that I ever forgot that I couldn't see anything. "No, Mom, I haven't. How about we make a deal? I promise to tell you if it happens again, and you promise not to ask about it, okay?"

"You don't have to get upset about it. I was just asking. You'll understand someday, when you have kids, that parents worry about their children no matter what their age and that all they want is for their kids to be happy."

Kids . . . Would I ever have kids? Every day something else came up that may be out of my reach. "I'm sorry, Mom. I know you're concerned. Truth be told so am I. I will let you know, okay? I'm going to go lie down before dinner. Oh, and I'm meeting a friend at *Parc Monceau* tomorrow for lunch."

"That's a lovely park. Who is this friend, and where did you meet her?"

Here goes. "She's a he and I met him at the café. I don't want you to worry. The waitress vouched for him, Frank saw him, and he seems like a decent guy. It's nice to have a friend, and he's really my only one here who is close to my age."

"That sounds wonderful, sweetheart. I'm sure you'll have fun. Just be careful."

I had to admit to myself that I was looking forward to it. I had spent so much time with Alex before my accident that I missed the company of a man. I hadn't realized how much, until I met Chance.

Chapter 24

I MADE MY WAY TO my room and pulled out my tablet. I decided to text Julie. The time difference was six hours, so it had to be about ten in the morning. I figured she would be at work, and if she wasn't at her desk, sitting in front of her computer, she would have her phone since it was always attached to her like an extra appendage.

4:14 p.m.—Hey stranger, I miss you. How are things?

My tablet made a ringing sound, indicating an instant message was coming through. I could talk into the tablet, and I could hear the other person, and it would type the words that I spoke. I had to admit, it was pretty cool. However, I decided to call Julie; I missed hearing her voice.

"Hey, lady! How are you? I am so glad you got a hold of me. I miss you so much. We all do!"

"I'm good actually. I saw a doctor today, and I'm having a scan next week. Fingers crossed that my vision will come back. I'm not going to get my hopes up, but I want to at least pray for a miracle."

"I agree; you need to have hope, Aubrey."

"You sound like Chance."

"Who's Chance?"

"He is a friend I met here while having coffee one day. He's really nice, and from the reaction of our waitress, he's good-looking too. Figures, right? And I can't see him." I laughed.

"I'm glad you found a friend, but don't forget me. I may not be some new, mysterious, hot guy, but I know your deep dark secrets." She giggled.

"You're funny, Julie. I'll let you go. Kiss Mark and Brett for me!"

"Okay, we all miss you!"

"I miss you all too. I love you."

"Love you too."

I rolled onto my side and held the tablet close to my heart. It made me feel closer to my friends. I was a little surprised that Julie didn't mention Alex. She probably didn't want me to break our pact of don't ask don't tell. *Who knows what he's doing?* I missed him so much that I ached all over. I dreamed about the times we made love, kissed, and danced. The man definitely had moves. I guess that comes with the territory of being a club owner. He must have had a lot of practice. Yup, as usual my head went there. I wish I could just erase all the bad memories and just keep the good ones. And really, there was only one truly bad memory; it just happened to be my last one.

I wish I was in a place where I could text him as I did Julie. He would be happy that I was using the tablet that he gave me. I wondered if he would be happy about my new friend, Chance; probably not, but that didn't matter.

Chance was a nice guy or at least he appeared to be. I really didn't know much about him. What was really funny was that everything he did epitomized romance, exactly what I was looking for. No way would I start keeping a journal about him; that's what got me into this predicament. My dreams of writing a romance novel were over, and I really didn't care.

Frank drove me to the park at noon. I was really excited to be out and about. Frank walked me toward the rotunda and it hit me. This was where Alex and I had come for our walk. I stopped walking and Frank did as well. "Miss Aubrey, is everything okay?"

What was I doing? Today was about spending time with my new friend. I needed to make new memories. I didn't want to replace the old ones; I just wanted to make new ones. "I'm fine, Frank; I just thought I heard something. That's all." Great. Now I was a liar, not only to myself but to Frank as well.

"We're here. Would you like me to stay with you until your friend shows up?"

"No, thank you, Frank. I'll be fine. I'm sure he'll be here soon." Frank left and told me to text him when I was ready to leave.

I stood still and listened to the sights and sounds of the park. It was really amazing. Apparently, when people said to take time and smell the roses, they weren't kidding. Since losing my sight, I really started appreciating the beauty of nature without seeing it: the sounds of the birds, the wind blowing through the leaves, and the trickling water in fountains. It wasn't that I hadn't heard these sounds before, it was just different now. My brain needed to think about them; before, I just took them for granted, along with a lot of other things. I never thought I wouldn't be able to see people, the sky, or a tree again, but that was my reality today. I suppose I could have been really depressed and sad about it, but I wasn't.

"There you are." I heard Chance. "I hope you weren't waiting too long. He kissed me on both cheeks." I was taken aback, but didn't say anything; I just took it as the European way of saying hello. I remembered when I was in Italy with Alex that everyone kissed hello. I wish he wasn't in every one of my thoughts.

"Nope, just a few minutes. I was just listening to everything." I could feel myself smiling. He told me that we were going to head straight and then to the left where he had laid a blanket on the grass for us to sit on.

I could feel the grass on my toes as my feet flip-flopped to the blanket. When I felt the warm cotton, I set my never-leave-home-without-it tote bag next to me and leaned back on my elbows. I was looking toward the sky and felt the sun on my face, so it must have been a clear sky.

"Chance, can you answer some questions for me?"

"Of course. I will answer them to the best of my ability."

"Is it a nice day out? I mean, I can feel the warmth of the sun on my skin, but are there clouds?"

"The sky is a pale blue. There are a few clouds, but they are the cotton-ball type."

I laughed. "When I was little, I used to think I saw things in the clouds like animals or cartoon characters. Once I swore I saw Mickey Mouse."

There was a pause. Was he looking at me as if I were nuts? Then he said, "Let's see. There is one cloud that could pass for a ship, which is pretty cool because the sky looks like water. Then there is another one that has a skinny little cloud coming out of it like a tail. I guess it looks like a puppy, and the next one just covered the sun, so that one I shall call a blanket."

I turned to him. "Thank you, Chance."

"You are welcome. I really did not do too much. I actually never thought about the clouds before. Okay, what is next? What else would you like to know?"

I could hear voices, young and old, male and female. "The people who are here, are there a lot of them? What are they wearing?" I felt myself having to squint. I sat up and rubbed my eyes.

"Are you okay? Do you need something?

"Did the sun just come back out from behind the blanket?"

"Yes, can you see it?" He sounded excited and scared at the same time.

"Not really, I saw a bright light, as if I'd been staring into the sun, but it's gone now."

"Did it hurt? Are you in pain?"

"No, I'm fine; really, I am. Okay, where were we? The people . . . What are they wearing?" People-watching was another one of my favorite hobbies, which I could no longer partake in.

Chance laughed. "Well, this man just walked by, and he was wearing pants that are not long and not short; I think you women call them capris. Growing up, we would get picked on for wearing those; kids would call them 'floods.' Now there is a woman—I guess she is in her mid-fifties—but apparently she did not get that memo. She is wearing a skirt that if she bends over right now, I am going to wish I was blind."

I burst into hysterics. I was laughing so hard that my stomach ached. "That's hilarious, Chance. That was a total visual that I could see blind or not. I'll be laughing about that forever; you're too funny!" I tried to catch my breath and wiped the tears that were streaming down my face due to my irrational laughter. I was taking deep breaths. I hadn't laughed like this in what seemed like forever.

I turned my head toward Chance. "How come you don't have a girlfriend? I know you said that you recently got out of a relationship, but you're a good guy, funny, and apparently good-looking for a kidnapper anyway." I winked. "And you keep your word, so you're trustworthy. Any woman would be lucky to have you."

I felt the cotton blanket we were sitting on shift. Was he leaving? I reached my arm out and my hand landed on his thigh. "Oh my God, I am so sorry. I didn't mean to touch you. I felt the blanket move and thought you left me. We don't have to talk about girlfriends or anything you don't want to. I was just curious. That's all."

"I would not leave you stranded in a park or anywhere for that matter. You are not the type of woman a sane man would walk away from."

"See that's what I mean. You say all the right things, and you have that amazingly sexy accent." I decided to get off the girlfriend subject. "Can you teach the French accent to me?"

"You seem to have an accent of your own."

"Ha-ha, yes, I'm from New York City, but we don't have an accent—other people do. Now about this hot French one, teach me some words I can say in English, but so I sound like you."

"Hmmm, try this. I like z feesh."

"Feesh? What is feesh?"

"You know feesh. They swim in the water."

"Oh, fish!" Laughter consumed me. Okay, this wasn't

going to work if I didn't stop laughing.

"How about we have lunch? You are having a hard enough time keeping it together today. Maybe you need some food in you; you might be getting delirious on me."

Chance unpacked the basket, telling me everything he was doing and where everything was located on the blanket. He did it the same way Frank did. The wine was at one o'clock, the fruit was at four o'clock, and so on. I was really enjoying myself.

"Thanks for doing all of this. I haven't laughed this hard in a very long time. I had a feeling today would be like this."

"What do you mean? Today would be like what?"

"Well, sadly my last visual memory was not a pleasant one. It's almost as painful to remember it as it is not to be able to replace it. But today, thanks to you, I have. Unfortunately, now it's a woman bending over in a miniskirt." I started laughing again. "I'm just kidding. My visuals are now clouds that look like puppies, blankets, and ships that sail on blue water surrounded by feesh."

Chance was the one laughing now. "That's eet!" He started tickling me, and I fell back onto the blanket.

Through my laughter and gasping for air, I said, "Eet? Do you mean 'it'?" He had a great laugh. It sounded a little muffled as if he was covering his mouth with his hand, but it was genuine. He was genuine. I pushed his hands away and sat up. My laughter stopped, and I felt tears instead, and not happy ones.

"I'm sorry, did I do something wrong? I did not mean to touch you anywhere personal. It was an accident if I did."

The memory came back as if it were yesterday. I was with Alex in my apartment, and he was tickling me, and that was such a great time in my life. I missed him terribly; I really wished I didn't, but I did. "It's okay. I just . . . the tickling reminded me of a time back home. I really like you, Chance, and you're my only friend here in France. I don't want to lose that. I just freaked out a little. That's all." What I really wanted to say was that I felt as if I were cheating on Alex, on my fairy tale romance, which was completely stupid because I'd been gone weeks and there was no way he was thinking about me and not sleeping with someone else.

"I have an idea. Is it okay if I look at your tablet?"

"I guess so; it's in my bag." I wondered what he wanted it for. I started to get nervous. I didn't think he would text or call anyone.

"Let's see. What about this one? *Disastrous* by E.L. Montes."

He was going to read to me? I missed my romance novels and the authors who'd written them. I felt so connected to them when I read. I tried to picture myself in their situation: what the characters were going to do and what I would do if I were in their position. Who knew that my life, which I wanted so badly to be like a romance novel, would turn into a tragedy?

"I was going to start that series before my accident, but I never had the time. I heard they were really great books, and I was really looking forward to the series."

"Well then, there is no time like the present."

He leaned me back until I was flat and my head was on his lap. I felt the warmth from the sky on my face and his warmth everywhere else. He read the first couple of chapters, and I didn't want him to stop. Not only was it a great book but I liked hearing him read it to me. It was the nicest thing anyone had done for me in a long time. The best part about it was he didn't seem as if he were doing it because he felt sorry for me or out of obligation or because I asked him to. It was just the kind of guy he was, sweet and genuine.

After about five chapters, Chance said, "To be continued."

I pouted. I always tried to read a book from beginning to end because I couldn't take the suspense.

"How about I pack up our picnic and we take a walk?"

He helped me up and told me he was packing up the blanket and picnic paraphernalia. I wished I could help, but I knew I couldn't. He took my elbow and guided me around what must have been other picnics.

A walk sounded great, and I wanted to spend more time with him, but my head hurt. "Actually, I'm getting tired and I have a headache. I don't mean a cliché headache. I mean a real one, and to be honest, it is starting to hurt a lot." I started rubbing my temples. I bent at the waist to lower my head, trying to alleviate the pain in some way. I felt his hand on my back, trying to steady me.

"Let us sit down; there is a bench about four feet to your right."

I sat down and felt Chance next to me. "I don't know what's wrong with me. I'm telling you I feel as though I live in someone else's body ever since my accident. I have these flashes, and I have no idea what they mean. Then I get these headaches that come on all of a sudden and I get tired. I never used to get tired in the middle of the day."

It dawned on me that I hadn't had a panic attack since my accident. I guess what I didn't see couldn't hurt me. There was no real explanation for it; I hadn't even thought about them. That was a good feeling.

"Would you like to call the doctor? Maybe he can answer your questions. Your headaches concern me. Maybe they have something to do with the flashes of light that you are getting. Do you always get headaches after seeing light?"

"No, it's random." I shook my head in hopes that would clear it and we could move on with our day. "I know that it doesn't appear this way, but I really had a good time today. This is the most fun I've had in a very long time. I'll remember it forever." And I truly would. Chance was definitely getting under my skin and slowly into my heart.

He walked me to the entrance, and I texted Frank to let him know I was ready.

"I think your ride is here because there is a large man glaring at me as if he wants to kill me."

I chuckled and pictured this burly man glaring at us, when I had no idea what he really looked like. "Yes, that would most likely be Frank. I don't want to send mixed signals here, Chance, but would it be okay if I hugged you good-bye?"

I was pulled into the side of his chest. It wasn't too tight; it was friendly. He let me go and rubbed the tops of my arms. "You have my number and email address, so please contact me if you have any more episodes or just want to talk."

"I have your number?"

"Yes, I programmed it in your tablet the other day at the café. I was hoping you would find it on your own. I hope you don't mind."

"No, of course not, I'll talk to you later then."

I got in the car with Frank and we went home.

Chapter 25

MORNING CAME QUICKLY, AND I didn't know what was in store for me that day. Every day was different in Paris because I didn't have a job to get to; my day was unstructured. I grabbed my tablet to check on the time and found it was only 6:00 a.m. I hated that I couldn't sleep past seven. It was almost comical since the sun or any form of light couldn't wake me up. The house was so quiet; I was left with my thoughts.

My picnic with Chance had been wonderful even after my freak out over being tickled and my headache. But he read to me. *Who does that? What guy does that?* No guy that I knew. Did Alex even enjoy reading? I didn't know the answer to that question. I thought about it for a while and about Chance. If I were ever going to get past Alex, I needed to move on. The sad thing was I didn't really want to get past Alex. I learned a lot about myself through him. I didn't want to forget about the good times we shared or my love for him. I would always have that. I didn't know what I wanted anymore; I felt confused. All I knew was that Chance meant something to me and I needed to tell him that.

Having my tablet in my hands, I decided to email him,

so I began speaking into my tablet's microphone.

Hi Chance,

I wanted to tell you what a wonderful time I had yesterday. Also, I wanted to apologize for my Sybil impression. I hate that I run hot and cold all the time. I love being your friend, and I'm so glad that you found me in the café. There are certain things about you that are so familiar and comforting that it makes me believe we were meant to meet that day.

There is so much I want to tell you about myself. I went to school and graduated with a Master's degree in English. I worked as a copywriter for a marketing company, but I really wanted to be an author: a romance novelist. Oddly enough, that led me to where I am today. So, when you started reading to me, you had no idea how wonderful that was.

I never had a real boyfriend, well, not before Alex. I wasn't expecting to meet Alex. I just wanted to find someone who could teach me what romance really was. For example, what types of things do men do for women and to women that are considered romantic? I kept a journal and made daily entries about some of my dates with Alex. In the beginning, I guess I did intend on using him a little, but that was short-lived. Please understand. I didn't know if he was using me.

When I first met Alex, he was a total player and didn't do relationships. They were "complicated," his words not mine. He owns a really nice nightclub and had women fawning all over him all the time—one in particular. I didn't like her at all, but he assured me that there wasn't anything going on between them, and I believed him. I needed to believe him. It was the only way I could imagine being with him. As time went on, I realized he wasn't the player I originally thought he was. We were together all the time. We even came here, to Paris.

Anyway, it ended because he found my journal. I'd never told him about it. Unfortunately, he only read the first part—the part that said I was going to use someone for romance. He didn't read the rest of it—the best part of it—the part that described my love for him. He believed what others had told him and not in our love. I think what hurt the most was that he intentionally hurt me. What was worse than seeing him with someone else, was the fact that he didn't believe that I loved him, but I did with all of my heart. I truly did.

I just wanted to tell you all of that because you have the right to know why I acted the way I did yesterday.

I enjoy being with you, but I have a lot of issues that need to be dealt with. Hopefully in time, this will get easier.

Aubrey

I put my tablet away and went to take a shower and get my day going. I decided I wanted to tell my mom about what happened at the park. I promised her I would be honest about seeing flashes. I just didn't want her to get too excited. It was hard enough for me to contain my energy; I didn't need to fuel hers.

I stepped out of the shower and grabbed my robe. I had nowhere to go, so I threw my hair up in a ponytail and tossed on a pair of sweats and my Yankees t-shirt. I could feel the number two on the back and knew it was my Jeter shirt. That was another thing I was going to miss—watching baseball games. I snatched my tablet off the nightstand because I wanted to pick up reading where Chance left off.

I headed to the kitchen and sat with my parents at the table. It smelled so good, like a French *patisserie*. "What are we having this morning?"

"We have blueberry and cinnamon scones and plain or chocolate croissants."

"Geez, Mom, how about having some fruit or yogurt every now and again? I'm going to get fat. It's a good thing I'm blind and I can't see myself in the mirror!" I giggled.

"That's not funny, Aubrey. You shouldn't say things like that!" Ooh, my mom was mad and did not like my humor.

"I'm sorry, Mom. It was a joke." I cleared my throat. "You'll be glad to know that I saw flashes of light yesterday while I was at the park. It was quick, but I plan on calling Dr. Beaumont today and checking if he has any available time today to see me."

My mom got up and hugged me. "That's wonderful, honey. Your dad and I will cancel our plans for today just in case the doctor is available."

"No, it's okay. I can do this on my own. Frank can take me. I'll be fine, really. The doctor may not be able to squeeze me in. I don't want you to change your plans."

"Okay, if you're sure . . ."

"I am." She kissed my forehead, and I headed to my room.

I called the doctor and set an appointment at two. My tablet rang indicating that I had an email. I found the button and opened it up. This tablet was great because it read for me. If I had to rely on my braille skills, it would have taken me a long time. I put on my headphones and listened.

8:30 a.m.

Good morning, Aubrey,

I received your email this morning. Thank you. I hope you are feeling well today and that your headache has not returned. If you need anything, please know that I am here for you.

In regards to your ex-boyfriend, you really don't owe me any explanations. I know that you had a life before you moved to Paris, and I am really happy being your friend. I am very pleased that you feel comfortable with me, as I do with you. I do not have many female friends that are just friends, especially when they are as beautiful as you are.

For the record, I think this Alex guy is an imbecile or, as you Americans say, an idiot for letting you go and hurting you so deeply. Although, as a man who has loved deeply and felt he didn't deserve it, sometimes it is easier to believe the negatives people say about you than the positives.

Could it be that when he read that you wanted to use him for your book that you hurt him? I don't want to make you feel bad about anything, because you are right: he should have talked to you about it and trusted in the love you shared. But keep in mind that you didn't trust him either.

Although, I agree that he shouldn't have purposely hurt you.

Anyway, enough writing about another man. I must be crazy! ☺ Let me know if you need anything today.

I hope all is well.

Chance XO

He was an amazing man, and I felt so lucky to have met him. I decided to call him and ask if he wanted to go to the doctor's with me.

The phone rang only once when I was greeted by his deep sexy voice. It sounded deeper. Maybe that was his morning voice. Some lucky woman would wake up with that someday.

"Hi, Chance, how are you?"

"Aubrey, it is good of you to call. I am fine, how are you? Feeling better?"

"Yes, and as a matter of fact I'm going to see the doctor today. Would you like to come with me?"

"Aren't your parents going?"

"No, they had plans, and I didn't want them to change them for me."

"Well then, I would more than happy to accompany you."

I was smiling. I knew he would want to come with me. "My appointment is at 1:00 p.m. Frank and I can pick you up."

"Thank you for thinking of me, Aubrey. I want to be able to help you."

"I know and I appreciate that. We'll pick you up at 12:30 p.m. *Au revoir.*"

I hung up the phone to get ready when it rang again.

"Hello."

"Hey, it's me, Mark."

"Hi, Mark!" I was so excited to talk to him. "What time is it there?"

"It's about three in the morning."

"Just getting home, are we?" I was laughing.

"No, actually Jess just called me from London and woke me up. I couldn't go back to sleep, so I thought I would call you."

"Jess called? Why? What did she say?"

"She wanted to tell me that she would be home for Christmas and she wants to get together. I don't know why she called tonight. Christmas is over a month away. It was really strange, Aubrey. I felt as if I were talking to a stranger. I don't even care that she'll be here. Why did she even bother calling?"

"I don't know, Mark; maybe she isn't happy and wanted to talk to you. She could have just used coming home as an excuse. How did you end the call?"

"I just said good-bye. I didn't thank her for calling because I wasn't thankful. It's confusing, you know? I'm finally in a good place; I have a great job and Valerie. I don't need Jessica coming home and screwing things up for me."

Work. I missed going to work and my job. I knew Mark had stepped in to cover my absence. "I'm glad that you're happy, Mark. You totally deserve to be. You're right; you are in a good place. Don't let the past make you not want to move forward. How is Valerie?"

"She's awesome. She really is."

"How's her father?"

"He's good, feeling much better. He's back at work, and I think that's the best medicine for him. Alex hired a nurse who goes to the restaurant every few days to check his vitals."

I didn't say anything. That was the first time anyone had mentioned Alex to me. "That was nice of Alex to do. I am glad he's feeling better."

"You're glad who is feeling better? Anthony or Alex?

Was Alex not feeling well? "What's wrong with Alex? Is he sick?"

"Alex is fine, I guess. Apparently, he was depressed, and for all I know, he still could be. I really don't care about his feelings. He's lucky I didn't coldcock him for what he did to you. I haven't seen him in a while, but Valerie said he asked about you, if we'd heard from you. Val and I don't go to the club much, and Brett has been working with Julie on any marketing-related items, so the only time I hear about him is from Valerie."

He asked about me? "Well, it's over between us, so it really doesn't matter. What are you going to do about Jessica? Does Valerie know about her?"

"Yes, I told her everything, and in a few hours I'll have to tell her that Jessica called."

"It's best to be honest. If not, it could come back to bite you in the ass. You should try to get some sleep and I need to get ready. I have a doctor's appointment soon."

"Good luck at the doctor's. Are you doing better? I worry about you."

"I am getting better; I've been seeing flashes of light, so that could be a good thing. Please don't worry about me. I appreciate it, but I'm learning to cope. I have a friend here who has helped me remember what it's like to have fun.

He's really nice; you two would get along well."

"Hmm. You met a guy, huh?"

"It's not like that. I'm not looking for more and neither is he. I better go because you need sleep and I'm meeting Chance for a cup of coffee before heading to the doctor's."

"His name is Chance?"

"Yes, why?"

"Nothing, just maybe it's a sign that you should take a chance."

"I don't believe in signs, but that's a good thought and why I love ya, Mark."

"Right back at ya. Don't be a stranger, okay?"

We hung up. I really missed Mark. I missed all my friends. Maybe a visit at Christmas would be nice. I wondered if my parents would want to go if I suggested it. I lay back on my pillow and thought about what a visit would be like. I'd probably be wondering where Alex was. At least the image of him with Leah was dissipating and being replaced with happy memories. Even if I didn't physically see them, I still imagined what they would look like.

I tried to imagine the picnic in the park with Chance, but instead pictured being in the park with Alex. When I really thought about it, we had good times together—more good than bad. Those were the memories that I needed to hold on to. I needed to be able to move on and let go of my romantic fantasies, since they were what got me into this mess. The problem was I loved romance, fantasies, and Alex. My heart hurt just thinking about him. I thought about texting him, but decided against it.

Chapter 26

CHANCE SAID HELLO TO FRANK as he got into the back of the car with me. We rode in silence to Dr. Beaumont's office building. Maybe Chance didn't want to talk in front of Frank. It was weird. We arrived at the office and walked into radiology. Chance wished me luck. The test took about an hour. Normally, I would have felt claustrophobic, but that was another sensation I was lacking since my loss of vision. The radiologist told me that I would hear something in a day or two. I thanked her, and she walked me to the reception area to where Chance was waiting for me.

I heard him thanking someone and saying that he would let her know if he had any questions. I wondered what that was about. He must have spotted me because he called out my name. The radiologist whispered in my ear, "Lucky girl, it looks as if you are in good hands." That was odd.

Chance and I walked outside. I loved the fall weather. Something about it felt so cleansing. Chance spotted Frank and told me he would lead me. I put my arm through his, and we started walking to the car when all of a sudden I was jerked back and landed on Chance's arm. "*Baiseur!*"

"What the hell was that?" One minute we were walking

and the next I was pulled back. Apparently, Chance was pissed. I knew "*baiseur*" meant "fucker."

"Are you okay, Aubrey? A car came really close to hitting you. I am so sorry. I never saw him coming. He flew around the corner at high speed. What an asshole!"

I could feel him shaking. "Chance, I'm fine. I'm just glad you were here with me. You saved my life." He let me hold on to him. It felt really good to be held by a man again, even if it was platonic.

"Here comes Frank. Let's get out of here and go get a drink or something."

"Okay, my treat though."

Frank came up to me and put his hands on my shoulders. "My God, Aubrey, are you okay? You have no idea how close that car was to hitting you." He was right; I had no idea.

"I'm fine thanks to Chance here." I smiled, but deep down that really scared me.

"I should have been at the curb, waiting for you. I did get his plate though and called it in to the police. He was driving as if he had been drinking. He didn't even slow down or notice you were there. He was reckless."

My thoughts went to Alex. I wasn't able to imagine him receiving the phone call that I was killed by a drunk driver.

"Let's go." Chance guided me into the back seat of the car. Frank asked if we needed to go anywhere else, and Chance asked him to take us to a restaurant so we could grab something to eat.

Chance's voice was still a little shaky. "So how did it go? Were you okay in the MRI machine?"

"It was okay, just really loud. Who were you talking too when I walked out?"

"Dr. Beaumont's nurse. She was talking to the receptionist, and I heard her mention your doctor. I asked her for some information about your condition. She retrieved some pamphlets for me."

"Why do you want to know about my condition?" I hated that I had a condition.

"I want to see if there is anything that we can do to help you. I am sorry if I overstepped."

Not wanting him to feel bad and knowing he just wanted to help, I smiled. "So, Dr. Chance . . ." I suddenly realized I didn't know his last name. "What's your last name?" It was weird that that bit of information was bypassed in all of our other conversations.

"My full name is Chance L'Amour."

"Your name is Chance Love?" I tried to suppress a giggle.

"Yes, I know. It sounds cheesy, right? Now we are here, so let's go eat, and I will tell you what is in these pamphlets."

We were seated in a booth, which I preferred. There were days when I felt that if I moved the wrong way my ass would fall off the chair. Booth seats were much more forgiving to my clumsiness. The waitress came to the table and started off in French naturally. Chance said something to her, and she converted over to very broken English.

"Your drinks? You know what you drink?"

Trying to contain a little chuckle at her question, I ordered a Perrier with lemon, and Chance ordered a beer.

"Maybe we should let her speak French. You can translate for me." I was smiling.

"No, she will be fine. Do you know what you want for lunch?"

"If I order the feesh, do you think she will know what I want?" We both laughed. "What are you doing right now?" I really wanted to see him. I willed my eyes to have him appear. It didn't work.

"What do you mean?"

"Well, you can see me, but you're just a shadow. You're a shadow! I see a shadow! Oh my God, Chance! I can see an outline. It's fuzzy, but it's there. Hold up your hand. I want to see if I see anything. Please, just humor me. Put your hand up, just for a minute. Come on, Chance. Please?"

"It's up, Aubrey."

Dropping my head, I could feel the tears starting to come forward. I couldn't see his hand, not even the outline or shadow of it.

Chance answered my question. "So what am I doing? I am looking at the most beautiful woman I have ever had the pleasure of being friends with. She is smart, honest, and one of the bravest people I know. She is a good friend and person, and I hope that she will want to sit across from me for many more years."

Looking up, I realized that the shadow was gone; it went as fast as the flash of light in the park. "Your shadow is gone. And for the record, I would love to sit across from you for many years, but someday you'll fall in love with someone, and she may not want me across from you." While waiting for his response, my tablet chimed. "That might be my mom; I never called her after the MRI." Holding the tablet in my hands and running my fingers over the screen, I started trembling. I read his name quickly; I excused myself for a minute and put my headphones on.

> ***Alex:** 3:13 p.m.—I'm worried about you. Are you doing okay? I miss you and love you more than anything in the world. Come back to me. Please. I downloaded music to your tablet; please listen to it. Listen for the wave.*

I put the tablet and headphones away, reached for my water, and took a sip. It had been months and he texted me now. He told me he added music to my tablet? I hadn't listened to any music . . . yet. And wave? What wave?

"Are you okay? You look pale."

I shook it off. "I'm fine. Where were we? Oh yeah, tell me about the pamphlets. Is there a miracle cure?" I sounded sarcastic and Chance was quiet. "I'm sorry, that was rude of me."

"I take it that wasn't your mom?"

Shaking my head, I said, "Please, tell me about the pamphlets; curiosity is getting the better of me." I didn't want to talk about the text from Alex.

"Well, it says that eating the right foods and vitamins are good for you: foods high in vitamins C and E, leafy vegetables, salmon, and citrus. There are quite a few things that keep your eyes healthy."

The waitress came and took our orders. "I can't read the menu, but if you have it, I'd like a spinach salad with grilled salmon and a glass of orange juice." Chance ordered the same meal. "Thank you." I reached across the table, searching for his hand. His found mine and he laid it on mine. "You have no idea how much you mean to me and how much you're helping me. Before meeting you . . ." Pulling his hand toward my lips, I kissed his palm.

He left his hand on my side of the table until our orders came. "You want to talk about that text you received?"

"There isn't much to talk about." I exhaled. "It was Alex. I haven't heard from him in weeks. Mark told me that Alex asked about me, but he's never contacted me before today."

"Did you want him to?" I tilted my head and lowered my brows. "Did you want him to contact you? You can try to deny it, but the look you got on your face when you heard the message says otherwise. We're friends. You can tell me. I won't judge you, ever."

Thinking about how I could phrase this was difficult for me because I really didn't know. "Yes, part of me has wondered why he hasn't contacted me. Unfortunately, as I always do, I assumed it meant he had found someone else and wasn't thinking of me. Pitiful, I know, but if you saw the flurry of female activity that I witnessed not just once but all the time, you'd feel the same way. To tell you the truth, it makes me sad, really sad. Loving and what I thought was being loved by Alex was everything to me, and in a blink of an eye, no pun intended, it was gone, and not just him but everything. My job, my friends, my apartment, and everything I went to school for and studied so hard to achieve were just gone. I don't blame him. That wouldn't be fair. This was my fault, all of it. What hurts the most is that he lied to me. He deliberately did something that he knew would crush me so deeply. Just thinking about it makes my chest hurt, and he did it anyway. I thought he loved me. That's not love, is it?"

He was very quiet. Maybe that was too much information to blurt out. Taking my hand out of his, I rubbed my chest, trying to get rid of the pain that was there. Although it was most likely emotional, it was felt physically. "Was that too much?"

"No, it wasn't. I'm just trying to figure out the right

thing to say. Unfortunately, I have been in his shoes. I hate that it needs to be said, but it is the truth. Losing someone not too long ago myself, I understand both sides. It makes me wonder if he felt just as hurt by you. My girlfriend did some things that I didn't agree with, and by pushing all her buttons the right way, I caused her to walk away. At the time, I thought it was a way of protecting myself, but now, seeing how hurt you are, I wish I had taken a different tack. It makes me second-guess my actions. Unfortunately, they cannot be taken back. We need to learn from them, accept them, and move on. We wouldn't be the people we are today if our past didn't happen."

I was really thinking about what he said. How different would I be if there'd never been an Alex and me? If he'd never entered my life, would it be better or worse? Eyesight aside, other than coming clean on the journal, which was really a non-issue because it wasn't even important and I honestly was starting to forget about it, my life was better because of him. Still, the hurt was there, and it didn't seem to want to leave my heart.

"I understand what you're saying, and I'm so sorry that you've endured the hurt that we're both feeling. The thing is he didn't just break my heart; he destroyed my heart . . . destroyed me. I'm not referring to my eyesight. If I could have him back, us back, before all of this happened, I'd give my eyes away, but that isn't the case." That was the truth too. Having my eyesight was nothing in comparison to having Alex. "Do you think I should text him back?"

"Why don't we eat lunch first since the waitress must have brought it without our realizing? You can think about whether that is something that you really want to do. I can't tell you what to do. My job as your friend is to listen, give my opinion when asked, and be there for you in good and bad times. I'll always have your back, no matter what."

The rest of our lunch was silent. I felt as if every word in my brain was expelled that day, and I was getting tired, so we went home after lunch. Frank dropped Chance back off at his place, and we agreed that we would take a day or two to relax at home, well, Chance at his and me at my parents' place.

Chapter 27

THERE WAS SO MUCH THAT I needed to think about. My parents weren't back yet. Bringing my tablet to the back patio and sitting on a chaise, I thought about my conversation with Chance. Maybe Chance had a point about the fact that I hadn't made contact with Alex. I felt so confused. I really wanted to email him. Maybe I would feel better and it would start to lead to some closure.

My feelings were all over the place. When I didn't hear from him, my heart hurt. When he sent me a text message, my heart hurt. When I heard his name, my heart hurt. I decided that I was screwed no matter how I looked at it, so I decided to email Alex rather than text him. I spoke into the mic and laid it out for him.

5:10 p.m.

Hi Alex,

I received your text. I'm doing well. Thank you. My parents' place is very comfortable and accommodating. There's no need for you to worry.

I can't say I wasn't surprised to get your text message, because it did surprise me. I don't want to rehash what happened the night of my accident. I know that I should have told you about my romance research, but we turned into so much more that it wasn't even important to me anymore. You were. I didn't even want to write about it. I didn't have to because I had you. I was living romance.

But, I'm tired, Alex. Losing you and trying to get over you is exhausting. There are days when I force myself to not think about it. But you need to know that it's over; we are over. I will always care about you and want the best for you, but the hurt and pain that you caused my heart is too much for me to get over right now, if ever. I'm trying to figure out why your first reaction was to do the one thing that you said you wouldn't do. I am not talking about the kiss; I am referring to the hurt.

Some say that loving and losing someone is better than never loving at all; and others say that if it is too good to be true it probably is. Those are the thoughts that plague me every day.

Take care,

Aubrey

I hit send and let out a deep breath along with tears. Alone again and lost in my thoughts, I knew that I would never get over him and that no one would ever be able to take his place. It always came back to the same question: How could I trust him again? And now it was worse because I couldn't even see if he was doing anything. Being blind makes you realize that trust is the most important thing in life. Aside from my parents, I trust Julie and Mark with my life, I trust Frank to drive me places, and I trust Chance with . . . everything. I did trust him just as I trusted

Julie and Mark. I wish that I could trust Alex that way; I did at one point. He convinced me that our love was real. Seeing him kiss Leah was bad enough, but the intent he had when he did it was difficult for me to comprehend.

I decided to explore my tablet in greater detail, now that I was able to read more braille. My instructor had showed me where the music app was and had told me that some songs had already been downloaded; I assumed they had come with the tablet. I never imagined that Alex put them there. I remembered Julie saying he had downloaded books, but I couldn't remember if she said music as well. I opened the app, put my headphones on, and played the first song. It was the song we danced to, the song about lovers who were separated by an ocean. Tears immediately came; the lyrics affected me in a way that they hadn't before. It wasn't my first time hearing this song, but now the lyrics meant more to me. Was this why he said, "Listen to the wave"? I felt as if Alex were singing it to me from across the Atlantic.

The rest of the songs followed suit. I dragged my fingers down the song titles to see what else was there, and as I passed the last one, I brought my fingers back up and slowly moved them over the title of the song. My heartbeat got stronger, and my hands started shaking. "The Way You Look Tonight" by Frank Sinatra. It was the song we danced to at the benefit. I rolled on my side, hit play, and wrapped my arms around myself, almost trying to remember what it felt like to be in his arms. The song didn't play right away; instead, I heard Alex's voice. I immediately sat up, feeling completely disoriented. For a moment, I thought he was here, but his voice was in my headphones. I lay back down, started the track over, and listened to the sound of his voice; it had been so long.

"Aubrey, I added this song to your playlist because it

reminds me of a very happy time, the night you accompanied me to the benefit dinner, a night I will never forget. Every other year that I'd attended the event I was sad. It reminded me of what I lost and the horrible way I lost her, lost them. This year I had you. I had you dancing in my arms, consuming my thoughts, and occupying my heart. That was a great night. I wish I could talk to you and try to make you forgive me, but I don't want to hurt you more than I have, so I won't let myself call you, and it is killing me."

"I am so sorry for everything—for not asking you about your journal before I assumed the worst, for drinking that night, and most of all for hurting you." I could hear his breathing changing as he was talking. "I broke my promise. I'm thinking about selling the club to Brett and Tyler. I don't want it anymore. I don't want anything else but you, Aubrey. Please forgive me. No other woman means anything to me; nothing does, only you." Tears streamed down my cheeks. "I have loved three women in my lifetime; my mom, my sister and you, please don't tell me I've lost them all."

I heard muffling, as if his hand were over the microphone. Was he crying? God, I hope not. He sounded so sad; there was no life in his voice, no buoyancy; it was just flat.

"I want you back. I'll show you the world through my eyes; we'll see it together. Please come back to me. You're everything to me. I hope you enjoy the song, I listen to it every day."

Then the song started playing. The next thing I knew, my tablet was on the bed, I was standing next to my bed with my hands in the dancing position, and I was swaying to the music, dancing by myself. I could feel his right hand on the small of my back, his thumb rubbing my spine, his left hand holding mine, not too tightly, but tight enough to know that he had a hold of me. I realized that he still had a hold on me. I could have tried to deny it, but it would have been no use. The song ended and I was still swaying. It was the last song on the list, so it was now eerily quiet.

I replayed his message. I didn't want him to sell the club. It was his, and now, with the addition of *Amoureux,* it was so beautiful. If he sold it, what would he do? I couldn't let him do that because of me. It was about twelve-thirty in the afternoon in New York, so I decide to call him.

My fingers were trembling as I tried to dial his number. As I heard the phone line connecting, I thought that maybe he wouldn't be there and that I could just leave a message.

One ring—that was all it took.

"Aubrey?"

"Hi, I listened to your message. Um, thank you for the songs." I pictured him pacing.

"You're welcome. I hope you liked them. How are you?"

"I'm okay, getting by, you know? I don't want to drag this out, so I am just going to say it." I grabbed a tissue because my eyes were watering, but I wasn't crying. I didn't understand my eyes anymore. "As I said, I listened to your message; I actually listened to it twice. I miss you too. I truly do." I heard him let out a breath. "That doesn't change anything, at least it doesn't right now. I know I lied and I am very sorry. I never used you, not even that first night. You shocked me that night. I think I started falling for you then. I know I was wrong not telling you, but it really wasn't a big deal since we were so much more than those words. It wasn't my *intent* to hurt you." And there it was. I made sure to stress "intent."

"I know that, Aubrey. I've told you over and over how sorry I am. I don't know what else to do."

"There isn't anything you can do."

"Okay, I understand. It doesn't mean I'll give up; I'll never stop loving you. I know you have your parents there, but if you ever need to talk, I know I wouldn't be your first choice, but I am here if you need me."

"Thank you, but I actually made a good friend here. He's helped me out a lot."

"Oh? He's a friend or is he more?"

"He's a friend, but I'm not going to lie to you. He's a good man. I think you would actually like him; he's a lot like you in some ways."

Chance would never take the place of Alex; no one would.

"Alex, for what it's worth, I don't think you should sell the club. You created that club and named it for your mom. It's you. Don't sell it."

I cleared my throat and wiped my eyes. I blinked a few times and saw the shadow of the bed, and then I saw a flower pattern that adorned the bedspread. What was happening? I could see light and color. This had never happened before. I needed to get off the phone.

"I should go. It was good talking to you. Take care."

"Wait, can I talk to you again? Can I call you sometime?

"Sure. Bye, Alex."

I sat down and looked around my room. I was dabbing my eyes with a tissue. I felt the need to lower my eyelids, but I was afraid that if I did, I would open them up to nothing. I could see a window and what looked like a tree outside. I saw the sun; it must have been starting to set, because it was low. I hadn't seen a sunset in so long. I never thought about it before. I saw a chair in the corner and a door on the opposite wall. I was taken aback by everything that is so normal to see on an everyday basis, but I hadn't seen in months.

I didn't understand what was happening, but I was alone in the house, so I decided to call Chance.

"Hello there."

"Chance, I just saw my bedspread. I saw shadows, light, color, and flowers. I could see them. I really could. It was fuzzy, but they were there! I saw the window and the chair. I think I even saw the sun!"

"That is amazing, Aubrey! Were you with your parents when it happened? Can you still see?"

I exhaled. "No, I was actually talking to Alex when it happened, and I am just seeing shadows right now."

"Oh. But you told your parents, right?"

"I'm home alone. Frank is off for the night; can you come over and pick me up? I want to go to the park." I wanted to be able to see things so badly.

"Give me the address, and I will be there as soon as I can. Aubrey, I am really happy for you."

I called my mom and told her I was going out for a bit. Then I walked out the main door and waited for Chance on the porch. It dawned on me that the first person I'd thought of calling was Chance and I'd already been talking to Alex. My heart broke a little at that thought. I wanted to give Alex a hug so badly when he sounded so sad, but when I had happy news, my thoughts went to Chance. I wished I could combine them; they were both amazing men. I guess the difference was Chance hadn't hurt me and I didn't think he would, or worse, I wouldn't give him the opportunity to. My heart was closed, and it would take a lot for it to open.

I heard a car pull up. I looked up and saw an outline of what looked like a sedan, and then a shadow was approaching me.

"Hi there, are you waiting for a handsome non-kidnapper to take you to the park?"

I laughed. "As a matter of fact I am."

"Well, here I *am*. Let's go."

We got in his car and the music was playing. I didn't know the song, but it sounded like something that would be played at a club. A club? Yeah, he would always be in my thoughts. "What song is this?"

"'The Big Bang' by Rock Mafia."

"I like the beat of it." I was shifting in my seat; it was as if there were ants in my pants. I couldn't wait to get to the park.

"You okay over there? Do you need the ladies' room?"

"Ha-ha. I'm fine. I just want to get to the park."

"What are you seeing now, anything?"

"Just moving lights. Do the cars have headlights on?"

"Yes, some do, yes. This is wonderful, Aubrey. Can you see me?"

I really wished I could see him. "No, I can't, just an outline."

He exhaled. Was he nervous about the way he looked? Maybe he was one of those metrosexual guys or whatever they are called who are very particular about their appearance.

I couldn't stop smiling. I felt as if I were beaming. I didn't want to get my hopes up, but I was. How could I not? The car came to a stop, and I heard Chance's door open and then mine. He touched my hand and led me out of the car. I paused for a moment to listen. "It's quiet here, are there many people here? I really wish I could see for myself."

"No, not many. The park might be closing soon."

I could listen to him talk all day. "Your accent is beyond hot. Have I ever mentioned that before?"

He laughed. "As a matter of fact, yes, you have, but you can keep telling me that. I packed us some dinner, nothing heavy, because I didn't know if you had eaten already."

He lowered me down to the familiar blanket, and I sat down and looked around. I felt Chance next to me.

"I am not going to constantly ask if you see something, because I don't want to make you feel bad if you don't."

"I won't feel bad, but right now it's still fuzzy. I'm going to call Dr. Beaumont tomorrow and make an appointment. I'm hoping my MRI results will be in soon too."

Chance was rubbing my arm. "Please call me and tell me what he says, okay?"

"I promise to call. Didn't you say something about dinner?" Chance informed me we were having tuna salad, grapefruit wedges, and carrots. "That's all the right food for my eyes, right?

"That is right." He laughed. "I have to do what I can."

"Chance, I've been thinking about something, but if you think it is too weird, let me know and I'll be fine with it."

"Okay, what is it?"

I took a deep breath and swallowed hard. "Will you kiss me?" He said nothing. The silence spoke volumes. "Never mind, I shouldn't have asked that. I just feel close to you right now, and I miss—"

"Shhh."

He took my face in his hands. I tried to focus on him, on his face, but I couldn't see anything, not even a shadow. He gave me a kiss on each cheek, then my nose, and a gentle one on my lips. I barely felt it. He rested his head on my shoulder. My hand grazed his back, and he flinched. I never thought that this might not be what he wanted, but I really wanted him. I didn't know what it was—my conversation with him earlier, the excitement of my eyesight doing weird things, or was it my conversation with Alex? He reminded me so much of Alex in the beginning of our relationship. All the good things that made me fall in love with him, I was feeling with Chance. What was I doing? "I am really sorry; I shouldn't have asked you to do that. It wasn't fair of me."

"It's fine; actually, that kiss was really fine."

I smiled. "Yes, it was, but it was wrong of me to ask it of you."

"You're not over him, are you?"

Was it that obvious? "No, I guess I'm not."

Would I ever be over Alex Logan? Did I want to be? I knew I needed to be. Crap! Get out of my head, Alex Logan!

He changed the subject. "Guess what I got? *Glace au citron.*"

"Lemon ice? Isn't it melting?"

"It isn't here; it is in my apartment. It's getting late. How about tomorrow night I will cook you dinner and we can have some fabulous frozen citrus treats?"

It dawned on me that he bought it because he read that citrus helped keep eyes healthy. He was really something. "That sounds wonderful."

Chapter 28

I CALLED DR. BEAUMONT, AND his receptionist told me that he had a cancellation at ten this morning and that I could come in then. I showered and got dressed, grabbed my tote bag and my necessities, and went find my mom. My dad was out to breakfast with his buddies this morning, so I knew she would be in the kitchen at the breakfast bar. I started seeing shadows after my shower, and I was hoping they would last this time. Using my walking stick, I made my way to the kitchen.

"Good morning, sweetheart. Would you like some breakfast?"

"Good morning." I kissed both her cheeks; I could see her shadow and what looked like a glass of orange juice in front of her.

"Have any more orange juice? It looks good."

"You can see my orange juice? This is the best day ever. I need to call your dad! We need to celebrate. We should go see Dr. Beaumont."

"Slow down." I couldn't help giggling. "I see shadows, outlines, some light, and some colors. It's fuzzy and it comes and goes. I already made an appointment to see the doctor; I was hoping you would come with me."

"Of course I will! Let me go change, and we'll have Frank take us into town. Then we're having a girls' day, and I'll make a wonderful dinner tonight."

"That sounds so wonderful, but I have dinner plans with my friend; he's cooking for me."

"I didn't want to say anything or interfere, but you've been spending a lot of time with him, and I don't even know much about him. I really haven't wanted to bring this up, but what about Alex? Are your feelings for him gone?"

"We really need to go. Can we talk about this on the way to the doctor's office?"

"Yes, but we will finish this." My heart was racing; I could hear my heartbeat in my ears.

As promised, the conversation commenced as soon as we pulled away from the house.

"So tell me, Aubrey. I want to know what you're feeling right now. When you were here with Alex, Julie, and that other nice young man, what was his name again?"

"Brett."

"Yes, Brett. You and Alex were head over heels for each other and everyone was happy. I know he hurt you, and believe me I am extremely upset with him, but I also saw him in the hospital. The desperation in his eyes when you wouldn't see him . . . He obviously loves you. A love like that doesn't just go away. Now there's this man, Chance. Do you have feelings for him? Does he have them for you? I just want to know what's happening, baby; I need to make sure you're safe. You don't want to hurt Chance the way Alex hurt you."

Holy barrage of questions! "Gee, Mom, let's see, where should I start? Chance and I are just friends, at least for now. I think he's a wonderful man and I feel close to him.

He even saved my life when I went for my MRI appointment." I knew I sounded irritated.

"What the hell happened? Saved your life how?"

"Apparently, a car almost hit us when we walked out of the office building. Chance pulled me back as the car sped by." Realization dawned on me. "Theoretically, he saved my life before that. He makes me laugh, he describes clouds for me, he listens, he talks, and he cares. So, yes, I like him very much, and as far as Alex goes, I will always love Alex, and I really don't know what to do about that."

"Let me ask you this. If Alex and Chance were standing side by side, who would you go to? Want to talk to? Spend time with?"

I had no idea. We pulled up at the doctor's office, and my mom took my hand in hers. "You don't have to answer that question. Just think about it. Think about how each makes you feel and how you feel about each of them."

Doctor Beaumont saw us shortly after we arrived. He looked at my eyes, and I could see the little light that he was using to look in my eyes. "Looking better, Aubrey, and I have your MRI results here. It looks as if the swelling is going down, but there is still some fluid that should be eliminated. It will relieve the pressure around the optic nerve. A diuretic will be administered during the procedure to prevent swelling and increase the absorption of cerebral fluid. Once the fluid is gone, the swelling should as well; you could regain some of your vision, if not all of it.

"Okay, sign me up. Tell me when and where, and I'll be there." I was dead serious. I didn't care if I had to go to Timbuktu, I wanted this and I wanted it yesterday!

"Well, my colleague that I generally refer patients to happens to be in the States. He is actually at NYU, teaching a fellowship class. Aren't you from New York?"

"Yes, I am. So if I go to New York, how soon could he do this?"

"I will contact him and get back to you by the end of the week. But if he can get the room, I am sure that he will take you right away."

Right away . . . I could be in New York right away? Holy shit! I asked my mom for guidance on what do to do, but she knew that I didn't need any guidance. There wasn't a chance in hell that I wasn't going home.

"We'll wait for your call and make the plans then. Thank you so much." My mom's voice was beaming as if the doctor had told her that her baby would be back to normal. On the one hand, I wanted to squash that thought so she wouldn't get her hopes up, but on the other hand, there was that chance that this would work. All I needed was to keep the faith and take this chance. Chance . . . I needed to tell him that I was going to be leaving soon.

We left the doctor's office and went to lunch. My mom was literally bouncing as she strode down the cobblestone path. "Honey, take my hand; this walkway is uneven." I did as she said and she led me into the café.

"Mom, thank you. I know this has been a difficult few months. First, my relationship with Alex, which I know you didn't approve of at first, then the accident and my vision loss." I wasn't going to cry. There was no reason to. With the exception that my heart broke when I thought of Alex, I had a serene feeling about this entire experience. *Should I call Alex and tell him?*

My mom sighed. "The only thing that matters to me is your health and happiness."

We had a delightful lunch and we went shopping. My mom wanted to get some traveling clothes for both of us. I was starting to wonder if I should just stay in New York after my surgery, especially if was successful. That was where my life was and my home. Brian said that he would take me back when I was ready, and there were Mark and Julie, not to mention Alex.

My mind was all over the place. I didn't want to get ahead of myself, but what would happen if I did go home? How different would things be? Would Chance visit me? I needed him, but sometimes I felt as if I needed Alex more. There was definitely a connection between Chance and me, but the love I had for Alex was fierce.

I decided to think this out. First, I should have never lied to Alex. Second, he should have talked to me, because he should have known I loved him. Lastly, he should have never kissed that slut or anyone else. I know it didn't mean anything; it was just the way it happened. Could I get past that? Did I want to?

"Aubrey, are you listening to me?

I hadn't heard a word my mom had said. "I'm so sorry. I was thinking of New York."

"I said your father and I are coming to New York with you. We'll stay in your spare bedroom until we figure out what comes next, okay?"

"Sure, okay."

We finished lunch, and my mom informed me we were going to shop Paris style. She sounded as happy as I was that my mom finally seemed more like herself. I realized that my injury affected everyone in my life. I tried to be understanding of that and made sure it wasn't all about me all the time.

We were walking arm in arm because my vision had returned to complete darkness. "Can you describe where we are? Just tell me what you're seeing." That reminded me of what I had asked Chance when we were at lunch, except he'd been looking at me. He'd called me beautiful. The only other man who ever called me that was Alex. My heart swelled and hurt every time I thought of him.

"Sure, honey, the stores are lined up along both sides of the street; picture New York, but a little cleaner." My mom laughed. "There are restaurants and cafes mixed in. You won't find a hot dog stand, but you will be able to purchase fresh foods. Right now, we are about to walk into Givenchy; I am going to spoil my baby today."

My mom had me trying on all sorts of things; I wasn't even sure what I had purchased. I told her that I wanted something pretty to wear to Chance's tonight. My mom had me try on a dress that felt incredible. I wasn't sure what the material was, but it felt amazing. It hit my legs just below my knees.

My mom started to sound like an announcer at a fashion show every time I tried something on; she was helping me with zippers and making sure that I had everything in the right place. Then she would leave the room and ask me to come out. "Aubrey is wearing a V-neck black sheath dress by Givenchy. It is sleeveless showing off her toned arms." I started laughing. "It fits her body perfectly, as if it were made for her."

"Does it look that good?"

"Oh, it sure does. You'll see someday soon."

"I hope so. What about shoes? I can't wear running shoes or flip flops. Can we look at a low-heeled pump?" I was accustomed to wearing high heels, but I didn't want to fall on my ass or break a leg, so I wanted to go with something lower, just not a flat. I needed to feel feminine.

"Of course, we'll go look after I pay for these purchases."

We left with apparently two shopping bags and a garment bag. I knew that Givenchy was not an inexpensive store, but my mom wouldn't let me put anything back or help pay for the purchases. We were on our way to find shoes, and my nose stopped me in my tracks. Yes, my nose. My mom was tugged back at my abrupt halt since we were arm in arm.

"What is that smell? Are we near a florist?"

"Actually, it's a flower vendor on the street." I started rubbing my wrist and my eyes filled up.

"What is it, Aubrey?" It must have dawned on her. "Where is your bracelet?"

I inhaled deeply. "I gave my bracelet back to Alex. I actually threw it at him." I wiped my eyes, which now had tears dripping out of them. I felt a tissue tap my cheeks. We started walking away from the scent, but I felt as if my skin had absorbed it.

Before we went looking for shoes, we sat down and had coffee. I needed to talk to someone about my feelings. "Mom, can we talk about something?"

"Of course, honey."

"I'm having such conflicting feelings right now. I really like Chance; he is amazing. He is sweet, caring, and right now my best friend. Part of me wants to pursue him, but I feel closed off and taken. I feel as though I still belong to Alex, that his hold on my heart is so strong that I can't get it back from him, even if I wanted to give it to someone else."

"Are you saying that this Chance fellow likes you? Do you like him?"

"I don't know, Mom. I do like him. I really do, but I love Alex. I really don't want to be with anyone else. I don't want to be a burden and bring him down with me." I dropped my head in my hands. "I'm so confused."

"As much as I would love to answer these questions, they're only for you to answer. But you need to ask yourself this: if you saw Alex right now, what would you do? Would you hug him? Would you want to kiss him or slap him? All I know is my little girl's heart is broken, but you need to decide who can fix that. Remember you are never a burden to someone who loves you."

I thanked my mom. She helped, but in some ways, I was more confused than before. We bought a pair of low-heeled shoes and went back home. I was getting tired, but I needed to get ready for dinner at Chance's. My mom brought in our purchases and hung them in the closet. She had my closet arranged in the order of tops, bottoms, sweaters, and jackets. She had my braille instructor make tags for the hangers so I knew what I was putting on.

"I laid the dress on your bed. Call me when you're ready, and I'll zip it up for you. Your shoes are on the floor at the foot of the bed."

I thanked her, and she left me to get ready.

Chapter 29

I NEEDED TO CALL JULIE; I was starting to feel my breathing accelerate.

"Hi, Aubrey!"

"Hi, Jules, I'm so glad you picked up."

"Are you okay? You sound weird."

"It has been a weird day. I have good news. I've had improvements in my vision. They're intermittent, but—

"Oh my God! Are you better? This is so great! What now? Can you come home?"

"What I was going to say before you ruptured my ear drums . . . You know, Jules, I don't need to add deafness to my ailments."

"I'm sorry. I got excited."

"I know. Anyway, I'm coming home to see a specialist, who happens to be there. I don't know when exactly, but hopefully it will be soon. Can I ask you something?"

"Of course, anything, you know that."

"Okay, but I need an honest answer. Don't think you need to spare my feelings, okay?"

"Yeah, geez, you know me better than that. Now spit it

out."

"How's Alex?"

There was silence, and for a minute, I thought I'd lost her. "Julie, are you still there?"

"Yes, I'm here. I don't know how he is because I refuse to see him for fear I'll kick him in the balls."

"Oh my God, Jules, wait, you don't see him? Not even at the club?"

"Nope, I don't know when he's there and when he isn't. I don't ask. I felt bad for him in the hospital, but I still want to kick his ass. Anyway, he pretty much has Brett and Tyler running it. Apparently, he makes his presence known when he needs to, but he told Brett that the club . . . well . . . that the club reminds him of you: where you met and where he lost you. He isn't in a good place, Aubrey. I know if I see him he'll want to get to you through me, so I refuse to see him. All ass-kicking aside, I know that I'd feel sorry for his ass, and I don't want to. He doesn't deserve it."

I hung my head. "I talked to him, you know. I started listening to the music on my tablet and realized that all the songs were about Alex and me. Not just the songs we listened to but the meanings behind them. Then I was completely thrown when I heard his voice. He recorded himself right before 'The Way You Look Tonight' played." I sniffed and tried to stifle my cry.

"I don't get it, why that song?"

"We danced to it at the benefit. Anyway, I was on the phone with him when my vision started returning. I didn't tell him, Julie. I should have. I know I should have, but I called Chance instead."

"Want to know why you didn't tell him?" I didn't answer. "I'll tell you why. Because you wanted to hurt him.

You know as soon as he finds out that it happened while you were talking to him and you kept your mouth shut about it he will be devastated just as you were when he kissed Leah, who by the way is always hanging on Tyler. I guess they're an item now."

"I should call him, right? I should tell him that I'm coming home?" I felt the octave in my voice changing. "And I should tell him that I was stupid. No, I should tell him my journal was stupid and that I fell in love with him and apparently that was stupid. That's what I should say, right?"

I was the one shouting now and becoming agitated.

"I thought that he loved me, and because of something I wrote, when I hardly knew him and I couldn't give a shit about now because I can't see the paper to write on, he had every right to fuck me over. Yup, that's what I'll say." I was in full blown hysterics. I thought for sure my mom was going to burst in my room and find me having a breakdown and an anxiety attack.

"Are you done, Aubrey?"

"Yes, I'm done." I enunciated the word "done" and started breathing as if I were doing Yoga to try to calm myself.

"No, that isn't what you should tell him, but you just told me a lot."

"Really! What is it that you think I told you?" I know I was sounding irritated and she didn't deserve that.

"First of all, this is me, your best friend, so table the pity party you're having right now and check your attitude at the Eiffel Tower. You love him, Aubrey. You aren't over him and he isn't over you. I may want to kill him for not talking to you before turning all stupid, but he's a guy; they do stupid shit without thinking."

Julie exhaled and paused. "I can't believe I'm going to say this, but maybe you need to get past this? I understand that you were hurt, and I don't want to say I told you so, but I did tell you to tell him about the journal. Yes, he should have come to you, and he should have read the whole godforsaken thing, but he didn't. And yes, he chose to listen to Leah and not ask you about it."

My heart singed and my brain clenched at Julie's words. "I know I should have said something, but I didn't, and as I said, I can be stupid. I still don't think I can forgive him, and even if I do, I'll never forget it. I have to go, Jules. I'm having dinner with Chance, and I need to get ready."

"You've been spending a lot of time with Chance. Do you like him? Is that why you can't forgive Alex, because it might ruin things for you and Chance?"

I'd never thought about it like that. "I don't know. He reminds me of the good parts of Alex, everything I fell in love with, and tonight I'm going to tell him that I'm leaving. It's just weird. I care about him a lot, and I think that if I wasn't so hurt I could fall for him. I just don't want to. I want to be on my own, especially if this surgery doesn't work. That way I won't be a burden. And if it does work, then I need to stand on my own before I can even think about anyone else." I paused and tried to calm my breathing. "Thank you. I love you for your honesty, even though it could use a little tact."

"I know. I'll work on that." She laughed. "I'm happy for you, Aubrey. Think about what I said though, okay? Guys like Alex Logan don't come along every day. You may be taking a bigger risk by not forgiving him."

"Okay." I understood but didn't agree with everything that Julie said. Feeling brave, I dialed Alex's number.

It rang three times. I didn't think he was going to answer; then I heard that voice.

"Hi." He sounded off.

"Are you okay? You sound weird."

"No, I'm not okay; I have a lot on my mind." He sounded as if he were moving around a lot, more than pacing, but not running. His breathing was ragged. Was he with someone? That thought sickened me, which should have told me a lot about where my feelings for him stood.

"Oh, okay, well, I won't keep you. I just thought you should know that I'll be coming home soon. My vision started coming back, and my doctor has a colleague who performs a procedure that could help me regain my sight, and he happens to be in New York at NYU."

"That's great, Aubrey." He didn't sound that excited, but a little relieved maybe? "When did your vision come back? Was all at once?"

"No, it was a little at a time and then . . . When I was on the phone with you, it was the most vivid that it had ever been. I'm sorry I didn't say anything. I was in shock."

"I'm just happy that your sight is improving and that you'll be coming home. I miss you. I miss my friend and my lover. Please let me be that again. I want to be by your side through this. I want to be with you, eyesight or not. I told you before that I'll show you the world through my eyes. We'll see things together." I heard him sniff as if he were crying. "Please, Aubrey, I am so sorry. You have no idea how sorry I am. I need you. I can't lose you; I can't lose us. We've lost so much time already. I'll prove to you how much you mean to me and how much I love you. Just give me a chance. You need to give us a chance. I'm not asking you to forget. Just forgive me."

you about something."

"Okay, but let's eat. I don't want this to get cold and then have it not rest on your palette correctly. I want you to experience my awesome cooking skills."

"Okay, well I wouldn't want that to happen, so I'll talk between bites." I was going to continue when he chimed in.

"Your plate is directly in front of you. Your beef is at six o'clock, the salad at eleven, and the potatoes at two."

He was so amazing. I loved that he thought to tell me that. "You're wonderful. Thank you for describing that to me." I tried again. "I need to tell you something."

"You can tell me anything."

I took a cleansing breath. "I went to Dr. Beaumont's office today, and he told me that my MRI scan showed improvement but there is still fluid in my brain and it may be preventing me from regaining either partial or my entire vision."

The next part I just needed to blurt out. I swallowed the most delicious piece of beef and said, "I'm going to New York to have the procedure performed. I don't know when I'm leaving or how long I'll be there, but I think I want to move back regardless of the outcome. It's my home, and I miss it and my friends." I didn't tell him I'd spoken to Alex and that my feelings regarding him were all over the place.

Silence. That's what came next. I set my fork down. I was finished eating.

After what felt like forever, he spoke, "I think it's wonderful that you have this opportunity that could possibly correct your vision. Are you done with your meal?" I heard his chair legs scrape against the tile floor and felt the table shift, so I assumed he stood up.

"Yes, thank you. It was delicious. Can I help you clean up?"

What was I thinking? Of course I couldn't. I hated not being able to do mundane tasks.

"No, you relax; I'm just going to set the plates aside."

I could hear him moving around the kitchen. Was he upset that I was leaving?

"Would you visit me in New York? I've loved the time I've spent with you. You're the best friend I have here, and I would love for my friends at home to meet you. I'd like them to meet the man who saved my life in more ways than one. You've made me laugh when I felt like crying, you've described clouds to me and read to me because I couldn't see to do it myself, and you've taken care of me." I'd never realized it until I said it out loud, but he'd done all the things Alex told me he wanted to do. "You're someone I care for . . . deeply."

I heard him moving closer and could see his shadow. He was tall.

"Sit with me so we can talk."

He took my hands in his and pulled me from the chair. My chest touched his and I froze. He turned me around and guided me to his sofa. I could feel the carpeting under my shoes, and then my knee gently grazed what felt like leather.

Still holding my hands, he said, "Have a seat; the sofa is right behind you."

My body was molded by soft leather; it almost felt like suede. My cushion dipped, and I felt Chance's hand rest on my knee. Surprisingly, I didn't make him move it. I missed being with a man; Alex had done that to me.

"Chance, look, I—"

"Let me say something first." His voice sounded almost desperate, so I nodded. "Ever since I met you, all I've wanted to do is be with you. You make me laugh and see things in a way I never thought I could. You appreciate life even though yours took a sharp turn that you didn't see coming. You are the most positive person, even when you could be negative. I am falling for you, and I want to be with you here in Paris, New York, or wherever we may end up. Life is too short; I think you know that better than most. I don't want 'what ifs.' I want you."

He was squeezing my right hand with his left and his other was still on my knee, but his thumb was moving back and forth. It soothed me.

He cleared his throat. "You're the best friend I have too, and I can't lose you, so if you still want me to go to New York with you, I will on one condition."

I wanted him to come with me so badly. I didn't care what anyone thought about it either. People might be stunned that I'd found a man that I was compatible with, someone who I felt as if I'd known forever, who makes me happy and who I was falling for. He helped me put my heart back together and I didn't even know it. Did I still love Alex? Yes, and I suppose I always would, but Chance found a new place in my heart. He wouldn't completely occupy the place in my heart that Alex owned, but I would make room for him.

I nervously replied, "Okay, what's your one condition?"

He pulled me up with the hand that was holding mine, making my knee a little jealous. He tilted my head up with his forefinger and thumb.

"Dance with me."

I heard the stereo's volume increase. He must have had a remote control for it.

A slow song started playing. Memories filled my brain and broke my heart. I immediately thought of Alex; he'd put this song on my tablet. My heart sunk and then began to race at the memory. Why did something always bring me back to him? I'd try to move on and then bam! I'd get blindsided again. I closed my eyes to absorb the present, not the past.

I could feel Chance's hand on the small of my back. I loved dancing. I hadn't danced since I lost my sight, since Alex. I was apprehensive, but if I wanted to move on, this was something I had to do.

He pulled me close, which was good since I was on shaky legs. I was nervous. I felt an odd connection to him. He led me to what seemed like an open space. I could see shadows, but I didn't have depth perception, so I didn't know how much room we had.

He must have sensed my apprehension. "I've got you. You won't bang into anything. I moved the coffee table out of the way. We have an open space."

That voice . . .

We moved to the beat of the song, but it was coming to an end and another immediately started. My breath hitched and my head spun as I heard Frank Sinatra singing "The Way You Look Tonight." I couldn't feel my legs, but Chance continued to guide me and glide me through half of the song. *What is going on?* I could feel my breathing change, and my chest ached at the memories that were flooding my brain.

He whispered in my ear, "I have something for you."

That voice . . .

"You do?" My heart raced.

"Yes, I do." He let go of my right hand, and I felt

something cool on my right wrist. He kissed the palm of my hand and let go of it. We stopped moving.

I touched my wrist.

I couldn't breathe.

My bracelet, my beautiful orchid bracelet . . .

My heart raced.

How? I looked up, still not seeing anyone, not even a shadow.

My breath hitched, and I found it hard to speak.

I staggered back.

Tears fell. It can't be.

"Alex?"

"Yes."

Alex and Aubrey's story concludes in ***My Chance.***

Acknowledgments

First and foremost, to my husband Dave and my wonderful sons, Nick and Zack, I love you. Thank you for putting up with me while I tucked myself away to write my first novel. I could not have done this without you guys. Along with my parents, your love, encouragement, and support carry me on and give me the strength to take on new challenges and smile while doing it.

A very special thank you to Vina Platania and Heather Ford—you two ladies were the first to take on the task of calming my nerves, reading and re-reading, even before there was an actual book to read. You were my sounding boards more times than I can remember. Your patience was unwavering, and I appreciate you more than any words could express. Thank you for putting up with my many versions, questions, and ideas. Most of all, thank you for your confidence in me. I will never forget it.

To beta readers, I can't thank you enough. Your feedback and comments were incredibly helpful. Thank you for putting up with my numerous IMs and phone calls. I'm sure I drove you nuts, and I appreciate your putting up with me.

To Barbi Garcia, Vicky Critchley, and Jeffrey Eichenlaub, thank you for your support and encouragement. You are amazing friends—the best! I am very blessed to have you in my life. You always have my back, and I will forever have yours. I love you!

This has been a new experience for me, and I couldn't have done it without inspiration, encouragement, and feedback, especially from authors Gail McHugh, Emmy Montes and Madeline Sheehan. Your words made me want to take this chance, and talking to you gave me the courage to do so. You all took the time to help someone you didn't know by answering questions, giving advice, and just being available. "Thank you" doesn't seem like enough, but it will have to suffice. You are amazing women who write amazing stories, and I feel very fortunate that you were there for me.

Emmy Montes, thank you for letting Chance read Disastrous to Aubrey. She loved it! ☺

To all the bloggers, thank you for everything that you do for authors and readers. I don't know what I would do without you!

Special thanks to my editor, Theresa Wegand. Thank you for your direction, kind words, and feedback. I have thoroughly enjoyed working with you.

Sommer Stein from Perfect Pear Creative Covers. Thank you so much for creating beautiful covers.

Thank you, Tami Norman from Integrity Formatting for making my book look pretty. You're the best!

A big thank you to Otilia Baker for taking the cover photo. I fell in love with it the moment I saw it.

Last, but certainly not least, to the wonderful Erik Fellows, thank you for being my cover model, my "teammate," my "calmer" and most importantly my friend. You're a great guy with a wonderful heart and I feel very blessed to know you.

About the Author

Originally from Rochester, New York, Joanne Schwehm now lives in Northern Virginia with her husband, Dave, her two teenage boys, Nick and Zack, and her cute Bichon, Torre, who is aptly nicknamed "Mommy's White Shadow." It's a good thing Torre only barks or she could give away many secrets!

Joanne loves spending time with her family and friends. She enjoys meeting new people, traveling, relaxing on a beach, and shopping . . . especially for shoes. She has a bit of a fetish.

She is an avid sports fan and loves the New York Yankees and the Dallas Cowboys. She also enjoys playing and watching golf.

Thank you for reading *Unexpected Chance*

If you enjoyed this book, please consider supporting this author by leaving a review. Reviews are a valuable resource in helping readers find other books they may enjoy.

Stay In

Touch

Facebook:

www.facebook.com/joanneschwehm

Twitter:

twitter.com/JSchwehmBooks

Goodreads Group Page:

www.goodreads.com/group/show/156533-joanne-schwehm-s-romantic-reading-friends

Facebook Reader's Group:

www.facebook.com/groups/joanneschwehmsreaders/

Subscribe to Joanne's **Newsletter**:

http://eepurl.com/bAKaDf

Books by

Joanne Schwehm

The Chance Series:

Unexpected Chance

My Chance

A Heart's Forgiveness – A Chance Novel

Standalone Novels:

Ryker

The Critic

The Prescott Series:

Incumbent

Gripped

CPSIA information can be obtained
at www.ICGtesting.com
Printed in the USA
FSOW03n0202190217
30875FS

9 781682 307830